DRUID ENFORCER

A NEW ADULT URBAN FANTASY NOVEL

M.D. MASSEY

MODERN DIGITAL PUBLISHING

ONE

"Here, birdy-birdy-birdy," I whispered as I made a cat-like landing on the ninety-year-old warehouse's hardwood floor. Although I landed softly, the aged wooden boards still creaked underfoot, protesting under the weight of my lean and muscular two-hundred-pound frame. That was okay, because I hoped to draw my prey out by alerting it to my presence. So long as I didn't attract any attention from the local human population, stealth didn't matter.

Earlier, I'd received an urgent text from my fae liaison, requesting that I deal with a rather unsavory creature who was abducting children in the Fredericksburg area. Fredericksburg was a well-known pit-stop and tourist trap nestled in the Texas wine country amidst verdant farmland, rolling hills, and clear, cold creeks and streams. It was a place where the affluent came to start second careers when they tired of the city life, a fact evidenced by the dozens of B&Bs, wineries, vineyards, breweries, boutiques, and antique stores that had infested the town and surrounding area.

One might wonder why a dangerous supernatural creature would end up here, but to a seasoned hunter, it was a familiar story. Germans had settled the area in the early to mid-1800s, and with them had come all manner of creatures from the old world, including every variety of Germanic fae, undead, and *other* species. The beast I currently hunted fell into the "other" category, and frankly I had no idea what to expect with regard to its magical powers and attributes. What I did know was that it liked to eat children, and two kids had gone missing over the last few days—reason enough for me to go half-cocked after it.

Besides, my job as druid justiciar was not just to maintain the peace accord that had been hammered out the night of my appointment. I'd also been tasked with keeping the supernatural world secret from mundane humans. There were a lot of fae living in the area, and since Queen Maeve didn't like it when creatures hunted near her subjects—missing children and mutilated corpses tended to draw attention, after all—she'd asked me to "deal with it."

And as the area's newly-appointed supernatural sheriff, how could I refuse?

Unfortunately, my entrance had failed to elicit a response, so I scanned the room for anything that might indicate the creature's presence. Moonlight shone through the oak and pecan trees outside, causing leafy shadows to play along the floor. Light from the big silver orb danced on motes of dust around me, the only movement my enhanced vision could detect. Gloomy darkness obscured the rafters high above, reaching down into the far corners of the building where even my enhanced vision couldn't see.

For the sake of thoroughness and self-preservation, I mumbled a spell as I made a few arcane gestures with my left hand. In an instant, my vision switched from visible light to the magical spectrum. Still, I couldn't detect any supernatural beings, and nothing stirred but the trees outside.

I was beginning to think I'd followed a trail gone cold when a cold draft blew up from the floorboards, carrying a scent that made the hairs on my arms stand up. The air in the diner-slash-antique-shop was heavily laden with the smells of mold, fried food, mothballs, dust, and some delicious baked goods that until this moment I'd planned to sample on my way out. But along with that peculiar olfactory mix, the musky odor of carrion and rot lay underneath. It was a scent that put a damper on my appetite... and my awareness on high alert.

The smell was old—much older than the antique furniture and junk arrayed around the outskirts of the large, open room. On the way in, I'd spotted a hand-carved hutch that had most certainly been brought over from the old country, perhaps two centuries ago or more. Yet this odor spoke of ages long past, dark memories that were best left forgotten in the time before man had built solid walls of wood and stone to keep its kind out.

I drew my sword, leaving my Glock holstered for fear of attracting the attention of the local police. This warehouse, while appearing dark and desolate on the inside, was within a stone's throw of half a dozen businesses, including two restaurants, a bar, a hotel, a bed and breakfast, not to mention the town's grocery store. The last thing I needed was to run afoul of the law out here in Gooberville, Texas. Rural cops weren't known to show leniency for city folk who disturbed the peace by shooting up their town. Hopefully, I could deal with this thing using only my blade and magic.

I skirted the edges of the room, treading lightly while keeping my eyes peeled and my ears tuned for any movement or sound. I'd soon walked the perimeter of the warehouse without seeing hide nor feather of my quarry, so I began again. Halfway through my second circuit, I sensed a strange and foreboding presence near the center of the room.

As I searched the area, my eyes landed on an old decrepit chair that had seen better days. The thing was made from stitched black velvet, rubbed smooth on the seat and arms, and it had a tufted, diamond patterned back adorned with thirteen matching buttons. Mold, mildew, and wear had eaten away the upholstery at the base, revealing dark shreds of stuffing between worn threads and frayed edges.

But is that stuffing… or feathers?

As I drew closer, step by cautious step toward the object that had attracted my attention, a sudden fear came over me. At twenty feet away, it was the barest suggestion testing the borders of my courage. At fifteen feet, it became a knot in my gut that told me to turn around and run. And at ten feet, I strove with my every gram of will against a desire to flee the premises and never look back.

Along with my fear, the shadows cast by the chair grew as well. They crept toward me, spreading outward until they took on the shape of a huge carrion crow—or, perhaps, a raven. The raven's talons reached for me across the darkened room, eight shadowy spears edging toward my chest, inch by harrowing inch.

As the shadows touched me, I was instantly frozen between fear and intent, unable to move forward or turn away—although I desperately wished to do the latter. I froze for the span of several heartbeats, until I felt a growing warmth in my hand. Straining to tear my eyes away from the shadowy source of terror ahead, my line of sight ticked by millimeters down to the object I held—the sword.

With my acknowledgement of the sword's presence, the warmth it produced increased. The sensation spread up my wrist and arm, through my shoulder and into my body, pushing the magically-induced fright out as the heat spread to the rest of my extremities. Once the sword's influence reached its terminus in my fingers and toes, the blade flared to life, filling the room with an intense light that chased the creeping darkness away.

FUCKING FEAR SPELL—AND a damned strong one. I touched the amulet that carried most of my wards as I murmured a spell to shore up my protection against fear magic. Hell if I'd let the thing surprise me like that again.

By the time I'd finished strengthening my wards, the sword's brilliant flames had almost completely cast the shadows from the room. No longer in its native element, the raven-shaped shadow shied away—and although it might have been a trick of light, I could swear I saw it cringe. Despite the reaction the fiery blade had caused, the shadow seemed to eat the light around it, like a black hole sucking in starlight and debris in deep space.

Suddenly, there was a sound like a flock of birds in flight, and before my eyes the dark throne began to unfold itself. The chair morphed like a life-sized work of origami done in wood and tattered cloth, rapidly undraping itself by limb and frame, feather and pinion, beak and claw. Layer by layer it grew, until a sinister and unholy thing stood in place of that old, battered chair—a nightmare amalgamation of shadow, cloth, wood, and metal.

The night raven cocked its head to the side, its crown nearly touching the warehouse rafters above. A black and empty eye socket regarded me—or, rather, I *felt* it did, just as I sensed the creature was anything but sightless. It spread its wings wide, the tattered ebony tips scraping the walls to either side. Then it cawed at me, a sound more like a Jurassic roar than an annoyed bird's retort.

"Sufferin' succotash," I muttered, "that sure ain't Tweety Bird."

The thing standing before me was definitely *not* a house pet, although seeing it made me wish I'd a brought a couple of pets with me to help take it down. Trained mountain lions, for example, or perhaps a liger. Not that I owned any trained mountain lions or ligers, mind you, but after tonight it was something I definitely planned to put on my druid to-do list.

Unfortunately, I'd chosen to hunt this thing solo, and considering its size and reach I knew I needed to get off the "X" in a hurry. I tried stepping back, but found my legs sluggish and my feet still rooted to the floorboards. I roared at the creature, a reactive response meant to chase the last traces of fear from my bones so I could spring into action.

And just in time, too. The *nachtkrapp* chose that moment to swing one of those tatterdemalion wings at me, one that happened to be equipped with a vestigial claw on the leading edge. I ducked underneath while swiping at the giant raven's plumage with my sword, hoping for an easy counter. Obviously wary of the flames that danced along the blade, the shadow creature snatched its appendage back with surprising speed, denying me a hit.

The nachtkrapp, or night raven, was a type of boogeyman that found its origin in southern Germany and Austria. While folklore often depicted it as a singular creature, like most supernatural creatures it existed as a race or type not limited to a single presence. I suspected this one had been trapped in the chair by a spell or curse, only to be released or awakened by the unsuspecting owners of this establishment. Antique dealers were always stumbling over shit they didn't understand, and I hoped it hadn't cost these poor people more than what they'd lose when I burned that fucking chair.

I didn't know much about night ravens, but I knew this one was big and fast. The only way to fight something that big was to attack it from a distance, or get in close to nullify its reach. Despite the generous dimensions of the warehouse, I still lacked the space necessary to stand back and blast the thing with magic. Besides, most of the spells I could use to strafe it were elemental in nature, and I didn't want to burn the place down.

That left getting up close and personal.

I rolled forward and to my right at a forty-five-degree angle, narrowly dodging another swipe of the raven's wing that came from that direction. Moving into an attack was typically not a natural response, but if I wanted to close the distance I needed to take risks. And, moving forward on the "V"—as it was known in Filipino martial arts—was often the best way to cut an angle on an attacker in order to hit it from the flank.

The nachtkrapp was fast and it had about ten feet of reach on me, but I was smaller and even quicker. The wing sliced the air where I'd stood a split second before, but my gamble paid off as I rolled to my feet behind it and within striking distance of the night raven's left leg. Not quite close enough for a slash, I opted instead for a thrust, committing to the attack in a deep lunge that drove six inches of fiery steel into the bird's thigh.

For a creature made from tattered cloth and shadow, it sure felt real when I hit it, much like stabbing a mattress or car seat. The nachtkrapp's reaction was real enough as well, responding with a shriek and a kick from that leg that might have disembow-eled me if I hadn't recovered from my lunge in time to pivot clear. Talons like iron-tipped ebony spears struck the floor as they missed, splintering wood.

But the creature had overcommitted, as large monsters often did. Before it could recover and spin to face me, I was slashing at the nachtkrapp's ragged tail feathers and back, alighting cloth, wood, and feathers with each stroke. Although the shadowy parts of the creature's body swirled and healed almost immedi-ately, the tattered material that comprised the rest of it did not. Fire began to flicker and catch everywhere my attacks hit solid material, as those areas proved to be quite combustible.

Within the span of three quick cuts, half its tail feathers and back were aflame, with those flames spreading rapidly to the rest of its body. The nachtkrapp released another cawing roar as it tried to turn and face me. I wasn't about to give up my superior position, so I stepped lightly and quickly to match its movements, staying in its blind spot. With each step I delivered yet another cut, catching it on fire in multiple places.

Although shadow creatures had little to fear from fire, this one obviously had a magical connection to the chair that had kept it trapped. The problem was, I didn't know whether destroying its physical body would release it or kill it. Lacking a better plan to take the thing out of commission, I kept hacking at it while hoping that the "burn it with fire" approach would do the trick.

SOON, the night raven's entire body was aflame, causing it to screech and caw in pain as it thrashed about. The shadow bird released one final cry before exploding into shadow, flame, and smoke with a loud *whoomp*. The pressure wave blew me back, sending me tumbling head over heels as my sword clattered across the floor. I picked myself up, searching for the weapon as I slapped at a few smoldering cinders that threatened to light my clothes on fire. Once I'd located my now-extinguished blade, I turned my attention back to the night raven.

Apparently, I'd been wrong about destroying the entity with fire. Where a giant *thing* made of wood, cloth, and metal had stood moments before, there now floated a creature of similar proportions made entirely of shadow and smoke. Thankfully, it seemed to want nothing to do with me, and I watched as it transformed into an inky flock of blackbirds that fluttered up into the shadows above.

"Uh-uh, you're not getting away that easily. Justice must be served and shit."

The shrill cacophony of an entire flock of ravens was the nachtkrapp's only reply to my threats.

I wove a quick pattern in the air with my free hand, matching the final stroke of the gesture with a command word. A brilliant ball of white light sprang from my hand toward the ceiling, where it stuck like the spit wads I used to shoot in my high school economics class. I covered my eyes with my arm just before the glowing orb flashed, releasing about 1,000 lumens of magical light into the room.

As the deepest and darkest corners of the ceiling above were bathed in brilliant white light, a shadowy flock of a hundred cawing blackbirds coalesced at the farthest end of the building. The shadow creature burst into action as the lot of them fluttered to and fro overhead, first heading for one open window and then the next. Each time the night raven tried to escape the building, blue light flared in front of it as the wards I'd set triggered in response to the creature's magic.

"I hate to tell you this, Big Bird, but you're locked in here with me." I paused as the cloud of bird-shaped shadows retreated as far away from my light orb as possible. "If you'll just tell me where the kids are, then maybe I'll end your miserable existence peacefully. But if you decide to drag this thing on, it won't go well for you."

In the far corner where the flock of shadow birds had retreated, they flapped about in a swirling, panicked mass of darkness. Soon, that shadowy mass spread into the room, a living cloud of black fog that fought against my illumination spell. The darkness pushed the light back like surf crashing against a shoreline, and soon the inky dimness reached the light orb I'd cast.

As the opposing magics touched, the nachtkrapp's magic

engulfed my own, leaving me as blind as Stevie Wonder in a vampire's casket.

"Aw, hell," I muttered, blinking and rubbing my eyes.

I spun in place, swinging my sword in random circles in a near panic as I felt the night raven's fear magic exerting its effects once more. Before the terror could take hold again my amulet flared, the wards responding to the influence of the night raven's fear spell. As the fear subsided, I quickly assessed the situation.

Besting the monster here and now was my chief and foremost concern. If I was forced to retreat, I'd necessarily have to break my containment wards as I exited the building, and that would allow the nachtkrapp to escape. Moreover, I was fighting a creature of a non-corporeal nature, which meant that my usual brute force approach was useless against it. With that in mind, I reviewed what limited options I had for either capturing or destroying the creature.

Option one, burn it. Tried and failed.

Option two, trap it with magic. Did that, and now I was stuck inside a creepy old warehouse with a creature made of shadow that radiated fear like a dead skunk put out stink. Not a complete fail—but not a solution, either.

Option three, figure out what hurts it and hit it with lots of that. That sounded like as good a plan as any. Considering that it was my only option as well, I decided to run with it.

So, Colin... fight fire with fire? Nope. *Fight shadow with light.*

I took a knee, holding the sword above me as I willed it to ignite. Once I had the sword's flame and light between me and my enemy, I extended my senses to locate what remained of my illumination spell. I was somewhat surprised to discover the spell was still active, but unfortunately it was quickly being smothered by the night raven's shadow magic. Soon, it would be extinguished completely, and I'd only prepared one such spell before heading out this evening.

Obviously, that meant I couldn't let the spell go out... but how was I supposed to bolster it? Druids worked with what they had on hand, namely ingredients and components taken from nature, along with the natural elements themselves. What I needed was more light, enough to turbocharge my little spell.

But as for light sources, I'd come woefully ill-prepared. I had a pocket flashlight somewhere, but I doubted the light it generated would do much to cancel out the nachtkrapp's powers. Same for my phone, and as for the sword right now, it was barely enough light to keep the night raven at bay.

Extending my senses further, I felt electricity humming through the building's wiring. But in order to light the place up I'd need to find and flip the light switch. Even I couldn't trace the wiring and jump an electrical circuit—at least, not in the little time I had before my spell faltered for good. And sure, there were street lamps here and there in the city, but it still wasn't enough to make a difference.

The only other light source was the ambient light outside cast by the moon and stars above. I thought about it—could that work? Sure, the light seemed faint, but that was only compared to the sunlight we humans craved. The fact was, there was an incredible amount of light hitting the earth at night, but it was so spread out as to appear quite dim.

Could I gather the light waves hitting the area around the warehouse? If so, maybe I could compress and focus them all through my spell.

Worth a shot.

It was either that or turn tail and run, which meant setting this thing loose to kill again. And that simply wasn't going to happen... not on my watch.

TWO

Slowing my breathing, I reached out with my mind beyond the walls of the warehouse. Formerly, I'd have needed to enter a druid trance to do this, but I'd been practicing a lot lately and could do it now without going under. Tuning into the light cast by the moon and stars, I focused on the area within a block or so around the building, which was about as far as my awareness could reach.

Once I was in tune with the light outside, I *pulled* on it, gathering it together by using my magic and force of will as a funnel. I wasn't actually refracting the light, but drawing its energy to me—like a magnet pulling iron filings to itself. As I collected every last bit of natural light over a roughly fifty-acre area, I felt the nachtkrapp's magic and presence closing in on me.

Mind taut and nerves frayed by my predicament, I strained against the forces of nature, struggling to force the light into a beam that I intended to focus on the building's roof—just above my little dying illumination spell. Perspiration broke out on my brow, and my muscles began to shake with tension and fatigue. Who knew that capturing moonlight could be so taxing?

Just when I thought I had it, the shadowy presence above pushed down against me like a giant hand, breaking my concentration. I cracked an eyelid and saw that darkness had gathered all around me, a black mass closing in on the sword's flame and light until it began to flicker and diminish. When it went out, I knew the nachtkrapp's fear magic would shatter my wards and fill me with enough fright to stop my heart. Or, it would fill my lungs with shadows made real and smother me, something I'd seen the wizard Crowley do once with his own shadow magic.

Either death was just as gruesome—and absolutely within the creature's purview, based on what I'd experienced of its power thus far. It was ancient and evil, and I'd come against it ill-prepared. If I couldn't stop it now, I might well and truly meet my end at the nachtkrapp's hands... or talons, as it were.

Lacking a better plan, I shut my eyes tight and focused on channeling all the light I'd gathered into one thin, silvery beam. I shuddered to think of what any bystanders might be witnessing at the moment; to them, it might look as though aliens were beaming someone up. Or, in this deeply religious town, the locals might think they were witnessing a heavenly visitation. No matter what unwanted attention my spell had gathered, I could deal with that later. Right now, I had an evil shadow spirit to kill.

The more I concentrated my will on focusing that beam of light, the more I sensed heat building on the tin roof of the warehouse. Finally, I heard a *whoosh* as the tiny beam of moon and starlight vaporized a small section of corrugated metal above my illumination spell. As the light I'd gathered hit my spell it was absorbed into it, and although I couldn't see it, I felt the orb expand against the thick dark mass above.

A loud screeching noise emanated from the cloud of shadow around me, then light from my spell broke through the dark mass like rays of sunlight breaking through heavy cloud cover.

My magic continued to burst through the cloak of darkness cast by the nachtkrapp's spell, and the light spread outward as it slowly chased the inky magic from the room. All the while, a hideous screeching and cawing echoed off the walls, fading out as the shadows dispersed.

Once my light spell had banished the gloom, it was easier to keep it running. I kept pouring energy into it until it filled the warehouse with a light so intense I had to shield my eyes from the glare. After my eyes adjusted to the radiant glow coming from above, I searched the room for the night raven.

Honestly, I had no idea if the supercharged light spell had killed it or if it had found someplace to hide. I did another circuit of the room, just as I'd done when I first entered the place. The faint sound of rustling feathers led me to a dilapidated divan, way off in an alcove between a china cabinet and an armoire where the light wasn't quite as strong.

Wary of another piece of junk furniture that might come to life, I approached the divan with caution, prodding it with the sword's tip at arm's length. When nothing happened, I knelt down to peer underneath the sofa. There below, nestled behind a bit of torn silk lining that hung off the bottom of the couch, sat what remained of the nachtkrapp.

Although still of an intimidating size, perhaps twenty inches from beak to claw, it was a pathetic-looking thing now that its magic had been negated and it had become fully corporeal. The thing was damned disheveled with its empty eye sockets, molting feathers, and diseased-looking skin on its feet and legs. It was funny how even the most terrifying monsters could be reduced to a sniveling heap once you took away their magic.

I reached for it, managing to grab it by the neck only after it had pecked a bleeding hole in the back of my hand. I squeezed tightly as I pulled it out, both as payback for the wound and to ensure it didn't get loose. I was exhausted, and in no mood to play hide and seek with this thing all night.

The nachtkrapp cracked its beak and spoke. "*Squawk!* The light, *jaeger*, the light... put it out, put it out, put it out!"

The bird's accent reminded me a bit of a parrot imitating Colonel Klink, and I had to make an effort to maintain a stoic demeanor as I replied. "'It burns us,' eh? Tell me why I shouldn't haul you over to that spell and stick your head in it until it turns you to ash."

The night raven flapped his wings and struggled against my grasp, to no avail. Finally, he settled down and turned one of those empty eye sockets on me.

"Because, *jaeger*—then you'll never find out where the children are. That is why you came, is it not? To save the little ones, yes?"

I rolled my eyes. "My patience with you wore thin about ten minutes ago, when I smelled a dead body under this building. You mean to tell me that's not a kid?"

"No rotting children—no, none at all. Only me, is what your nose detected."

I squeezed even harder. "You lie."

The raven shook his head. "*Squawk!* No, I would not lie. Just as the fae are bound, so are my kind compelled to only speak the truth. The children live, *jaeger*. And I will lead you to them, if you spare me."

"Nope, no deal. If they're really alive, I'll find them." I plucked a single, oily feather from the bird's wing, tucking it inside my Craneskin Bag. "Wherever you have those kids hidden, that feather will lead me to them with a little magic. Your time has run out, I'm afraid."

"A divination, then! A portent! One that speaks of *your* future, and that of those you love. Dark days lie ahead for you, *jaeger*, dark days. Allow me to share what I know, and if you deem it worth one small, miserable bird's life, then you'll spare me. Agreed?"

ALTHOUGH COMMON SENSE told me to just kill the damned thing, instead I considered his offer. Typically, supernatural creatures didn't rattle off prophecies lightly. For one, entities that could divine *probable* futures had to expend a lot of energy to do so, which in itself was reason for most to avoid it.

Also, divination required the fortune teller to astrally project down various paths of probability, a dangerous proposition by any measure. I knew little about it, but from what I understood, even the most powerful beings could become lost while casting a divination. And if gone too long, their physical body would wither away while their astral selves would be left to wander the endless bifurcations of the twisted paths for all eternity.

If this creature was offering to tell my future—or at least, my probable future—he was desperate indeed. To be honest, his desperation couldn't have come at a better time. I had a lot on my mind at the moment—questions that needed to be answered. Terrible and unusual things had happened recently, events that had made me doubt decisions and feelings I'd once considered a done deal.

For one, my Uncle Ed had been murdered by Cold Iron Circle operatives, and at least one responsible party was still at large. I'd dealt with the actual killers when I'd taken out the Circle bigwig whose team had carried the murder out. And although I'd gotten retribution against Commander Gunnarson and his followers, I still longed to confront the person who'd given the order—Gunnarson's anonymous benefactor on the Circle's High Council—to bring them to justice. Weeks later, I was still reeling from the loss, and thoughts of revenge weighed heavily on my mind.

Second on my list of Things That Were Giving Me Ulcers was my recent appointment as druid justiciar, a kind of supernatural Texas Ranger with the same sort of wide-reaching jurisdiction and authority. And while that appointment was supposed to have simplified my life considerably, instead it had complicated it immensely. Granted, the various supernatural factions and players in the Austin area no longer had the authority to push me around. But despite my change in status, I still found myself doing their bidding as they turned to me to solve various supernatural problems and interspecies squabbles. In short, I'd become more of an enforcer than an investigator, and I wanted to make that stop.

Last but not least, my deceased ex-girlfriend Jesse had shown up again—and I wasn't talking about her ghost. No, she'd found a way to come back from the dead, in a real life, flesh and blood version of her old self.

Flesh and blood—now that was a funny term. It didn't quite describe her current state, but the fact remained there *was* a walking, talking facsimile of my dead ex back at the junkyard, and I had no idea how to deal with her—or rather, *it.* I'd been loath to speak with Finnegas about the situation, because I knew he'd hit the roof if he found out. Or, worse, he'd ask to see her and get used to her presence all over again.

That would be a problem, considering I was pretty sure I was going to have to banish her at some point.

Oh, joy.

To say I was confused by recent events was an understatement. And while I didn't trust the nachtkrapp, I wasn't about to look a gift-raven in the mouth.

I extinguished the sword's blade, laying it across my other wrist, near the raven's throat. Despite having been on fire for most of the last ten minutes, the metal was strangely cool to the touch—a unique property of the magic it held. One of these days, I'd need to figure out where it came from and what it was all about. But that was a puzzle that could wait for another day.

"First, your name. And if you even think about saying 'nevermore,' I swear I'll end you."

"*Namenlos*," the night raven answered with a cackle.

I slid the blade against the night raven's throat and looked directly into his dead, empty eye socket. "Nameless? You are seriously trying my patience, raven!"

The bird flapped his wings frantically. "I do not lie! *Namenlos* is my name—all my brethren were given ambiguous names by our maker. I swear it!"

Names were power, and the foul entity that had birthed these creatures knew it. Giving them slippery names was a definite "fuck you" to any magicians who might wish to bind them into service—or banish them into eternity. I'd intended to use the thing's name to cast a compulsion on it, but it looked like I'd have to do things the old-fashioned way.

"I'll not kill you, but only if you agree to three stipulations. You'll speak the truth of my divination, plain and simple. You'll cast no curse or spell in the telling. And, you'll also lead me to all the children you abducted during the last seven days. Do these things and I'll spare your life. Agreed?"

"Agreed!" the night raven replied. "Ready yourself, *jaeger*. I have three tellings for you, no more, no less."

"Just get on with it," I muttered as I placed the sword inside my Craneskin Bag.

THE RAVEN KIND of half-squawked and half-cawed, a noise that I assumed was meant to clear his throat. I'd have already killed the annoying little shit if I didn't think he was telling the truth about the kids. I doubted that destroying his physical body would end his life completely, but it would at least banish him from the mortal realm for a century or two. My foot tapped an impatient rhythm as the bird shook himself, unruffling his feathers despite the fact that I still held him by the throat.

Then, he spoke.

"The first telling: Beauty binds and beauty blinds, when beauty clashes, old bonds die. After winter spring will rise, the truth revealed in serpent's eyes."

I frowned and scratched my head. "Well, that's sort of obvious, except for the last part. If Bells finds out about Jesse, I'll be in a world of hurt—and there's no doubt those two will clash. But what's this shit about snake eyes? You'd best do better than that with the next two tellings, raven."

The bird squirmed a bit in my hand. "Perhaps if you loosened your grip? It is difficult to concentrate while being throttled by a bipedal moose like yourself."

"I don't think so. Speak."

The bird cleared his throat again with a weak little squawk. "The second telling: Weed killer."

I knuckled my forehead, trying hard to keep myself from snapping the bird's neck. "'Weed killer'? Are you serious? What the hell kind of divination is that?"

The raven cocked his head to the side. "I can only share what I see—it's up to you to determine the meaning behind the words I speak."

"Fine... but this last one better be good."

"The third telling: Three ravens you must face, two in battle, the third in chase. Something precious will you lose, but what is lost you will choose."

I sighed. "I take it you're one of those three ravens?"

If a raven could shrug, this one did. "That is rather obvious, is it not?"

"I don't suppose you'd care to elaborate on when and where I'm supposed to meet with these other two ravens? Considering that they'll probably be buddies of yours?"

Nameless twitched his tail feathers. "Just because I'm a supernatural creature who takes the form of a raven, that doesn't mean I know every magical bird on this plane of existence. Not to mention consorting with them. It's not like I fly around with an entire conspiracy of my kind—birds of a feather do not always flock together, *jaeger*."

"A conspiracy—that's what they call a flock of ravens, right? Fitting, all things considered." The bird eyed me, or at least I thought it did, what with the empty eye sockets and all. "Well, you've proven yourself to be damned useless, so now I have to figure out what to do with you."

"Release me!" he cawed in an avian imitation of Werner Klemperer. "We had a deal."

I rustled around in my Bag, looking for something I could use to detain the bird temporarily. No way was I going to turn him loose, uh-uh. "You still have to lead me to the children, remember? And I only promised to spare your life—I didn't say a damned thing about letting you go."

"Trickster! Liar! Deceiver, perjurer, prevaricator, pseudologue!"

"Alright, Mr. Thesaurus. I've had about enough of you."

I pulled out the silver thumbcuffs I'd been looking for, snapping one side around the bird's neck. I squeezed the cuff shut, narrowing the opening click by click until I was certain the bird couldn't slip out. Then, I pulled out a permanent marker and etched a few symbols on the surface for good measure, a spell to keep the creature bound. Finally, I taped his beak shut and pinned his wings to his side with electrical tape, tying a length of paracord to the other end of the thumbcuffs as a makeshift leash.

"There. Now, where did you leave those kids again?"

The night raven responded with something like, "Mrfle, wrfle blrfle yrfle erfle."

I ripped the tape off his beak. "What was that?"

"I said, 'My, what a bastard you are.'" I reached out to wrap his beak again. "Stop! I promise I'll not insult you anymore... today, at least. Besides, I need to vocalize in order to lead you to my secret roost."

The sound of sirens echoed in the distance, bringing me to my senses—cops would be here soon. I looked around the warehouse at the mess we'd made. There was a hole in the roof, the chair that had bound the raven had been reduced to a few smoldering pieces, other furniture had been smashed, and the floor where we'd fought had deep, ragged scratches several feet long, and a few scorch marks as well.

I might be able to hide my weapons and other contraband I carried inside my Craneskin Bag, but I had no idea how I was going to explain the damage to the place—never mind the raven.

"At least I didn't burn it down," I muttered.

"There is that," Nameless replied.

"Bird, do you have any magic that can hide us while we get out of here?" I asked.

The nachtkrapp cawed softly. "I suppose I can scrape together a few shreds of shadow to conceal our departure."

"Alright then, let's boogie—just as soon as I grab a lemon bar from that case." I dashed over to the counter with the bird tucked under my arm and grabbed two for good measure. I slid them into a paper sack I pulled off the counter, slapping a tenner down on the counter and securing it with a coffee cup.

"You aren't going to pay for the damages?" the raven asked. I arched an eyebrow at the mangy bird, and he squawked. "I may be a lot of things, but I'm no vandal."

"Great, a bogeyman with a sense of honor. Go figure. Just get us out of here without being seen—I'll send someone to clean up, once the cops have left."

"Your wish is my command," Nameless said.

"If only," I muttered. Shadows filtered up from between the floorboards, wrapping us in sufficient darkness to conceal our movements. Once the raven had draped us in shadow, I ducked out the back door, slipping away unseen by human eyes.

THREE

Nameless had tucked the kids away in a long-forgotten cellar, hiding them from prying eyes underneath one of the historic buildings at Fort Martin Scott. To access it, I had to drop into the old well on the property and swim down a hidden passage that led to the underground chamber. Not trusting my makeshift collar enough to leave the night raven unattended, I held on to the nachtkrapp as I made my descent.

The bird was none too pleased that I'd dragged him along. After we'd emerged from the water into a small cavern, he fussed endlessly about his damp feathers until I taped his beak shut again. I had no idea how the creature had accessed the space without getting wet before, and suspected there was another way to access the room that didn't involve water. My suspicions were proven true upon finding the children safe and sound, just where the raven had left them.

Although the kids nearly had a fit when I showed up—sopping wet, with a mangy old raven tucked under my arm—I eventually convinced them I was there to help. An adjacent tunnel exited at the far reaches of the property, and once I'd gained their trust, the raven's abductees were more than happy to point it out to me. After removing the barrier spell Nameless had used to keep the kids in, I ushered them outside.

As we headed back to the parking lot, I assured the children that yes, the raven I carried was the same one that abducted them, and yes, I'd rendered him harmless. I even allowed them to take turns throwing stones at him. It was the least I could do, considering what the nachtkrapp had intended for them.

Besides, they wouldn't remember much of anything about their ordeal—the liaison Maeve had assigned me would make sure of it. I had called Sabine and asked her to meet us at the fort, which was blessedly dark and deserted at three in the morning. She'd been dispatched by Maeve to assist me earlier, but considering our recent history, I'd decided to wait until it was absolutely necessary before summoning her to my location.

I had the children stay by my car while I walked out to greet her; they didn't need to hear what Sabine and I were about to discuss. The night raven was inside the vehicle, tied to the seat and safely restrained by lots of paracord and the wards I'd placed on the Gremlin. That which was designed to keep things out could also keep things in, I'd found. I glanced back to make sure the children were okay, verifying they were with a snort. The two of them were taking turns poking the bird with a stick through the partially rolled-down window, and even with his beak taped shut, Nameless was making quite a fuss.

After the employees at the junkyard had surprised me by fixing my car, it had taken me a week of all-nighters to replace the spell work on the little street rod. Apparently, my newly-inherited staff wanted to express how grateful they were that I hadn't sold the junkyard after Uncle Ed's passing. Thus the extensive body work on my main set of wheels, which I'd wrecked during the whole shit-show with Commander Gunnarson.

Of course, I couldn't tell them they'd sanded down and

painted over about a hundred hours of spell work when they'd repaired the vehicle. And I wouldn't have had the heart to tell them, even if I could reveal such secrets. Despite having to replace all my wards, I was still incredibly happy to have my Gremlin back. When people did things like that for you, you just accepted it as-is, with no fuss and all the graciousness you could muster.

My life might have been a hot mess at the moment, but I was still carrying on my uncle's legacy. That much was right in the world, at least.

Minutes passed before Sabine pulled up in a late model Toyota, a nondescript sedan with stock wheels and boring silver paint. It was the type of car that could blend in and be instantly forgotten, even without the use of magic. The fact that she'd placed a look away spell on it meant that nobody but an adept would notice her driving by. Smart.

I nodded at her as she got out of the car. "Sabine."

"Druid." She glanced at me, stone-faced, then peered over my shoulder at the kids and the highly-agitated raven tied to the headrest in the passenger seat of the Gremlin. "I see you managed to retrieve the children unharmed. Will they need to be mind-wiped?"

Before responding, I took a moment to assess the differences I saw in the half-fae girl who stood before me. Something had changed in her during our trip to Underhill. She'd become more confident and self-assured, leaving her former self-conscious-ness in the dust. Where the old Sabine would have stood with eyes downcast and shoulders slumped, avoiding eye contact while hiding behind appearance-altering magic, this new version of my estranged friend was no shrinking violet.

The girl had always been a supernatural beauty, but before she'd hidden her allure with magic because she was self-conscious about how she looked. She was basically a blonde

Christina Hendricks, but prettier due to her fae heritage. When I'd first met her, she'd concealed her figure under loose clothing and a reverse glamour spell. Yet this new Sabine was obviously proud of her looks, that much was clear.

As I quickly took the new Sabine in, her stance was pure confidence—shoulders back, head up, and eyes fixed on mine, as if she were challenging me to make a comment. Her hair had been cut and styled into a severe but flattering bob à la Taylor Swift, which framed her heart-shaped face and sapphire-blue eyes nicely. She wore knee-high riding boots with tights, a lacy tunic dress that hit mid-thigh, and a short leather jacket. Even with minimal makeup, her beauty was on full display. She was stunning.

Were we on better terms I'd have complimented her, but considering our currently strained relationship, I was afraid she'd take it the wrong way. So instead, I chose to focus on the mission.

"Yes, both of them. It was a creature of shadow that took them, one that uses fear magic to subdue its victims. I nearly succumbed to it, actually—"

Sabine cut me off mid-sentence, her voice flat as she responded. "I'll take care of the children and get them back to their families. I already cleaned up the mess back at the antique shop as well. You'll want to contact Maeve to let her know the job is done. As I understand it, the factions must each pay you a stipend for your services, and the queen wants to know her money isn't being wasted."

"How did you—?"

"I followed the police sirens. You've always been anything but subtle, druid." She glanced at the children, who were hard at work sharpening their stick on a flat stone. "I need to attend to the children. Nightmare creatures have a way of turning good people to evil, and the influence gets stronger the longer they're in the creature's presence. You should leave, and take that thing with you."

She walked off without giving me a second glance, her Coach boots crunching the gravel underfoot. I opened my mouth to say something, anything, then I stopped myself. What would I say that hadn't already been said? First, I'd unintentionally broken her heart, although she was too proud to admit it. Then, I'd betrayed her queen and potentially doomed her race to extinction by cutting off their connection to Underhill. All things considered, I really didn't blame her for hating me.

Still, I had to try. I called out to her, willing as much contrition into my voice as possible. "Sabine, wait."

She paused and raised her right hand, looking over her shoulder without actually making eye contact. "Please, druid. I may have to work with you, but I don't have to like it. And we certainly don't need to be friends to accomplish whatever tasks Maeve requests of you. Save your apologies for someone who cares."

I exhaled heavily. "If it's what you want, then I'll keep things on a professional level between us."

Sabine nodded once, then she approached the children, kneeling as she explained that she was there to take them back to their parents. She radiated a different kind of glamour as she spoke, one that enhanced her beauty and instilled trust. Once the children had relaxed, she wove a spell over each of them, erasing all memory of the past few days and putting them into a deep, restful sleep. I helped her carry the children to her car, strapping them into the back seat. Then, I watched as she hopped in the front seat without a word and drove off into the night.

THERE WAS no way I was going to report to Maeve in person. I'd done her bidding for long enough, back before I'd gotten this ambiguous title and all the dubious responsibilities that came with it. Besides, my last visit to her home had been less than cordial, and I wasn't in the mood to tangle with her pet assassins, Eliandres and Lucindras. I was dead tired, and taking on a couple of high fae stone killers was just not on the menu for the evening.

So, I sent a message to her through "channels," as she liked to call them. Meaning, I dialed up some stupid answering service she'd set up and left a message with them. *Tell Maeve it's been handled. Click.* Fuck you, Maeve.

When I got back to the junkyard I crashed hard, but woke up a few hours later due to the noise the morning crew made. Growling in frustration, I pulled a pillow over my head, then eventually I gave in to the inevitable and opened my eyes. Although being woken up by an air chisel at nine in the morning was annoying, the shop sounds were also comforting to me. The staccato rattling of an air wrench, the hiss of a cutting torch, the clang of a hundred-pound chrome bumper hitting the shop floor—it was all routine, and routine was what I needed right now.

Still, the hardest part of my day was walking into the office and not seeing Ed there.

May as well face it. I rolled out of bed, dressed in jeans, a t-shirt, and boots, and headed to the restroom to wash my face and brush my teeth. Once my daily ablutions were done I headed for the office, stopping along the way to say hello to the morning crew. Ed had always made a habit of greeting everyone by name, no matter how new they were. I felt obligated to do the same.

It took an effort, though, because lately I'd been feeling angrier than usual. At first, I'd chalked it up to my uncle's murder and the senseless killing of Elmo, the world's gentlest ogre. But considering the intensity of my mood swings, I couldn't help but wonder if there was something else going on.

Once I'd checked in on the staff, I headed to the office. Before I walked in I paused for a second, just as I always did lately, bracing myself for Ed's absence. I let out a deep breath as I opened the door. If I hadn't known any better, I'd have said my uncle *hadn't* been shot down here just weeks before. The bullet holes in the walls had been expertly patched, the blood stains magically removed, and the damaged furniture repaired or replaced. Most of that was Maureen's doing, half-fae angel that she was—or angel of death, some might say.

She was sitting behind Ed's desk, working on the accounts or something. I had no idea how to run a business, so Maureen had agreed to work on our books and manage the office until I could find someone trustworthy to handle it.

"Morning, Maureen."

The half-kelpie handed me a steaming cup of coffee in a to-go cup without looking away from the computer monitor in front of her. "Books have been balanced, but it looks like you'll be short on payroll Friday, unless you can move some of your used inventory. Oh, and there's a shadow creature taped and tied to your front seat. The thing shat all over your upholstery, by the way."

"Shit!"

Maureen brushed a strand of fiery red hair behind her ear. "S'what I said. Hope you weren't attached to those bucket seats. What I can't understand is why you didn't kill the thing and banish it back across the Veil in the first place. Something I should know?"

I took a long pull off the coffee; it was hot and sweet, just how I liked it. How Maureen managed to have a hot cup waiting every day was a mystery to me. I suspected she either kept it warm for me by magical means or conjured it on the spot. Either way, it was a welcome gesture.

"Good coffee."

She kept typing away at the keyboard while she spoke. "And again, don't mention it. Yer bound ta' slip one of these days and thank me for it, and where would that leave us?" She stopped to pencil a note on the desk blotter in front of her. "Now, what's the story with the raven?"

"I sort of made a deal with the thing—its life, in exchange for a divination." I winced when I said it, expecting an ass-chewing.

Maureen kept typing, but she glanced at me briefly with those emerald green eyes. "Ya damn well know better than that, Colin McCool. Hope it was worth it."

"That's to be determined."

She crossed her arms and swiveled her chair to face me. "And what do you propose to do with it, now that you've agreed to spare the damned thing? Ya sure can't leave it taped to the front seat of that car, that's fer sure. Lucky I showed up early today, in time to cast a glamour on it ta' hide it from the morning crew."

"Yeah, I was bushed last night when I got in and sort of forgot about it."

"So, where will you keep it? Ya' can't just let it go, and it's yer responsibility now."

"I was kind of thinking about leaving it inside the tree," I said with a sheepish grin and a half-shrug.

Maureen chewed her lip. "Well, it's as good a solution as any, but you still haven't dealt with that situation, either. The girl needs to be banished, Colin. She died, and it ain't natural, her coming back in another form."

"I know, and I'll deal with it. I just have a lot on my mind right now."

Maureen harrumphed loudly. "Oh, woe is me! Lad, do ya'

think yer the only one who ever lost someone? Try living a few centuries, and then come crying to me." Her expression softened a bit, perhaps because I glanced down at Ed's chair. "Ah, I know it's hard, but life goes on. You need ta' suck it up, because your problems are only going ta' get worse while yer busy crying in yer panties."

I started to get pissy, but had to laugh. "Oh, Maureen—how I've missed these little pep talks."

"If you think I'm mean, you should've seen the Seer back in his heyday. My, but that man could scream." She smiled and winked at me. "Give it time, lad, and yer heart will heal. Now, I suggest you go take care of that foul creature—and spend some time thinking on how to deal with yer recently resurrected ex while yer at it."

WHEN I OPENED the door to retrieve Nameless from the car, it was worse than Maureen had indicated. White, green, and brown goopy shit was all over the passenger seat, and the smell was just plain hideous—like urine and rotten eggs.

My eyes did a quick sweep of our parking lot to make certain none of the employees or customers were around. Once I was assured of privacy, I cut the bird loose with my hunting knife, rousing him from his sleep as I grabbed him by the neck and ripped the tape from his beak.

"*Squawk!* Is it necessary to be so rough, *jaeger*? I am captured and completely at your disposal, am I not?"

"First off, I might be impulsive, but I'm not stupid enough to think you're not going to try to escape or double-cross me. Second, you're cleaning this up. Now."

The bird flapped his wings in protest, then stilled his movements—whether as a sign of resignation or exhaustion, I couldn't be sure. The damned thing looked even more haggard than he had the night previous. Nameless still had the spine to glare at me, however, at least as much as he could glare with those eyeless sockets he had.

"Fine!" he squawked. "But you can't blame me for the mess. Birds have short alimentary tracts, you know, and since we can't chew our food we rely on digestive juices to do the job. Thus, the constant need to defecate."

I squeezed the bird by his neck. "If I want a zoology lesson, I'll watch Jeff Corwin. I only promised to spare your life, Nameless, so clean my seat now or I break something."

The nachtkrapp complied without further comment, and smoky tendrils of shadow oozed out of him. The raven's magic swept the inside of my vehicle like the tentacles of an octopus, reminding me of my part-time ally and full-time frenemy, the wizard Crowley. *He practices shadow magic,* I thought. *Wonder if he'd be willing to take this crap machine off my hands.*

Moments later, the car was clean—if still a little smelly. "Disguise yourself," I muttered under my breath as a car pulled up in the lot. I sensed a spell being cast, and before my eyes the raven transformed himself into a large, plump rooster.

Now I have to explain to everyone why I'm bringing live-stock into the yard. Fan-fucking-tastic. I wasn't about to give Nameless the benefit of knowing he was getting under my skin, so I remained silent as I marched his tattered ass to the druid tree.

Under any other circumstances, the sudden appearance of a thirty-meter-tall oak tree in the middle of a junkyard might have raised a few eyebrows. Apparently, however, when you planted a druid grove it came with its own built-in magical stealth system. Not that the tree was invisible—far from it. Strangely, from the moment it had sprung into existence, everyone who came in viewing range of it simply ignored it, or acted as if it had always been there.

Everyone but me, that is, and a few select confidantes of mine. How the tree knew who was kosher and who wasn't remained a complete mystery. But that wasn't the weirdest part about it; the really strange thing about the giant oak tree was what it concealed.

The tree itself was a good ten feet in diameter at the base, with limbs that spread far out from its center and up to the sky above. Where once there had been stacks of cars twelve feet high, the area where I'd planted the Dagda's acorn was now a grassy open space some fifty feet across. The tree had simply swallowed the cars up as it grew, sucking them into the soil beneath it where its roots could slowly break down the iron and other metals, returning them to the earth.

To access the grove, I walked three circuits of the oak's trunk, widdershins, with my left hand in constant contact with its rough bark. As soon as I started the ritual required to enter the grove, the raven went batshit crazy. Apparently, shadow creatures wanted nothing to do with druid groves.

"*Squawk!* Don't take me in there, *jaeger*, I beg of you. Better for you to send me back across the Veil. Whatever you ask, I'll give it to you—just don't make me go to that place!"

I squeezed his neck until he stilled, then I ignored him. I'd instinctively known how to access the grove from the moment the acorn had sprouted, and just as instinctively I knew that losing my concentration during the ritual could have disastrous consequences. On the third loop, the world around me changed completely as I rounded the trunk a final time.

One moment I was in a junkyard, and the next I stood in a sunny wooded grove. Light shone through the leaves above, dappling the loamy forest floor below, and insects, birds, and small animals frittered, flitted, and fluttered about, oblivious to my presence. The druid tree was at the center of the space, and the whole damned thing looked like a Disney movie. The overall effect kind of creeped me out, because it was too perfect, and it reminded me a bit of Underhill. Pretty, until you looked beneath the surface.

But the worst was yet to come.

"Hi, Colin."

It was her voice, but it wasn't, as some quality about it had changed. That voice had never been so mellifluous; she'd always been a bit of a tomboy, with a slightly raspy voice to match. I turned around, suddenly forgetting the night raven that squirmed and flapped in my right hand.

"Hello, Jesse."

FOUR

She was leaning out from behind a maple tree, her lower body half-hidden by the trunk. Or at least, a facsimile of her. While the thing in front of me resembled Jesse and spoke like Jesse, I wasn't convinced that it *was* Jesse. Not my Jesse, not by a long shot.

Her skin was smooth as silk in some places, rough and bark-like in others—but somehow it worked, making her even more beautiful than she had been in her human life. The flowing mane adorning her head was a living thing made of green, leafy vines and small red leaves that rustled and swayed with every movement and toss of her head. And her eyes—oh, those eyes. Shiny, dark orbs pierced me, each of such a deep hue of green as to be hypnotizing if I stared at them too long.

Jesse's body was very nearly the same as ever, if of varying colors and textures. Her face, neck, and shoulders were a pale, earthy green, fading to brown and grey over the random, symmetrical patches of bark that covered her skin here and there. Her figure was as lean and athletic as she'd been in life, but she now moved with a playful sinuousness that *my* Jesse had never possessed. And, in a strange show of modesty for a dryad

—because that's what she was—a thick growth of leaves covered her breasts and pelvic area, in a manner reminiscent of Poison Ivy from the Batman comics.

Just as on my previous visits to the druid grove, her presence brought an entire range of emotions with it. Elation, trepidation, guilt, nervousness, impatience, and most of all, a sickening feeling deep in my gut that her presence was just *wrong* at the most basic level.

"You came back," she said. The strange, harmonious layers of her voice put me on edge, but I tried not to show it. "Were you gone long?"

Jesse had no way to tell time inside this place, this eldritch pocket dimension created by Tuatha magic. It was convenient for me at least, because it meant I didn't have to explain my absences.

"Not long," I lied. "Jesse, I need a favor."

"Ask, my love," she said with a toothy, slightly unsettling smile.

"I need somewhere to keep this bird—someplace safe."

She looked down at the nachtkrapp with a sneer. He was now making a soft crying noise, like the sound of a baby wailing in the distance.

"I could kill it for you—shall I kill it? It doesn't belong here, you know. This place is life personified." She gestured lazily at the night raven. "Its kind knows only death."

That was one of the reasons why I was so concerned about the new incarnation of my ex. From the moment I'd found her wandering the grove, she'd demonstrated a fickle, mercurial side that the real Jesse had never possessed. It was an alien characteristic that reminded me way too much of the fae, and out of all the idiosyncrasies she possessed, it creeped me out the most.

"No, Jess, I can't kill it, and I can't let it go. I need a place to keep it, something that will prevent its escape. Can you do that for me?"

Jesse's eyes sparkled, and a smile played across her smooth brown lips. "Of course I can. As I've told you before, I'm your helpmate now, Colin—it's what I was created for. Or, at least, it's what this body was meant to do. And as I am bound to it now, I'm bound to you. The master of the grove commands and the spirit obeys, always."

A small tree sprang from the ground a few feet from me, and its branches wove themselves into the rough approximation of a large bird cage. I didn't see a door, but one look at Jesse's face told me I didn't need one. Experimentally, I extended my hand toward the cage. Its branches spread apart of their own accord, leaving enough space for me to deposit Nameless inside.

The bird remained on his side where I placed him at the bottom of the cage, cradled in the notch made at the point where all the branches split. At first I thought he was dead, but then he lifted his head slightly to speak.

"You've doomed me, *jaeger*," the bird croaked. Then, he laid his head down and was still.

Jesse whispered in my ear, "It won't die here, but it won't live, either."

I jumped slightly, not expecting her to be standing next to me. Early on, I'd found she could make herself appear and disappear anywhere within the grove. I'd also discovered she had a habit of popping up out of nowhere, right at my elbow in most cases.

"Damn it, I told you to stop doing that!" I said as I took a step away from her.

Jesse looked hurt, but I couldn't tell if it was a ruse or a real emotion. I had the sneaking suspicion that she didn't feel emotions the same way I did anymore. Either the time she'd spent as a ghost had changed her, or the process of possessing the dryad had. I couldn't be certain of the cause, but she was defective, that much was clear.

Jesse hung her head and gave me a wicked look beneath her hooded eyes. "You're unhappy that I returned. It's that other girl, isn't it? I can make her go away—then we'll be happy together, you'll see."

"No, Jesse. That's not what I want."

"You don't want me?" She moved toward me, hips swaying, eyes hungry. Her scent was intoxicating—a combination of jasmine, forest loam, and musk. I suspected she was releasing pheromones without even realizing it.

I stood there, paralyzed between disgust and desire. Jesse laid her palm on my chest, over my heart, and I felt her skin warm at the contact.

"I... I don't know what I want, Jesse. Just give me time."

"Your heart is pounding." She looked up at me. Those unnatural, deep-green doe eyes were like spring-fed woodland ponds I could fall into, forever. "I told you, we have all the time in the world now. We were meant to be together, silly. And now we can be, for all eternity."

MY HEART WAS RACING, and some survival instinct deep within me set off an alarm in my head. *Danger, Will Robinson, danger!* I shoved her away from me—not violently, but with enough force to break contact.

"Jesse, stop it! I know what you're doing to me, and it won't work. I've been on the receiving end of enough glamour and seduction magic to know how to resist it. So please, just stop."

Her eyes were downcast again, and the guile I'd seen there earlier had been replaced by genuine hurt. On one hand, I felt terrible for rebuffing her advances. Jesse had been my first love, my first kiss, my first everything. Even in death, she'd stuck by me through my darkest times, and in a sense she'd saved me more than once. My heart told me I owed her more than this.

But on the other hand, *this* was the problem. The whole situation was wrong; I knew it cognitively and intuitively. Jesse had never been meant to inhabit the body she currently possessed. Whether due to the fae magic she'd melded with, or the time she'd spent as a ghost, she'd changed. And, she was dangerous.

"Don't you love me?" she asked, like a child who'd just been denied a cookie before dinner.

"I..." *Shit. How do I respond to that?* "Of course I love you—but I'm not digging this version of you, Jesse. You've changed, and not for the better."

She looked up at me, and that same treacherous look was back again. Her face split into a wicked grin. "Perhaps you'd prefer me like this."

In an instant, Jesse morphed into an exact likeness of Belladonna, nude as the day she was born. The resemblance was perfect, right down to the last beauty mark, curve, and scar. If I hadn't seen her shift I'd have sworn it was Bells, and not my recently-dead ex.

My voice was low and serious as I replied. "No, Jesse—not at all. Change back, and don't ever do that again."

She shifted back into her dryad body with fury in her eyes. Her lips drew into a tight, thin line, her feet spread apart, and her arms were tense and straight at her sides. Jesse's entire body shook with rage. Her tangled, leafy head of hair danced and swayed in a halo around her head like Medusa's tresses.

"LIAR!" she screamed, revealing the mercurial side of her I'd come to fear. Her voice echoed all around, and a strong gust of wind whipped at the leaves and branches around us. The forest floor trembled and shook, and for a moment I staggered, finally catching my balance against the night raven's cage.

She began to close the distance between us, step by perilous step, hatred in her eyes like I'd never seen her display in her previous life.

"Jesse, don't..." I pleaded.

She ignored me, fully possessed by the rage she directed at me. I suspected if I allowed her to, she'd end me here and now. As dangerous as she was, I hadn't a clue how to banish her—and even if I did, I had no idea what that might do to the druid grove.

From what I'd gathered thus far, the body she'd inhabited was supposed to be the avatar of the grove, a spirit made manifest that was meant to help me with—well, druid stuff. I worried that if I hurt her or banished her, it would endanger the grove. It being the last of its kind, I couldn't bear to see that happen. Besides, this place was meant to be a sanctuary for me—a place to recharge my batteries, train my skills in druidry, and retreat when danger was near. I had a feeling I was going to need it for whatever might lie ahead.

So, burning it to the ground wasn't an option. But then again, neither was being ripped to shreds by my reincarnated ex-girlfriend.

I reached into my Craneskin Bag and pulled out the one thing I knew she feared. The sword burst into flames as soon as I drew it out, and it radiated a heat that I'd never felt before. I extended the sword and pointed the tip at her chest. Jesse immediately shied away from the blaze.

A moment before, she was ready to kill me. Now look at her. Jesse had sunk into a squat, cowering away from the sword—and me. She shielded her face and head with her hands and arms, looking for all the world like an abused child shying away from a beating.

I extinguished the sword, but kept it at hand. "I'm leaving." I headed for the druid tree, the exit point from the grove.

"No, don't go! I'm sorry, Colin. I'll be good, I swear—just don't leave me. I've been alone too long, way too long."

I paused to look back at her. "Jesse, you've become dangerous and unpredictable, and I don't care to be around you when you're like this. Look, I want to help you—"

"Then stay," she begged in a whisper.

"—but I don't know how." My hand gripped the handle of the sword, squeezing it so hard my knuckles cracked. "Just—just give me some time to figure things out. Alright?"

"I love you, Colin. I hope you know that."

"The problem is, Jesse, I don't even know if you're capable of love anymore."

Her only reply was an angry screech. I ran to the tree, touching the bark and willing it to lead me back to the mortal realm. I did a quick circuit around the trunk, thankful that it was easier to return from the grove than it was to get there—a single walk around the tree was enough. Once I'd rounded it completely, I was back in the junkyard.

I hung my head and leaned against the tree, exhausted by the brief encounter and despondent about what had happened to the love of my life. I heard someone approach, so I hid the sword behind my leg and looked up to greet them.

"Hey there, loverboy! Maureen said I'd find you back here—"

She stopped mid-sentence, her face blanched and her eyes wide as she stared at something over my shoulder.

"Colin Edward McCool... what in the actual fuck is that?"

I FELT a pair of arms wrap around my waist as cool, soft lips laid a kiss on my cheek. I quickly snapped my head around, knowing what I'd see. Jesse was already ducking behind the tree and out of sight, the damage she'd intended to do already done.

Shit, I had no idea she could leave the grove. This could pose a serious problem.

I turned back around to explain myself, but Belladonna was already stomping her way toward the parking lot.

"Bells, wait!" I shouted, tossing the sword into my Bag as I jogged to catch up to her.

She raised a hand over her shoulder, not even looking at me as I dogged her steps. "I don't want to hear it. Whatever that thing is—and if it's a golem, you should know that you're one sick fuck—you should have told me about it the moment it happened."

"Belladonna, it's not—" I laid a hand on her arm as I spoke. Big mistake. Next thing I knew, Bells grabbed my hand, locked my wrist, and threw me into a nearby truck with a textbook *kote-gaeshi*. I had my bell rung as I collided with the truck's door, and took a few seconds to recover. By the time I gathered my senses enough to stand, she was exiting the front gate.

I sprinted after her, only weaving slightly despite the mild concussion I'd sustained. It only took me a few seconds to reach the parking lot, but I arrived just in time to watch Belladonna's Harley drive off into the distance.

Shit! I stood there for a moment with my hands on my hips, unsure of how to proceed.

"Smooth move, Ex-Lax. What'd you do to piss her off?"

As I spun around I saw a whip-thin thirteen-year-old boy leaning against the fence—feet propped, arms crossed, and collar popped on his surplus Army jacket like a modern James Dean. He had braces, a mild case of acne, and wore a t-shirt that said, "Make Love, Not Horcruxes." He kicked off the fence and whistled.

"Looks like she kicked your ass, too." He pointed at my face. "You're going to have a shiner for sure. Remind me to never go to you for dating advice."

"Hello, Kenny," I replied, probing the rapidly swelling area around my eye. "Shouldn't you be in school right now? And how'd you get here, anyway?"

"Duh, public transportation. And don't worry, I'm home-schooled now. Mom got tired of me getting into fights, so no more public school for me. I do this online thing—takes me about an hour a day to get through my lessons. After that, I usually take the bus to the comic store and hang out until the fat-ass behind the counter makes me leave."

"An hour a day? Is that because you're that smart, or because it's that easy?" I asked, genuinely intrigued.

He smirked. "What do you think? Now, as much as I'd love to chat with you about the wonders of modern education, I came here because I need your help."

"Kenny, I already told you that you're not old enough to start training yet."

He pointed a finger at me. "First off, you said one year, and that year is almost up. Second, I didn't come here for that."

"You better not be messing with the fae again. I already told you, they're dangerous. That stunt you pulled on Rocko's boys could've got you killed, you know."

"They were leaning on Mr. Paljor! That old man never hurt no one, and they were extorting him for protection money."

I poked at my cheekbone again. It was going to need some ice, and soon. "'Never hurt anyone,' Kenny. And besides, I told you that was between him and Rocko. Mr. Paljor can take care of himself."

"Yeah, yeah—he's some sort of werecat. Heard you the first time."

"A pantherathrope, to be exact. Trust me, he's a lot more

dangerous than he looks." Mr. Paljor was a were, alright, of the snow leopard variety to be exact. He was also a political refugee, which was why he was trying to fly under the radar. I'd had to smooth things over between the Pack and the Red Caps after Kenny and Derp had pulled a number on Rocko's crew.

"But he's too nice to stand up for himself, so we did it for him."

I laughed, because Kenny was a master of understatement. "You blew up a delivery van, Kenny... with two of Rocko's boys in it."

"It was just a little bomb," he demurred. "Just enough to scare them, you know?"

"What it did is piss them off, and it made them think Mr. Paljor hired someone to take them out. If I hadn't stepped in, the Pack would've been forced to intervene. And that might have ended the peace accord between the Pack and the fae. Next time, listen to me when I tell you not to get involved."

Kenny dismissed me with a wave. "Aw, you're no fun."

"So I've been told. Now, do you want to tell me why you're here?"

The kid stuck out his lower lip and huffed, blowing a stray lock of hair out of his eyes. Kenny had a Mallen streak on the back of his head that stuck out like a sore thumb, but he owned it like a boss. He'd taken to wearing his dark brown mop skate-punk style since I'd last seen him—long in the front and shaved on the sides and back.

"You see, McCool? This why you're having girlfriend problems—you never listen. Shit, man, I've been trying to tell you that since I got here."

"And?" I asked as I checked a non-existent watch on my wrist.

"It's Derp, Colin. He's gone missing, and I'm pretty sure the goblins took him."

FIVE

"Damn it, Kenny! Why didn't you say so in the first place? That's kind of an important piece of information to leave out."

He rolled his eyes in that practiced, nonchalant manner all teens possessed. "Um, because you've been busting my balls for the last five minutes, remember?"

"Yes, but..." I remembered I was talking to a fourteen-year-old and thought better of arguing with him. "Never mind, there's no sense in wasting time. Hop in my car—you can explain it on the way."

Kenny glanced around, confused. "What, did you finally get rid of that shit heap you call a hot rod?"

"Naw, I still have it," I said as I opened the driver's side door and snagged the keys from under the visor. "And it's not a shit heap."

Kenny's eyes went wide as he realized my car had been there the whole time. "Whoa... that is cool! Invisibility spell?"

"Uh-uh. Just a compulsion that makes mundane people overlook it."

"Normally, I'd make a smart-ass remark about polishing a turd, but the shit heap actually looks a little better with the new paint and rims." He opened the driver's side door, started to get in, then backed out gagging. "Ugh! I changed my mind. This thing is obviously a piece of shit and that stench proves it. What died in here?"

"A magical bird crapped all over the front seat. Just hop in the back, the smell's not as bad there."

The kid held his nose, feigning that the smell was much worse than it was. I drove while he filled me in, his mouth moving a hundred miles an hour while his arms and hands gesticulated wildly for emphasis.

"You see, it's like this. Derp and I were monitoring the police channels and we kept hearing dispatch sending units to check out missing persons reports downtown. So, Derp and I decided to go check it out, and we agreed to meet each other at Sixth and Congress after school, which is near where most of the missing people had been seen last. I mean we were going to meet after he got out of school, but—"

"Whoa, slow down. You guys went to Sixth Street by yourselves?"

Kenny's head bobbed up and down. "Yeah—I mean no. Well, Derp went, but I ended up not getting to go on account of my mom not having any money for the bus that day, 'cause she spent it on lottery tickets the night before—you know that's how the state collects taxes on poor people, right? Anyway, I tried calling Derp to tell him that I wasn't going to make it because my mom can't resist being a sucker, but it just went to voicemail."

I tapped a finger on the steering wheel, then stopped myself. Wouldn't do to let Kenny see I was nervous. "When was this?"

"Last night. I stopped by Derp's house on the way here, just to make sure he wasn't at home sick or something, and there was a police car there and his mom was crying. I told them I hadn't seen him, and I stole some money from Mrs. Martin's purse—

that's Derp's mom—and slipped out the back. Then, I took the bus downtown to look for Derp. All I found there was this."

Kenny pulled a red plastic card from his pocket and handed it to me from the back seat. It was a Capital Metro bus pass. I gave it a quick look and handed it back to him.

"How do you know this is his, Kenny?"

He flipped it over and shoved it in front of my face. "Because Derp is a dork, that's how. Look." The bus pass had a Charizard decal on the back. "Derp loves Pokémon, even though he won't admit it. That's his bus pass, I'm sure of it."

"Alright, I believe you—and put your seat belt on. Cops may not be able to see this thing, but you can still get ejected through the windshield if we have an accident."

"Sheesh, you sound like my mom. I bet you play the lottery too."

"Never," I lied. "Tell me about the missing persons cases."

"Don't you watch the news? Damn, but you live in a bubble. Alright, so these young, single men have been disappearing for the last few months. All of them were last seen downtown near Sixth Street and Congress Avenue, around expensive restaurants and bars where they serve Manhattans and Appletinis with little umbrellas and crap. You know—the Garage, Firehouse, The Roaring Fork, that sort of place."

"How do you know what kinds of drinks they serve at those places?"

"Duh, bonehead—I looked it up." I glanced in the rearview mirror in time to see Kenny typing with his thumbs on a make-believe phone. "We have this thing called Google now, maybe you've heard of it? Anyway, the strange thing is these guys were always alone. That's weird, right? A guy goes to a fancy restaurant or bar and just sits there eating and drinking by himself?"

"Well, that depends on his social skills."

"And you'd know, right? Man, you sure must've messed

things up with your girlfriend. I mean, I kind of worshipped you after I saw her, 'cause she's a high eight, maybe even a solid nine. But you had to go and ruin it. Geez, I can't even look at you right now."

"Um, what you just said was all kinds of wrong. C'mon, Kenny—rating women on a ten-scale? That's for lame-ass wannabe pickup artists. If you want to impress women, you need to show them respect."

"I dunno, man. Seems like nice guys always get the big chili."

I laughed. "The what?"

"You know, the big chili." I looked at him in the rearview again, and he made a circle with his thumb and forefinger and stuck his other index finger through it. "Up the ass, doofus."

I shook my head. "You need to stop watching Internet porn."

He gave me the strawberries. "I live in a trailer park with my single mom. How else am I going to learn about sex and stuff?"

"Kenny, that is *not* the way you want to learn about sex. Gah, I can't believe I'm having this conversation with you. But trust me when I say that pornography depicts a distorted view of sexuality."

"Oh, so you never watch it?"

I didn't have an appropriate answer for that. "Hey, look, we're here." I pulled over to the curb. "Take me to where you found Derp's bus pass."

KENNY WAS WALKING with a lot more skip in his step than I'd have expected of someone who thought his best friend had been abducted. It made me more than a little suspicious, because these boys were always up to something.

"Kid, you don't seem too worried about Derp. Care to explain why that is?"

He screwed his lips to one side and shrugged. "What do you want me to say? We're not the same scared, stupid kids who got nabbed by the goblins last year, Colin. While you've been putting off teaching us how to defend ourselves, we've been doing—stuff."

"Kenny..."

His cheeks flushed and his eyes grew hard as he spoke. "Aw, c'mon, Colin. What did you expect us to do, just sit around and wait to get taken again? We seriously pissed those goblins off, and you and I both know they were going to come back for us eventually. But you decided to leave us hanging. Well, we did something about it."

My temper was rising again, forcing me to push it down with an effort of will. I counted to ten before I spoke. "Like what, Kenny? Spill."

He stopped on a dime and turned on me, arms crossed as he locked eyes with mine. "We started teaching ourselves magic, is all." I opened my mouth to respond, but he cut me off. "See, I knew you'd get all bent out of shape. It wasn't anything serious, just warding runes and charms. You know, stuff to scratch on our window frames and door sills, to keep *them* out."

Last year, after the whole carnival fiasco, I'd made a deal with Maeve, asking her to tell the goblins to leave the boys alone. She'd assured me it would be done. Still, I should have thought about warding their homes, and maybe even crafting them some protective charms. Even though I'd told the boys not to mess with things in the world beneath until I said they were ready for it, I couldn't blame them for wanting to protect themselves.

Bottom line? I didn't have the right to chew Kenny out for doing what I should have done. I pinched the bridge of my nose and took a few deep breaths, waiting until the tension went out of my shoulders before I spoke.

"You guys were right to do what you did."

"Yeah, well fuck y—huh?" Kenny arched an eyebrow and cocked his head. "Wait a minute, did I hear that correctly? Did Colin McCool just say I did something right?"

"Don't let it go to your head, alright? Runes and wards are fine for protection when you're at home, or when you have time to set up a barrier or protection spell. But putting runes and wards on your house isn't going to save you when you're out in the field. Plus, even minor magic can draw the attention of things you don't want hanging around. Sometimes it's better to pretend like you don't know about the world beneath our own, so you can fly under the radar and avoid catching the eye of something that might be more than you can handle."

The kid's face was all smirk now. "Hah! Derp won't believe it when I tell him you ate your words! Man, I can't wait until I see him."

"We'd better get busy finding him then." The kid had led us behind a very trendy and expensive restaurant, the type of place you took a date when you really wanted to impress them. "Is this it, then?"

Kenny nodded. "Yeah, I found his card right over there." He pointed at a pile of produce boxes that sat by the kitchen entrance of the restaurant. The scent of garlic and basil mingled with the odor of cat piss and human feces, making my nose itch and my skin crawl.

I looked around for a possible witness, but the closest I got was an unoccupied cardboard pallet behind a trash dumpster. The city had a huge homeless population, a result of non-existent vagrancy laws, plenty of resources for the homeless downtown, and a thriving illegal drug trade. It wasn't uncommon to see junkies begging for change right outside a $200 a plate restaurant. Austin was nothing if not a dichotomy of class and privilege.

It was a given that I wanted to take in every detail of the alley, so I cast a cantrip to sharpen my already highly-tuned senses. I took a deep whiff of air, regretting it instantly. A faint breeze carried the pleasant bouquet of human feces, cat urine, rancid grease... and goblins.

A quick visual scan of the alley revealed there were no security cameras, making it the perfect place for an abduction—or a murder. I looked for clues in the magical spectrum and found none, not a single trace of magic. From what I could tell, nothing had been erased either. I did a more thorough pattern search of the alley, looking for scuff marks, blood, or anything else that might indicate a struggle had occurred here, but I found nothing.

The scene was way too clean. If goblins had abducted Derp in that alley, whoever had done it was either very stealthy or the kid had gone with them willingly.

"Find anything?" Kenny asked, looking over my shoulder as I squatted down by the trash dumpster.

"Not much—definitely no sign of struggle, which is puzzling. There are no cameras back here, and I don't see any witnesses around, so it's hard to say what happened."

"What about the goblins? Any sign of them?"

I sucked air through my teeth as I looked around. "Goblins have been through here, but that doesn't necessarily mean they took Derp. They're habitual dumpster divers, so they could have simply been here to grab a meal."

"Some mystical detective you are," Kenny sulked.

"Hang on, there's still one thing I haven't tried." I nodded toward a single concrete step that sat by the building's back entrance, and pointed to a gap between the slab and the brick wall behind it. In the darkness beyond, a pair of feline eyes stared out at us. "I may not have a clue regarding what happened here—but I bet she does."

"KITTY, KITTY, KITTY," I cooed. "Here kitty." My overtures were met with a hiss, as well as the faint mewling cries of kittens in the background. "Looks like mama cat's not having it. Time for plan B."

Kenny tapped his foot. "You know, I like animals as much as the next guy, but is now really the time to be rescuing stray kittens?"

I reached into my pocket and pulled out a twenty, handing it to Kenny. "Do me a favor. Go to that restaurant over there, find someone in the kitchen, and ask them if you can buy some of their meat scraps."

"I could just sneak in and steal some food, you know."

"Druids are not thieves, Kenny. Do as I ask. It'll help us find Derp."

The kid grumbled a bit, but he did as requested, returning in short order with a paper sack full of fat trimmings and chicken skin. I dumped the meal out in front of the mama cat's den, then backed up and motioned for Kenny to do the same. Minutes later, she sauntered out of the hole—a lean, somewhat scruffy-looking Siamese mix with chocolate points, thick fur, and bright blue eyes. She sniffed at the food, then started wolfing it down.

"How's this helping us find Derp?" Kenny whispered.

I held a finger to my lips, then knelt in *seiza* position, just like my old karate instructor used to make us do at the beginning and end of class. I closed my eyes and slowed my breathing, extending my senses into the area around me. Besides the cat and her kittens, there were a couple of rats keeping their distance, as well as an anole hiding from the grackles and pigeons overhead.

I ignored the other animals, focusing in on the mama cat. In the weeks since I'd discovered the druid ability of communing with animals, I'd learned that some species were more susceptible than others. Some were willing to follow suggestions and allow an intrusion into their mind and memories, while others would resist it—feral cats being chief among creatures who did not want anyone poking around in their brains.

Once the cat had finished feasting, I knew she'd return to her den and feed her young. I waited, still and silent, while Kenny fidgeted nearby. Soon, I heard him tapping away at his phone screen, but I kept my awareness mostly focused on the mama cat. As I'd expected, a full belly and nursing kittens had put her right to sleep.

Ever so carefully, I began prying at the edges of her consciousness, easing around her defenses until I was able to slip in unnoticed. I chuckled as her feline dreams registered in my mind—mostly impressions of successful hunts, chasing off rivals who wanted her hunting territory and protecting her kittens. I went deeper, looking for recent memories of the night before.

I sifted through her mind, following along with her in reverse chronological order as she hunted, fed, and slept earlier in the day. The emotions that accompanied those memories were mostly pleasure, with a healthy dose of caution and a wee bit of self-congratulation—typical for a cat.

Going a little deeper, I caught a whiff of a memory that had disturbed the mama cat immensely. Something had happened outside her den late the night before, arousing her from her sleep and sending her protection and survival instincts into overdrive. I watched the memory unfold as she was awoken from her sleep not by a sound or scent, but by a feeling of wrongness.

A predator lurked nearby. Something dark and dangerous. Mama cat's instincts told her to remain quiet and hidden, but her natural curiosity overwhelmed her sense of caution. Besides, she needed to know what type of threat she faced. If it could reach her kittens, she'd need to start moving them to another location. Sometimes survival required saving part of a litter, while leaving one or two behind in sacrifice. If that were necessary, it would pain her to do so, but she would do what she must to save the strongest of her kittens.

She crept, inch by inch, to the opening of her den. A thing, large and cloaked in shadow, was wrapping its prey in—what was that? String? No, silk. Spider silk, but not like the kind mama cat sometimes got stuck in her fur. These strands were thick—large enough to capture a man, perhaps.

And that's exactly what the creature was doing. Click, click, click, skrikt, skrikt, skrikt, went the thing's legs. Mama cat couldn't see clearly as shadows strangely obscured the predator from sight. However, she could see four huge spider legs, spinning and wrapping the creature's silk around a man-sized figure. Yes, that's what it was—a man. The spider-creature had enjoyed a successful hunt this evening.

Mama cat was about to inch back into her den, secure in the knowledge that the predator wouldn't be hunting her or her kittens tonight. Just as she began her quiet retreat, a can clattered across the alleyway. At the noise, the spider-thing paused in its task. Mama cat held her breath, because she knew what was coming.

In the flash of a sparrow's wings, the spider-creature dropped the silk-wrapped package it held and leapt across the alleyway, sinking its fangs into a fat man-child who had been hiding behind some trash cans nearby. The child yelped, then twitched and spasmed. Finally, he was still. The spider-thing dragged him back into the alley, where it began to wrap this newer, smaller, juicier prey in silk as well.

Mama cat crept back into her den and snuggled up to her kittens. She remained alert long after the presence left her alley, and did not sleep until the sun rose again.

SIX

"Gah!" I snapped out of my trance and back to reality with a start, the fear and trepidation the mama cat had felt still gripping me. My mouth was dry, my palms sweaty, and my heart was beating faster than normal. The poor cat had been terrified, and after sharing her memories, I could see why.

Kenny stood in front of me, leaning forward with his hands on his knees. "Did you astrally project? You did, right—I mean, leave your body? What did you see? Did you see where Derp went?"

I stuck my hand, palm out, in his face. "No, I didn't astrally project. Astral projection is dangerous and it's a bit beyond my current skills. I simply took a peek inside the cat's mind, so I could sift through her memories."

"You can do that, like read minds and stuff? Do you talk to animals too, like Dr. Doolittle?"

"Do you ever shut up?" I barked, still on edge from living through the cat's brush with whatever had taken Derp. The look on Kenny's face instantly made me regret losing my temper. *This is not like you, Colin, not at all.* "I'm sorry, I didn't mean to snap at you. Just—just give me a minute."

Kenny stood, half turning away from me. "Derp's in trouble, isn't he?"

"It's not looking good, Kenny. Whatever took him is bad news."

"What did it look like?"

I had no intention of giving him details. Doing so would only give him rope to hang himself. "I—didn't get a good look at it."

"Can't you put out some sort of mystical APB on it? Or a magical BOLO on Derp? Maybe get your fairy friends to help?"

"They're not my friends, and they don't like to be called fairies. They consider it demeaning, a racial slur. And no, nothing like that exists. Let me think for a minute." I needed to give him something useful to do, to keep him out of trouble. "Kenny, can you get me a couple strands of Derp's hair? If so, I might be able to cook up a locator spell. Also, did Derp's phone have a tracker on it?"

"The hair thing I can do, but tracking the phone is a dead end. Derp's parents already tried using the 'find my phone' thing, but they couldn't get a location on it. Either Derp turned off his GPS or someone pulled his SIM card from his phone when they took him."

I sucked on my teeth and tapped my chin with a knuckle. "Well, that's what I would do if I was abducting someone. Kind of funny that a supernatural creature would be that tech-savvy, though."

"Freeze, Austin Police!"

Shit. There were two uniformed Austin PD officers standing at the end of the alley. One had his hand on his service weapon as he approached me, and the other was calling it in on their radio.

"Dispatch, this is patrol unit 29. We're 10-23 at the last

known location of the Martin child, and currently 10-26 on a potential 10-31 involving another child. Over."

"Understood, unit 29. Sending additional units to your 10-20 now," was APD dispatch's reply.

The cop who was approaching me looked pretty damned serious. "Sir, step away from the child and put your hands in the air—now!"

I did as he asked, slowly raising my hands as I turned to face him. "Officer, this isn't what it looks like. Kenny is friends with Derp—I mean, the Martin kid—and we're just trying to help find him."

The officer wasn't having it. "Sir, turn around and face the wall!"

"I've never met this man in my life, officer," Kenny said, suppressing a grin. "He offered me some candy, and told me it was hidden here in this alley."

"Kenny!" I snapped as I turned to look at him. "Stop it, this is serious!"

The kid stifled a laugh. "He said he wanted to touch me in the butt, officer."

"Kenny, stop!"

The officer had his eyes locked on mine. "Sir, turn around and place your hands on the wall, or I will use force!"

"Seriously, officer, this isn't what it appears. My young friend here is trying to play a joke on me." I looked at Kenny. "A very serious joke, I might add."

"Last warning, sir!" the cop yelled.

"But I—" I didn't have a chance to finish that thought, because the cop pulled out his taser and lit me up. I did the hokey-pokey on my feet for a moment, then dropped like a rock and did the fish flop on the ground. I could still see Kenny from where I'd fallen, and noted with quite a bit of resentment that he was recording the whole thing on his phone.

"Holy shit," he squealed. "This is absolutely the most awesome thing I've ever seen."

Mercifully, the cop stopped zapping me a few seconds later, and I allowed them to cuff me and put me in the back of their cruiser. Kenny gave the cops a statement, and while I couldn't hear the entire thing, he did actually admit that he knew me.

Unfortunately, the cops didn't know what to believe at that point. They had a missing kid on their hands, and they'd found his best friend with a strange adult in the alley where the missing kid's cell phone had last pinged a GPS signal. All told, I must've have looked like the biggest Chester in the world to them.

Kenny glanced over at me, sitting uncomfortably in the back seat of the cruiser with my hands cuffed behind me. When the cops weren't looking, I silently mouthed *I'm going to kill you* at him. He flipped me off while brushing the hair out of his face, so the cops wouldn't see.

Fifteen minutes later, Sergeant Klein showed up on scene. After a brief discussion with the uniformed officers who'd arrested me, and a longer discussion with Kenny, she sauntered over to the black and white and opened the back door.

Klein looked at me over the door with an inscrutable expression. I couldn't tell if she was upset or about to crack up laughing.

"Colin McCool—if anyone was going to piss in my cornflakes this morning, it was bound to be you." She drummed her fingers on the top of the window, frowning. "You may as well climb out of there so I can uncuff you and find out what the hell is really going on."

SERGEANT KLEIN SENT the uniformed officers on their

way, then she led us around the corner to a coffee shop so we could chat. Klein had been the officer we'd turned to when we'd broken up a massive fae child sex trafficking ring. Necessarily, she'd been clued into the world beneath, and Maeve's people had set it up so she'd get all the credit for finding the kids.

Understandably, she was a bit of a local celebrity now, and while her fifteen minutes of fame were over she was still APD's golden child. So, when she told the officers to let me go, they obeyed without question. It was fortunate that she'd heard my name over the radio, else I might have spent an uncomfortable night in jail.

I grabbed us a few coffees—decaf for Kenny, of course— while Klein snagged us a table in the back corner of the shop. It was a franchise, so the coffee wasn't nearly as good as it was at Luther's, but I was feeling cranky after getting tasered so virtually any source sugar and caffeine would do. As I headed back to the table, I saw that Klein had sat with her back to the wall, just like all cops tended to do.

Klein frowned as I sat down next to Kenny, glaring at each of us in turn. Finally, she ran a hand over her close-cropped hair and heaved a sigh. "Alright, McCool, let's get this over with. Go ahead and fuck up my day by telling me why you were at a crime scene with this juvenile delinquent. And please don't tell me that the fae took this kid's friend."

"It wasn't the fae, it was goblins," Kenny interjected.

Klein shot him a cross look, raising a finger in front of his face. "Shut your trap, Harris—I'll get to you in a minute," she growled.

"You two know each other?" I asked, taking a sip of my coffee. The java was acrid, bitter, and it smelled like shoe polish, which was pretty much everything I expected from a corporate coffee conglomerate. It was sad when even Mickey-D's could brew a better cup of joe than the biggest coffee shop chain in the world. I tore open four packets of sugar and poured them in as Klein dished on Kenny.

"Oh yeah, we've met. Kenny here used to like to shoplift. I picked him up for it back when I was on the beat. Kid actually tried to steal a game console from a Target, can you believe it? He waited until the store employee opened the case, then he lit a smoke bomb and tossed it in the center of electronics to distract everyone. Might have gotten away with it, if he'd thought to remove the security tag before leaving the store."

Kenny rolled his eyes. "I was eight, give me a break. You think I'd make that mistake twice?"

Klein actually chuckled. "Not when you can use stolen credit card numbers to order whatever you want online," she replied. Where moments before Kenny had defiantly met her gaze, now his eyes looked anywhere but at the cop. "That's right, Harris. I've been keeping tabs on you."

I crossed my arms and leaned back in my seat. "Do tell."

Klein tsked at Kenny before turning to me. "Back when I was partnered with Erskine, we were assigned to the Commercial Burglary division. We got a tip from an online retailer who'd sent an order of electronics and video games to the kid's neighbor's house, only to get charged back by the credit card company after the order had been delivered. Since Mrs. Thompson is seventy-two years old and can barely dial in NPR on her console stereo, we connected the dots pretty quick. Eventually, some of the shit ended up in a local pawn shop—but since Harris here isn't old enough to take out a loan we could never pin it on him."

Kenny squirmed in his chair. "I plead the fizzith."

"Smart move," I replied. "And don't think we're not going to have a talk about this later, young man." Kenny waited until I was looking at Klein before mocking me. I ignored him, deciding it was best to choose my battles. That's what my mom had always said when I was his age.

"Enough about our future license plate maker here," Klein said. "I want to know what the hell happened to the Martin boy."

"She means Derp," Kenny said.

Klein slapped a hand on the table, hard enough to shake the condiments. "And I told you to shut your trap," she snapped at Kenny before turning back to me. "So, what's the scoop, McCool? Did the fae take him, or was it 'goblins' like dipshit here said?"

"Honestly? I'm not sure what took him, Sergeant Klein. But I know it wasn't anything human. I also know that your people aren't going to get very far in tracking him down, because the thing that took him was smart. It didn't leave a trace of evidence in that alley, not a single clue—although Kenny here did find Derp's bus pass by a dumpster in the alley. Show her, Kenny."

"Okay, but I want it back." He tossed it on the table in front of the detective.

Klein pulled out a plastic bag and slid the card into it with her pen. "It's evidence, kid—might have prints on it, so I'm handing it over to Missing Persons."

"It won't have anything on it," I said.

"I still need to turn it in," Klein replied.

"Man, I was going to use that to get home," Kenny sulked.

"Anything else I need to know?" Sergeant Klein asked. "This isn't my case, but I can make it my case real quick if you need some space to work. Your name is going to get back to whoever is working it, and they *will* follow up by questioning you."

"I'd certainly appreciate it if you could keep them off my back. One last bit of info that I failed to mention—I think that whatever took Derp is responsible for abducting the young men that have been going missing downtown. That's actually why he was down here, because Kenny and Derp were looking into things that are better left alone."

"Speaking of which," Klein remarked, "how are these two kids clued in? Do I even want to know?"

I sipped my coffee, wincing at the taste before taking another sip. "Long story short? Last year I rescued them from a tribe of juggalo goblins who planned to sacrifice them to their evil clown god."

Klein clasped her hands in front of her and hung her head. "Nope, I didn't want to know that. Shit, McCool, how deep does this myths and legends stuff go? I mean, how much of it is true?"

"Pretty much all of it, Sergeant Klein. Most of the folklore and fairy tales you've read or heard have some basis in the truth."

"Except for orcs, the Loch Ness monster, and Bigfoot," Kenny stated. "That stuff is total bullshit."

"What a relief," Sergeant Klein deadpanned as she stood. "Look, I'm going to go snag this case from Missing Persons so I can run interference for you. Just do me a favor and don't get arrested again, alright? There's only so much I can do to keep you out of trouble."

"Thanks, Sergeant Klein."

"You can thank me by finding the kid," she said.

I nodded. "Consider it done."

As Klein headed for the door, she stopped to address me one last time. "And, McCool? Don't make me regret this."

AFTER SERGEANT KLEIN LEFT, I grabbed a fiver out of my wallet and handed it to Kenny. "Listen up—you need to take the bus home and stay there. No looking for Derp, no checking out clues and leads, and definitely no more credit card fraud."

"Aw, you're no fun. Besides, I wasn't the one who stole the numbers. I just agreed to grab the packages when they arrived at Mrs. Thompson's house. She's always asleep in the afternoons when they deliver, so I knew I wouldn't get caught."

I leaned over the table and got in Kenny's face to make sure he was hearing me. "Kenny, you need to listen to me and listen good. Becoming a druid-trained hunter gives a person a lot of power. I know it sounds corny, but it comes with a ton of responsibility, and it's not something you teach to people who don't practice a moral code. If I even think you're doing anything illegal, there is no freaking way I'm going to train you or recommend you to anyone else. Am I clear?"

He popped a dent in his plastic cup and let it pop out again several times, avoiding eye contact. "Yeah, I get it. But you don't know how hard it is, living with a single mom on welfare in a trailer park. If I don't come up with extra money, bills don't get paid and sometimes we don't eat. You can talk about morals and right and wrong all you want, but when your stomach's empty all that crap goes out the window."

"I am not going to discuss moral relativity with you, because this is not a negotiation. If you need to make extra money, I'll give you a part-time job at the junkyard. But—"

Kenny's eyes lit up as he cut me off. "You're giving me a job? At the junkyard? That's freaking awesome!"

"Hang on and let me finish. What I was going to say was that school comes first, and since you're only thirteen it'll have to be odd jobs for cash. And it's not going to be easy work."

"Say no more, I can handle it. When do I start?"

"After I find Derp. Now, go home, stay out of trouble, and contact me if you hear anything that can help me track him down."

Kenny stood, pocketing the five-dollar bill I'd given him. "Done. See ya around, McCool."

As he was leaving the café, I yelled after him. "And don't think I've forgiven you for getting me tasered and arrested!" A couple of patrons in the shop gave me nervous glances, making me wish I'd used my indoor voice. After the day I'd had, I felt like flipping them off, but instead I ignored them as I gathered my things and headed out the door.

On the way to my car, I took a shortcut through an alley as I typed out a quick text to Belladonna. *Sry bout bout wot hapnd. pls caL me so I cn explain.* I kept checking my phone to see if she'd replied, a habit that Finnegas and Maureen often chastised me about. Situational awareness was a big issue for hunters, because you never knew when something was going to jump out of the sewers or shadows and try to eat you.

Despite the risks, sometimes I let my guard down when I wasn't on the job anyway, because being at DEFCON 1 all the time was exhausting. Imagine having to live every second of your life on edge, alert for danger around every corner. It'll make you crazy, believe me. Considering the day I was having I should have known better, but I still had my face in my phone when I felt the eerie tingle of a spell being spooled up.

I ducked as I reached into my Bag for my sword. That was a mistake, because I got hit full in the face by a push spell cast with bad intent. A push spell wasn't true telekinesis, because it was damned hard to lift or otherwise control organic matter with your mind. Instead, the spell controlled air molecules to send a tightly-focused microburst of air at the target.

In this case, the target had been my stomach, but since I'd ducked it nailed me in the head. It pretty much felt like you'd expect—as if a young Arnold Schwarzenegger had hit me in the skull with an old-school New York City phone book. And believe me, being hit in the head with a phone book is no picnic.

A second later, I found myself laying flat on my back in an alley, looking up at four very large, very angry-looking men who wore an assortment of tacti-cool clothing. You know, the stuff they sell at sporting goods stores that's supposed to help you blend in when you're carrying concealed, but in reality it screams "ex-military" or "off-duty cop." It was like an unspoken dress code for wannabe pipe hitters or something.

Each of them wore some version of combat or tactical boots, cargo pants, and military-style jackets over lycra shirts or Henleys. A couple wore baseball caps—not team caps like a normal human, mind you. These hats came in digital camo, desert tan, and olive drab, with matching U.S. flag patches or firearms manufacturer logos on the front. And, of course, they all had aviators on—every last one of them.

I spat blood to the side as I addressed my attackers. "Did you guys pick those outfits on purpose, or do you just throw darts at a 5.11 catalog and order whatever you hit?"

Their only reply was a boot heel to the face. And to that, I responded by blacking out.

SEVEN

An indeterminate amount of time later, I woke up tied to a chair with a bag over my head. Rather than stir and let my captors know I was awake, I chose to remain still and silent so I could gather information on my surroundings. The last thing I wanted was for them to come in and start working me over before I had an idea of my odds for escape.

I'd already surmised that one of the Cold Iron Circle's tactical teams had abducted me. For one, no one else dressed like that outside military and police circles, and to my knowledge special forces and SWAT operators didn't use magic when they renditioned a suspect. Even units that were clued in preferred to use breaching explosives, bean bag guns, flash bang grenades, and the like over spell work, because the results were much more predictable.

I wondered if these guys had been loyal to Gunnarson. If so, I was fucked.

Time to get to work, McCool.

When it came to gathering information, Finnegas had taught me that most people rely on their eyesight way too much. As a druid, I was trained to use all my senses, and part of my training was going through Finnegas' version of SERE school—which stood for Survival, Evasion, Resistance, and Escape. More than once, Finnegas had "abducted" me and put me in various restraints and confines, forcing me to devise ways to escape.

I'd hated it at the time, but right now I was glad the old man had been such a hard ass during my early training. I began to inventory everything my other four senses were picking up, starting with taste and smell. The room stank of commercial detergents or disinfectants, combined with my own sweat and blood. I also detected a faint whiff of engine oil, gas, and exhaust.

Interesting.

Next, I carefully and gently tested my restraints. I'd been duct taped and not zip-tied, which wasn't necessarily a bad thing. However, my captors had seen fit to restrain my hands behind the chair. They'd also taped my ankles to the chair legs, and my chest to the chair back. I had to hand it to them; these Circle dickheads did thorough job of it.

Once I had a handle on how I'd been restrained, I listened to my surroundings. Traffic noise echoed in the distance. In an adjoining room, someone was watching an old spaghetti Western—*The Good, The Bad, and The Ugly*, based on the musical score. There were footsteps in at least two—no, three—directions.

Still outnumbered. Not good.

So, I was in some sort of garage or warehouse that likely housed a carpet cleaning or pressure washing business. All my captors had stuck around to keep an eye on me. I was still in the city, that much was clear. But chances were good they'd brought me here because they needed privacy, either to question me, torture me, or both.

Why they'd taken me was anyone's guess, but I suspected it

had to do with me killing their leader a while back. If so, they weren't going to treat me with kid gloves. I needed to escape quickly, before they decided to do their worst.

I was just about to start heating up my restraints when a door slammed somewhere in the building. Faint sounds of conversation carried through the walls. Two men were talking, but I couldn't tell what they were discussing. I cast a cantrip to enhance my senses and tuned in to what they were saying.

"Is he here? Did he agree to come?" It was a man's voice, high and uptight.

The second speaker had a deeper, gruffer voice. "Yeah, we got him."

"What do you mean, 'you got him'?" There was a pregnant pause. "Holy hell! You mean to tell me you lunkheads brought him here *by force?* Are you fucking insane? If he snaps, he could rip you idiots in half and level this building without breaking a sweat."

Gruff voice cleared his throat and spat. "He doesn't look so tough. One spell and a boot to the face, and we had him."

High voice actually went up a few octaves as he replied. "Did you jackasses even read his dossier? Intelligence classifies him as a Class Seven supernatural threat. Class fucking Seven! If you managed to abduct him without any casualties, either you got lucky or he let you take him."

Yeah, that second one... let's go with that.

"Geez, McCracken," gruff voice replied. "I don't see why you're getting all bent out of shape. It's not like we water-boarded your pet hipster or something."

Hipster? Seriously? Now I was really getting pissed.

"That's Lieutenant McCracken to you, Keane, and you'd do well to remember that. Commander Gunnarson isn't here anymore, and the person you assaulted and abducted is the one who took him out. While you might have thought it'd be cute to get a little revenge for Gunnarson and your dead buddies, you had no authority to take liberties with the parameters of this mission."

Keane started to protest, but McCracken didn't allow him a word edgewise. "Not one fucking peep, Keane! Just take me to him, and you'd better hope you didn't fuck this up for me, because if you did I'll see to it your whole team gets assigned to a werebear monitoring station in Alaska."

I decided to play like I was still unconscious. Soon, footsteps approached, a door opened nearby, and two people entered the room.

"Son of a bitch, would you look at him? Keane, you are a world-class fuck-up," McCracken hissed. Silence followed, presumably because Keane knew when to shut up and take an ass-chewing. "Well, don't just fucking stand there, you walking steroid commercial—go cut him loose!"

"But if he's as dangerous as you say, I think—"

"No one pays you to fucking think!" McCracken shrieked. "If he kills you it'll be your own damn fault. Cut him loose."

Heavy footsteps crossed the room. I heard the *snikt* of an automatic knife, then someone began cutting the tape that restrained me. Finally, they pulled the bag off my face... and that's when I sprang into action.

I GRABBED the chair for balance as I stomped the inside of Keane's knee. Not hard enough to buckle it completely, but just enough to get him to drop his weight forward and bend at the waist. As I stood, I grabbed the hand that held the knife, and in the same movement I hit him with a nasty palm-heel strike that snapped his head back.

Since his head was coming down when I hit him, it should

have knocked him out. Unfortunately, the guy was a dead ringer for Stone Cold Steve Austin and had a neck like a bull, so the blow merely stunned him. Despite getting less than the intended result from my attack, it was enough to allow me to disarm him. I spun him around while he was still dazed, using him as a shield with the knife at his throat.

"My Bag, now! Or I open Keane's jugular and bleed him like a pig."

McCracken was staring at me with eyes like saucers, and his hands were open and up in front of him. "Please, Mr. McCool—I can assure you, this has all just been a misunderstanding."

Several sets of footsteps echoed outside, and three other Circle operatives rushed into the room. One had a sidearm drawn and pointed at me, and the other two had spells at the ready. Of the two magicians, lightning crackled between the first magic-user's fingers. The other was forming a fireball in the air between his hands.

I felt Keane tense as he realized the deep pile of shit he'd stepped in, so I pressed the side of the blade against his neck. Having sharp, cold steel at your throat tended to make you think twice about fighting back. The guy knew better than to make a move on me, so instead he barked orders at his teammates.

"Shoot this fucker or fry him, now!" His teammates looked at each other, unsure if they could take me out without endangering their leader. "Damn it, that's an order!"

McCracken's voice was taut as he yelled at Keane's teammates, all while keeping his eyes on me. "Belay that order! Stand down, before you get us all killed!"

Keane's team looked back and forth between him and McCracken, who obviously didn't have as much authority here as he thought. Finally, the magic-user spinning up the lightning spell lowered his hands.

"Stand down," he said as the ozone smell of lightning magic

faded away. The others complied, banishing the fireball and holstering the pistol.

"You just got us all killed, Smithson," Keane declared.

I punched him in the back of the head, finding that his switchblade made a nice fist load. "Shut up, Keane. He just saved your life."

Keane's legs buckled slightly from the blow, but he managed to remain standing. "You should've just killed me, McCool," he said. "Because I'm going to stomp a mudhole in your ass when this is all over."

"Hmm, sounds kinky, but I'll have to decline." I looked at McCracken. "My Bag, if you don't mind."

McCracken looked at fireball guy. "Don't just stand there— do what he says. Now, Cullen!" Cullen ran out of the room while McCracken continued to speak. "Mr. McCool, I apologize for how you were treated. I promise, these operatives were only supposed to deliver a message to you, and that was it. They were not authorized to undertake this"—he gave Keane and his team a contemptuous look—"well, this cluster-fuck. I have the full authority of the High Council behind me, and I can assure you they'll all be reprimanded accordingly."

Unlike the rest of these assholes, McCracken didn't have that ex-military look about him. He was short, maybe five-foot-eight, and slight of build, although he obviously stayed in shape. With his conservative haircut, casual dress shoes, slacks, preppy windbreaker, and polo shirt, he looked more like an accountant than a field agent. If I had to guess, I'd say he was an analyst, a desk jockey. But that didn't mean he was harmless, and it definitely didn't mean he was on my side.

"I'm touched, McCracken—really, I am. The thing is, I don't take too kindly to being ambushed and abducted, so you'll have to forgive my skepticism."

Cullen ran back into the room carrying my Bag. He slid it

across the floor in a lame attempt to get me to expose myself. I didn't fall for it, of course. Instead of giving up control of Keane to grab it, I stopped the Bag with my foot, kicking it behind me.

"Alright, that's a start," I growled. "Now that we're developing rapport, let's keep it going. I know you cock-juggling thunder cunts have some zip-tie restraints around here. McCracken, I want you to disarm these morons, then I want you to cuff them together, back-to-back."

"I can assure you, Mr. McCool, that isn't—"

"Now, motherfucker!" I roared, accidentally nicking Keane with the knife as I tensed up in anger. *Settle down, cowboy. You lose control and you might do something you'll regret.*

Keane winced as blood began to trickle from his neck. McCracken squeezed his eyes shut as he exhaled in frustration, then he complied with my request. He removed an assortment of knives, sidearms, and back-up weapons from the team, then cuffed them and tied their cuffs together with more zip-tie restraints.

"You three, have a seat," I said to Keane's teammates.

Cullen looked confused. "How the hell do you expect us to do that?"

"I don't know, just figure it the fuck out already," I replied, exasperated. They tried to lean on each other to squat on a three-count, but fell on their asses instead. I fought the urge to crack a smile. "Alright, McCracken, zip-tie their ankles."

"He's going to kill us, once you comply," Keane muttered. McCracken did what I asked, ignoring his subordinate's warning.

"Now, hand Keane some zip-cuffs and turn around," I commanded.

"McCool, this really isn't necessary," McCracken said.

I tsked. "We'll see. Better do it fast, because this knife is getting awful heavy. I'm getting the urge to stab it into something so I can rest my arm."

Once Keane had cuffed McCracken, I punched the steroid jockey as hard as I could at the base of his skull, just to the side of his spine so it wouldn't paralyze him. I was feeling a lot angrier than my normal self, but I hadn't completely lost control, after all. He collapsed like a slinky, to which I gave a satisfied grunt.

I closed the knife and pocketed it, then dragged Keane over to his buddies and zip-cuffed him to the group. My next few minutes were invested in doing a more thorough pat-down of Keane's team, all while keeping McCracken in view. The search turned up a few neck knives, a Beretta Pico .380 that McCracken had somehow missed, and a few razor blades concealed in waistbands and paracord bracelets.

Clever.

Once done, I stood and searched McCracken, relieving him of an Emerson CQC combat folder and a stock Colt .45 caliber semi-auto pistol, both of which I kept. Keane's teammates were starting to give each other looks, so I figured I'd better take care of the magic users before they decided to get cute. I grabbed the roll of duct tape they'd used on me and taped all their mouths shut, then taped their fingers together.

"Try spelling your way out of that shit." I turned to McCracken. "Have a seat, asshole—since you went through all that trouble to get me here, I may as well hear what you have to say."

MCCRACKEN SAT in a folding metal chair, hands cuffed behind his back, looking up at me. I leaned against the wall a few feet away from him, arms crossed with my Glock in my hand.

"What do you want to know?" he asked.

"It's obvious you're the High Council's butt boy," I said, "but that doesn't explain why these clowns abducted me or what you want with me."

"I'm here to help you," he exclaimed. "Isn't that obvious?"

I rolled my eyes. "Oh, plain as day." Then it hit me. "Wait a minute—you're my liaison?"

"Those are my orders," he replied. He nodded at Keane's team. "Before these dipshits screwed it up, that is. They were only supposed to deliver a message, to ask you to come here for an initial meeting. Unfortunately, they took it upon themselves to get a little payback. They're no Gunnarson loyalists, mind you, but they had friends who were killed in that battle."

I rubbed my jaw where I'd gotten kicked. "Haven't you idiots ever heard of electronic communications? A phone call, email, or text would have sufficed."

McCracken shook his head. "Uh-uh, not after we found out the fae are monitoring all our communications. Magical wiretaps are hard to root out. It's not like you can ward an entire cell network. That's why the Council ordered me to only communicate with you face-to-face and in private."

I tapped the muzzle end of the Glock's slide on my arm. "Makes sense, I guess. Not much sense, but for a clandestine organization run by paranoid xenophobes, ostensibly dedicated to eradicating all supernatural threats from the earth—I can see why you'd choose to go that route." The truth was, I probably wouldn't have taken the call. I'd been avoiding the Cold Iron Circle like the plague since I'd been appointed as druid justiciar... lucky me. "Still doesn't explain why you sent these geniuses to speak with me."

McCracken blushed. "They've, uh, been *assigned* to keep

an eye on you. It made sense to have them reach out."

I rubbed the cold metal of the Glock's slide against my forehead and sighed. "You guys just don't learn, do you? When are you going to figure out that I'm not a threat to humanity?"

McCracken cleared his throat, but his voice still cracked as he replied. "In all fairness, the Circle named you as a Class Seven threat for good reason."

"Hold up—what does 'Class Seven threat' even mean?"

The lieutenant perked up at my question—obviously, this was his wheelhouse. "Oh, that's easy enough to explain. Logically, there are ten levels on our threat scale."

"At least you didn't assign me a color code," I quipped.

McCracken laughed nervously. "We started with a color code system, but it got too confusing. Operatives and analysts argued over how many colors we should include, whether there should be different hues at each level to denote which entities were more dangerous, that sort of thing. So, we scuttled it and went with the ten-point system."

"Fascinating," I said, standing up to kick Cullen in the ribs. He was getting fidgety, and I didn't want him getting any ideas. I sat on the desk again facing McCracken, whose face had considerably blanched. "You were saying?"

"Um, yes—yes, of course. So, ten levels, with Level One being the weakest and more or less benevolent creatures. You know, Japanese *baku*, jackalopes, halcyon birds—that sort of thing. Levels Two through Four mostly consist of more dangerous cryptids and your lower-order fae. 'Thropes, wyverns, red caps, selkies, and so on, as well as vampires less than two centuries old. But Levels Five and Six—well, that's where it gets interesting. Most higher fae are considered to be Level Five, with the older ones being classified Level Six due to their proficiency with magic. Older vamps and 'thropes are usually classified as Level Five or Six as well."

"Wait a minute... you guys consider me a greater threat than Maeve?"

McCracken shook his head. "Oh no, she's definitely a Class Eight or Nine, for sure. But she's also a special case. For decades, we've suspected that she was one of the Tuatha, but we haven't been able to prove it."

McCracken looked at me expectantly, but I maintained a poker face and kept my mouth shut. I might not have been on good terms with Maeve, but I wasn't a snitch, either. Besides, she'd never dish on me to anyone who might wish me harm... at least, I didn't think she would. If Maeve wanted me taken out, she'd do it herself.

McCracken frowned at my reticence and continued. "But as for you, well—you've certainly proven yourself to be more than a match for most higher-order fae, and most anything Class Six or below, really. There were those Germans—you took care of them quite handily, as I recall. I'd be remiss to leave out that Norse demi-god—don't think that didn't raise a few eyebrows among our analysts. And then there was the matter of the Mayan deity's avatar. Oh, now that was an impressive kill, I have to tell you. I've watched the footage of that battle at least a dozen times, and it gets better every time."

"You have that on video? How? I have it under good authority that the vamps had taken precautions against that sort of thing."

McCracken cleared his throat again, a nervous tick that was obviously his tell. "Well, yes—magically-enhanced satellite photography trumps most magical counter-surveillance measures. But we only have one copy of the event—on our secure servers at headquarters, of course. The firewalls are top of the line, so there's no need to be worried about the footage getting into the hands of, say, the CIA's Cerberus Project—or those nasty 'military science' people, heaven forbid."

"Uh-huh. So, what you're saying is, you clowns consider me to be a high-level threat, and you've been surveilling me for some time now because of it."

McCracken nodded enthusiastically. "Yes, I think that covers it."

"Which means you also likely have a plan for taking me out—a sort of doomsday scenario, in case my Hyde-side jumps the prison-yard fence."

"I wouldn't put it that way, exactly—"

I didn't bother letting him finish that thought, instead rolling right over him as I continued. "And the fact that you even have that plan pretty much empowers any Cold Iron Circle operative or team leader with a hard-on for killing supernaturals to take a crack at me—which is exactly what Keane's team did."

McCracken's eyes blinked rapidly, and he cleared his throat every few seconds as he spoke. "Well, uh—*cough*—I mean, that is to say—*cough*—rather, it's not how it looks—"

"Pathetic. You pricks can't even fess up when you're caught dead to rights. And you want me to cooperate with you? No, I don't think so." I stood, pulling my Craneskin Bag's strap over my head and holstering my pistol. The duct tape was on the desk nearby, so I snagged it and tore off a long strip. "I'm sure someone will be along to check on you jokers"—I checked my imaginary watch—"oh, in a day or two."

"Wait, Mr. McCool, I can help you mmrrff—"

Taping McCracken's mouth shut and leaving him there with his team was the most satisfying thing I'd done all day. He didn't seem like a bad guy, but a boy scout like that working for the Circle couldn't be trusted—not after everything that had happened. And at the moment, there just wasn't any upside to giving him a chance to prove himself.

Come to think of it, if Bells hadn't been so damned cute and charming, I'd probably have never given her a chance, either.

I turned the lights off as I left the room and shut the door behind me. The Circle operatives responded with a chorus of muffled protests, which I casually ignored.

Bells. Damn it. I needed to find her and make things right, and figure out what I was going to do with Jesse—or whatever she'd become.

But my first priority was finding Derp. And for that task, I needed better intel.

EIGHT

I'd tangled with giant spiders before, but they weren't intelligent enough to hunt without leaving a trace. For that reason, I doubted a giant spider had taken Derp. In fact, it was quite possible that what the cat *thought* she saw and what had really been there were two entirely different things.

I hadn't accumulated much experience with reading animal memories, because it was a relatively new skill for me. But from what I'd gathered thus far, they often remembered things much differently than how they occurred. Animals were champs at conflating threats, a side effect of tens of thousands of years of evolutionary survival. That meant the thing that took Derp could've been a human casting odd shadows on the wall, or some other multi-limbed supernatural creature, or two humanoids standing close together—there were any number of possibilities.

I was merely speculating, but when it came to the supernatural I'd found it paid to keep an open mind while gathering as much information as possible. What I needed was someone who had more experience with creatures that hunted in darkness, someone who had been around long enough to encounter a wide variety of night-stalking monsters. Someone who was, in fact, a night-stalking monster himself.

In short, I needed to speak with Luther. If anyone would have insights regarding what the cat had seen, it'd be him. Not only could he pull a mean cappuccino, but he was also the oldest vampire in the central Texas region. With the day I was having, I'd gladly take my intel with a side of caffeine and sugar, thank you very much. After cleaning up in a convenience store restroom—blood tended to freak mundane citizens out, after all —I took a rideshare to Luther's cafe.

Out of all the supernaturals in town and of all the major players, Luther was the one I trusted most. He'd never led me wrong, and when I needed help he was always there for me. But Luther wasn't against trading a favor for a favor, either, and that meant I was likely to get tasked with some errand in exchange for whatever help he might provide.

Still, I didn't mind. For one, Luther had always paid me for my time, unlike Maeve. It probably rankled her that she'd have to pay me a stipend now, as the fae hated giving up anything to mortals in any bargain—especially money. But Luther was like most older vamps in that money wasn't a big deal to him. Besides that, I got free coffee whenever he was working the counter.

It was late in the afternoon by the time I finished dealing with McCracken and Keane, and already getting dark when I walked into Luther's coffee shop. At this time of day, the place was empty. It was too late in the day for humans and too early for vamps and other supernaturals. Luther was standing at the end of the counter, holding hands and close-talking with Mateo, another older vamp I'd recently met. It appeared to be a private moment, so I stood by until they were done.

Mateo released Luther's hands, then gave me a sideways glance. As usual, he was impeccably dressed in a double-breasted wool blazer over a cable-knit cashmere sweater and white button-down shirt. Despite the time of year, he wore light-tan slacks pegged over deck shoes with no socks. It was a look few people could pull off who weren't on a modeling agency's roster, but Mateo wore it with style.

Luther, on the other hand, had stuck with his usual dark silk shirt and simple, if expensive, jeans and sneakers. He was trying a little too hard to be understated, if you asked me.

"Well hello, druid," Mateo trilled. "Slain any gods lately?"

"Hey, Mateo, Luther." I nodded to each of them in turn. "Naw, I've been trying to avoid altercations with higher-order beings lately. They tend to hold a grudge."

Luther looked me up and down as he headed for the espresso machine. "And how's that working out for you, hmm?"

"Oh, you noticed the bruises? I promise you, these are all human-made." I watched him pull and mix a double-shot mocha in a to-go cup, savoring the pungent, familiar smell of pressure-brewed coffee, steamed milk, and chocolate. "So, I'd say it's working out fine... more or less."

Luther passed me the mocha, smiling knowingly as he crossed his arms and flipped a dish rag over his shoulder. "Uh-huh. I keep telling you, the more enemies you make, the less peace and quiet you'll get. You're going to have to start using some diplomacy, Colin, if you ever want to have a moment's rest."

"Yeah? Well, it's not like I *could* rest, even if I wanted to. Ever since I got this stinking justiciar gig, it's been nothing but long nights and longer days." I tipped my cup to him. "Thanks for that."

Mateo cleared his throat from the end of the coffee bar. "I sense a lot of boring business talk coming. Not that I'm not fascinated by"—he twirled his index finger in lazy circles at me —"whatever it is you druids do. But I have an appointment with my tailor at eight, and my aesthetician is arriving at nine, so I'll leave you boys to your fun." He gave Luther a wicked smile. "I'll be free after midnight, of course."

Luther avoided my eyes as Mateo left, instead busying himself with cleaning the espresso machine and wiping down the dark and worn wooden counter. I waited for him to speak, but that was a losing battle—he *was* semi-immortal, after all. He could wait a decade if he wanted and not bat an eye.

"So... you and Mateo? What happened to his boyfriend, the landscaper?"

Luther continued to avoid eye contact, obviously uncomfortable with the topic of conversation. "We're trying something new. In the past, each of us have preferred to date humans, with disastrous results. So, we decided to see if dating our own kind might work out better."

I nodded. "Well, I'm happy for you. I hope it works out, Luther."

He finally looked at me, narrowing his eyes. "Really? Not a single smart-assed remark?"

"Nope, none. I'm not even going to comment on the fact that you are suspiciously chipper today," I replied, pursing my lips to avoid cracking a smile.

"I knew you couldn't resist being a smart ass," he said. "You'd better tell me what brought you here this evening before I lose my patience and kick you out."

"Kick me out?" I laid a hand on my chest, doing my best pearl-clutching maiden impression. "I'm hurt, Luther. Really, I am."

"As it so happens, I do have a job for you, so kicking you out isn't an option at the moment. But keep it up and I'll start making you pay for your coffee."

"As druid justiciar, I live to serve," I said, my voice dripping with sarcasm. "Anyway, here's the situation..."

BY THE TIME I'd nearly finished my story, Luther was eyeing me with keen interest. When the old vamp stared, it was more than a bit unnerving, because he tended to forget his human mannerisms when lost in his thoughts. Having someone look at you without blinking, breathing, or twitching for several minutes was freaky as all hell, but I'd gotten used to it.

Eventually, I wrapped up my account of what had happened with Derp, Kenny, and the alley cat. Luther kept up his wax figure bit for a few more seconds, then took a sudden, sharp breath. I was expecting it, but still nearly pissed my pants.

"Tell me again about what the cat saw?" he asked. I described the vision once more, and this time around he had the good grace to nod along as I spoke. "I see. Incidentally, that's one hell of a talent to have, tactically speaking. Can all druids do that—read the minds of animals, I mean—or just you?"

"I dunno, to be honest. I assumed all druids could do it, but since it's just me and Finnegas, I have no idea."

Luther crossed his arms and tapped a finger on his lips. "I'd find out, just for curiosity's sake. As for this mystery creature, there are a few possibilities regarding what it might be."

"Hit me—I'm all ears."

Luther informally leaned an elbow on the bar, but his tone of voice was anything but casual. "First, you should know that for the last several weeks, my people have been finding male human bodies that have been drained of blood. These corpses have been carelessly left in the open for anyone to find. Thankfully, the smell of human blood has alerted my coven members to the presence of each body thus far, and we've avoided an incident. However, it's only a matter of time before the authorities find a body before we do."

"I'm going to take a wild stab and say that the identities of these corpses were those of the missing men—am I right?"

"You're correct. It would seem that your young friend ran afoul of whatever has been killing male humans in my territory. Whether the culprit is intentionally trying to cause trouble for the Coven, or if it's just sloppy work, who can say? But I do need this problem taken care of immediately. And since I believe it to be a fae creature and not one of my kind, well—this job would seem to fall within the purview of our new justiciar, yes?"

I scrubbed my face with my hands, wincing when I rubbed my jawline. "Oh, joy. What makes you say it's not a vamp?"

Luther's nose twitched slightly, an uncharacteristic gesture for him. He was miffed about the interloper, but trying not to show it. "I didn't say that it wasn't a vamp—I merely said it wasn't one of *my* kind. Meaning, not a conventional vampire, but instead of a different species entirely."

"What, a *nosferatu*, like that old one we tangled with a while back?"

"Actually, no. Nosferatu are distant cousins—albeit an older, less-evolved branch of the family. This creature, on the other hand, is entirely unrelated to my kind. It doesn't hunt the same, and it certainly doesn't kill the same. The kills have been way too clean, indicating that the bodies were wiped of evidence somehow, perhaps by magical means."

"Interesting that you mention that," I remarked. "The crime scene I saw showed no signs of struggle. I was thinking that the killer uses hypnosis on its victims, or maybe some sort of paralyzing agent."

"I couldn't say, as we've only seen corpses. However, I do know this thing kills for the joy of it, apparently driven by some dark compulsion. My kind could be called evil by most measures of morality, and rightly so, but even nosferatu only hunt when they need to feed. Killing more often goes against our survival instincts, because it invites way too much attention from humankind."

I nodded. "Hunters do tend to notice such things."

"Indeed, you do. Thus, we've learned to feed out of necessity first and pleasure second. This is the vampire way. Those who don't follow such conventions are hunted down by my kind because they threaten our way of life."

"Okay, so it's not your standard, garden-variety vamp. Then what is it?"

Luther blinked, just once. *Creepy.* "I have a few theories. As I said, I believe it could be a fae creature, perhaps *baobhan sith*, *empousai*, or even a *mandurugo*—the *baobhan sith* being the most likely scenario. That would certainly explain the lack of evidence on the corpses."

"I suppose that's possible. Been a long time since I ran into one, though. Sabine once told me that Maeve doesn't care for them, so she chases *baobhan sith* out of her demesne whenever they try to settle here. *Empousai* like to devour the entire bodies of their victims, and that tends to leave a mess, which rules them out. *Aswangs* and *manananggal* prefer to prey on pregnant women, which likewise eliminates their kind from our list of suspects. But a *mandurugo* might fit the bill. Did anyone happen to look inside the victims' mouths for wounds?"

"I did, in fact," a seductive female voice replied from behind me.

I ONLY BARELY RESISTED GIVING IN to my startle reflex, and forced myself to glance over my shoulder with as much nonchalance as I could muster. Chances were good this was one of Luther's coven members, and showing fear to a vampire was like limping away from a lion. Not that I was afraid—far from it. I mostly just didn't want to let on that I'd allowed something to sneak up on me. I had a reputation to uphold, after all.

Standing behind me was the blonde who'd accompanied Luther to the Conclave a few weeks earlier. She was tall, maybe six feet, and built like a long jumper—with shoulders that bordered on manly, a slim waist, and narrow, boyish hips. Now that I got a good look at her, I noticed that her eyes were heterochromatic—one was blue, the other, hazel. That was a common trait among European royals, a result of marriages between close relatives.

She was pretty, but something about her rubbed me the wrong way, something in her carriage. Arrogance, that's what it was. The female vamp looked me up and down as she wrinkled her nose in distaste.

Yep, I'm sure of it. I hate her.

I turned to address Luther. "Your new guard dog?"

Luther winced slightly at my remark. "Trouble-shooter, actually, on loan from another coven." He leaned over to look past my shoulder. "Sophia, thank you for coming. Now that you've practically given poor Colin here a heart attack, why don't you introduce yourself like a civilized vampire so we can continue our discussion?"

The female vamp stepped up to the bar, wedging herself into my personal space. "Sophia Doroshenko," she said with her arms crossed over her flat, athletic chest. "And you are the famed druid apprentice and 'god-killer.' You do not look so impressive to me." She pronounced every "s" with a "z" sound, and her "l's" were formed in the back of her mouth.

Slavic, definitely. How cliché.

I gave her a look that was halfway between a frown and a smirk. "Meh, people say a lot of things—doesn't mean they're all true. Still, looks can be deceiving. For example, I'd never have thought someone as big as you could move so silently."

The pretty blonde vampire leaned in, glaring and clenching her jaw as she spoke. "What do you mean, 'big'?"

"Manners, Sophia," Luther chided. "Colin has proven himself to be quite capable many times over, and he's a valued ally of this coven. If possible, I'd prefer that you two get along."

"Pompous American oaf," Sophia Doroshenko muttered under her breath, knowing full-well that Luther and I both heard. She sneered at me, then tossed her hair as she took a seat at the bar with vampire-level alacrity. I noted that she made nary a sound, despite the speed at which she sat down.

"The silent movement thing... your talent, I presume?" I asked.

"Indeed," she said. "I've always been able to move quietly, since I was turned."

"Good talent to have when you're trying to avoid a fight," I remarked.

Sophia began to stand again, her eyes ablaze. "Are you insinuating that I am a coward, druid?"

Luther slapped his hand on the counter, hard enough for the sound to reverberate through the room. "Children, please! We have business to discuss, and I'd like to get done before the evening crowd arrives. If you could find it within yourselves to stop quibbling, perhaps we might conclude this discussion and surmise a plan of action?"

"She started it," I sulked.

Sophia Doroshenko tsked at me, then pulled herself up to her full height as she sat ramrod straight on the barstool, eyes locked on Luther. "My apologies, Luther. Please, continue."

"Suck up," I whispered, garnering a sigh and an eye roll from Luther. Sophia pursed her lips as she ignored me. I smirked, knowing I'd gotten the last word. It was petty, but then again so was I. "As I was saying, a *mandurugo* would leave a mark on the inside of the victim's mouth after feeding. You say you checked inside each victim's mouth, Sophia?"

"I did. I can assure you, my examination of each body was very thorough. I saw no evidence of a wound on the inside of the mouth, nor on their neck or limbs."

I rubbed my chin. "Hmm... did you happen to check their genitalia and groin area?"

Luther nodded. "You're thinking it could be a succubus or some similar creature?"

I tilted my head. "Maybe." I turned to Sophia. "Any marks down below on any of the victims?"

"I—I did not think to look there," she said, her face a mask.

I arched an eyebrow at Luther. "Tell me you still have the bodies lying around."

He shook his head. "Too risky—those few we found were disposed of immediately. The last thing we need is for the authorities to find a body on a coven member's property."

I clucked my tongue. "That's a shame. Be sure to call me if another stiff pops up. In the meantime, I'd like to check out the most recent site where a victim was found."

Luther's lips curled into a grin. "Absolutely. In fact, I'll have your new liaison accompany you to the location."

"I'd appreciate it, Luther, especially since I'm on foot at the moment. Incidentally, who is my liaison? Mateo, maybe?"

Sophia Doroshenko raised her hand. "Ahem... that would be me."

I thrust my jaw out slightly and blew hair from my eyes. *Just when I thought my day couldn't get any worse.*

NINE

A few minutes later, I was riding shotgun in a jet-black Corvette ZR-1 as it zipped in and out of traffic on Loop 360, which in fact wasn't a loop at all but a north-south thoroughfare on the west side of town. Sophia Doroshenko gripped the wheel tightly, her driving gloves making small squeaking noises as she turned each corner at speed. I noted that she worked the clutch and gearshift expertly, hitting the precise RPMs needed to smoothly change gears without grinding the clutch or causing the engine to stutter and jerk. This was a woman who took her driving seriously.

"Do you enjoy driving American sports cars?" I asked.

She kept her eyes on the road as she responded. "They are adequate for the task. This is the automobile my host coven has provided, so it is what I use."

I combed my fingers through my hair with a grunt. "Look, maybe we should start over, since we're going to be working together and all. Allow me to begin by apologizing for my behavior earlier."

The tall, blonde vampire shifted gears, sparing me a brief

sideways glance before speaking. "I should not have insulted you before evaluating your worth. Luther is no fool, and he chooses his allies carefully. Perhaps there is something to you, after all."

I chuckled good-naturedly. "Well, I'll say this much—I like the way you drive."

She snorted softly. "The KGB prepared its operatives well."

"You're Russian?"

Sophia shook her head slightly. "Ukrainian, actually. Cossack, if you want to be specific."

"So, what brings a nice Ukrainian girl like you to Austin, Texas?"

Her expression darkened. "Coven business. I am *resheniye problema* for the covens, a problem solver. Where there is trouble, I am sent to intervene, to prevent exposure of our kind."

"Huh. You were sent to help Luther find the thing that's leaving dead bodies everywhere."

"That, and other things." She remained tight-lipped after that, so I decided to sit back and enjoy the ride.

Minutes later, after crossing the 360 Bridge heading north, Sophia made a sharp U-turn at Courtyard Drive. She floored it before screeching to a halt just off the shoulder, in an area where people typically parked when hiking up the Pennybacker Overlook. It was a popular place for couples to watch the sun set over the hills, plus the bridge and the Colorado River made a stunning backdrop for snaps and profile pics.

Sophia shifted the car into neutral and set the parking brake. "We are here," she stated unceremoniously as she exited the car.

I followed suit, jogging to catch up. The vampire's boots crunched the gravel underfoot at a steady and rapid pace, her bearing rigid as she proceeded toward the river.

"What, did they leave the body under the bridge?"

Sophia Doroshenko shook her head. "No, on the cliff above."

"Man, they really *did* want the body to be found."

"Yes. Come, I will show you."

Her tall legs ate up the trail, and although she was moving slowly on my account, I had to struggle to keep up. When we reached the top, there were a few people there drinking beer and chatting. Sophia pulled out a flashlight, shining it in their eyes as she flashed a badge at them.

"Police business, please be on your way," she commanded. The hikers complied, grumbling about Nazis and fascists as they left. Sophia Doroshenko stood with her hands on her hips as she watched them go.

"Americans, pfah!" she spat.

"Well, you can't blame them," I commented. "We did ruin their evening, after all."

"Your people have no idea what fascism is, druid, and no appreciation for the freedoms they possess. They cry that they are oppressed, when they live in the most free society in the world."

"Actually, last I checked, we were ranked seventeenth or something. I think Switzerland gets the prize for providing the most freedom to their citizens."

Sophia sniffed. "Perhaps you should try living under Soviet rule, eh? Then you see what oppression is about."

"Nope, I'm good," I replied. "Now, can you show me where that last body was found?" I asked, hoping to change the subject. I hated discussing politics with people. It always ended up being an argument, which made it a complete waste of time. Besides, I had a case to solve and a fourteen-year-old to find.

"Yes, it was left there." She pointed to the corner of the cliff, at a spot that put the 360 Bridge in the background. It was where just about everyone and their cousin posed for pictures when visiting the site.

"Damn, that's bold." I walked over and squatted near the area she'd indicated, touching the limestone bedrock beneath my feet. There was no sign of violence, and the smell of death had long since dissipated. However, I sensed something else here—a "disturbance in the force" of sorts.

"We are wasting our time, druid," Sophia commented. "We should be out looking for another body, or trying to determine a pattern in the killings."

I held one finger up. "Give me a second. We druids have methods of gaining information that are somewhat unconventional, and I'd like to try one of them."

"Pfft. If you insist," she replied.

I knelt, ignoring the jagged edges of rock that dug into my knees as I settled in. I planted my hands on my hips, then slowed my breathing as I extended my senses and awareness outward. All I needed was one small animal nearby that might have seen the killer, just one.

Sounds of cars passing below blended with the whine of an outboard motor in the distance. Underlying the harsh noise of civilization, I detected the soft lapping of water against the shoreline below, and the wind whistling through the juniper trees nearby. The air smelled of exhaust fumes, river water, cedar, and earth. I lowered my hands to the bedrock beneath me, extending my senses further into the night.

Bats and swallows whistled overhead, but none of them had seen anything. Field mice rustled in the leaves a few yards distant, but they had a habit of keeping their eyes on the skies and their next meal, so I didn't bother with them. A rabbit laid curled up in its den down the hill, fearful of meeting its end in the jaws of a fox or coyote. It stayed in its burrow after dark, and thus made a poor witness to nocturnal events. A further scan revealed that no large predators were near enough to query, and none of the fauna here had witnessed anything of note.

I was just about to give up when I noticed that strange *disturbance* again. And this time, it noticed me as well.

I OPENED MY EYES, because I knew instinctively that this presence wasn't natural. My breath caught in my chest as a dim glow appeared just over the edge of the cliff. Suddenly, a pale white hand clawed its way over the edge, its black fingernails raking the stone with an unsettling *skritching* noise. Next rose a shock of black, disheveled hair, followed by a likewise pale hand and arm that pulled the creature over the side of the cliff and into view.

Scuttling over the cliff's edge like a spider, its limbs canted at impossible angles, was a young Asian man with ghostly-white skin dressed in similarly pale rags. His eyes were the color of midnight, and his lips curled back in a wicked sneer that revealed crooked, black teeth. The thing's feet were bare, and he rocked this way and that as he observed me where I knelt a few feet away.

"What is that thing?" Sophia asked.

I kept my eyes on it as I responded. "A ghost, I think." Typically, when spirits remained on this plane after death it was for some purpose, and often that purpose was to see their killer brought to justice. I addressed the ghostly figure directly, hoping it might reveal its killer. "Am I right? Are you the ghost of the young man who was found here?"

"*Fukushū...*" it moaned in response.

"I don't know what that means," I said. "Do you speak English?"

The thing opened its mouth impossibly wide as it let out a screech that pierced the night. "*Fukushū!*" it wailed.

I felt Sophia's cold, firm hand on my shoulder. "Vengeance, druid. The ghost cries for vengeance. We should go."

"No—if it wants revenge, maybe it will tell us who its killer was so we can help it find peace."

Sophia squeezed my shoulder tightly. "While your logic is sound, druid, your judgment is not. Somehow, I do not think this ghost knows the difference between friend and foe."

I looked up at Sophia. "Oh, come on, it's clearly asking for help—"

My words were cut off as a screeching white blur tackled me at about fifty miles an hour. I bowled over backwards, and found myself pinned to the ground by the ghost. Its hands were on my wrists, and it perched over me with its feet on my hips. Strangely, it felt heavy on me, more like the weight of an automobile than an ethereal being. Wherever it touched me cold seeped into my body, draining me of strength.

I struggled against its grip and weight, but I might as well have been trying to move a dump truck. Being in contact with it seemed to slowly be sucking the life out of me, and moment by moment I felt my limbs growing weaker. The thing kept screeching all the while, and slavered some sort of ectoplasm on my chest as it cried its misery to the night sky.

Sophia stood nearby, a mixture of amusement and concern on her face. "So, it just wants our help, eh?" she gloated.

"I could use a little help here myself, if you don't mind?" I asked, with only a small bit of panic in my voice.

She chortled as she stepped forward to grab the ghost. Being no stranger to vampire strength, I fully expected her to pick the thing up and toss it off the cliff. To our mutual surprise, her hands slipped right through the ghost's body. Even more surprising, it turned its head around one-hundred-eighty degrees like an owl, fixing her with that black-eyed stare. Then, it backhanded her across the chest, hard enough to send her sailing into the trees.

"Damn it, there goes my ride."

I continued to struggle as I watched the ghost turn its head back around in a sort of ratcheting motion. It was altogether creepy and hypnotizing in a macabre, "train wreck happening right in front of me" sort of way. However, I didn't start crapping my pants until it looked at me and opened its mouth wide enough to drive a mid-sized sedan down its throat.

"Fuck me sideways," I hissed. "Damn it, dude, I am *not* your enemy!" I yelled as the ghost began to slowly lower its mouth to my neck. "Okay, fine then—have it your way."

Recently dead ghosts were often befuddled and frustrated by their situation, which made them dangerous to deal with. Worse, it often took days or weeks for their memories to coalesce enough for them to focus on their purpose and stop poltergeisting the shit out of random people. While this ghost might eventually be able to tell friendlies from serial killers, right now it was angry and bewildered enough to kill anything that caught its attention, including me.

Knowing I had just one means of getting out of this predicament, I flipped my inner switch, shifting as far into my Fomorian form as I thought I safely could. Bones shifted and joints popped as my body rearranged itself into a larger, sturdier version of me. My skeleton lengthened, my skin thickened, and my muscles swelled as I gained mass and size.

The further the change progressed, the greater the urge I felt to *rip-maim-tear-claw-dismember-kill*. It was like a voice in the back of my head telling me to do terrible things—my Hyde-side, trying to take the driver's seat. I pushed the urges down, ignoring them as I took stock of my situation.

I wasn't sure how strong I was when I went one hundred percent Hyde-side, but if I had to guess, it was somewhere between Kraven the Hunter and Beast on the comic book scale of strength. However, in my half-shifted form, I could just barely bench the back end of a compact car, which equated to about a five hundred-pound press. I knew, because I'd tried it back at the junkyard, just to test the limits of what I could do when partially transformed.

But despite my considerable, if limited, strength, I still couldn't toss the ghost off me. Obviously, it was using some otherworldly power that defied physics to hold me down, because technically an ethereal creature had no mass. It occurred to me that, if I didn't do something immediately, it would breach my thickened skin with its teeth and suck the life force right out of my body.

If that happened, my Hyde-side might take over to save us... er, me. And that always led to bad things.

But I wasn't completely down and out. It was going to suck, but I had an ace up my sleeve that this ghost didn't know I could play.

EYE, you there?

As the "voice" I'd come to associate with Balor's Eye replied, it sounded like it was calling to me from a great distance. Even so, it was a welcome presence.

-It is difficult for me to communicate with you in your partially-transformed state, but yes, I am here.-

That's good news, because I need your help. Tell me, how well does that heat blast of yours work against ethereal creatures?

-Such as the shade that is currently preparing to drain your life force?-

That'd be what I was getting at, yes.

-Considering that I am, in effect, an inter-dimensional being myself, I am capable of altering a release of energy such that it affects beings and objects that are out of phase with this dimension.-

Give it to me in English, if you don't mind.

-To use an expression from your own vernacular, I am fully capable of 'blasting the living shit' out of this ghost. Since the blast will be out of phase with your dimension, it shouldn't harm you in the slightest.-

Will it kill the thing? I don't really want to destroy it. I just want it off me so I can find its killer and help it pass on to the next life.

-No. It will merely disperse its energies. I estimate the entity will fully coalesce again within the span of one or two earth days.-

Do it.

I sensed rather than felt the Eye's presence somewhere behind my eyeballs. Turning my eyes downward, I craned my neck to focus the Eye's energy blast directly at the ghost's head. The space between its gaping jaws was now a vast, dark pit that seemingly threatened to swallow me whole. Despite the grotesquery of its appearance, I felt bad for the thing, considering how it had presumably suffered as it died. However, I trusted that the Eye knew its business. A blast wouldn't kill the ghost or prevent it from passing into the beyond.

As soon as I had my eyes fully focused on the ghost's head, Balor's Eye released its considerable energies at the specter. A beam of heatless light escaped from my eye sockets, hitting the ghost square in the face. Unlike past occasions when the Eye had blasted someone while I was in my half-Formorian form, my eyeballs didn't melt out of my skull. Instead, I merely felt a tingling sensation that caused my eyeballs to itch.

Despite the lack of damage to my own physiology, the effect on the ghost was immediate and dramatic. In short, its head disintegrated in a puff of pale white sparkles and moondust. The thing's body immediately followed suit. As the image of the haunt disappeared, all that was left was a keening, mournful wail that faded off into the night.

I stood and brushed myself off, unwittingly getting the ghost's ectoplasmic slobber all over my hands. Since my jeans were shredded anyway due to increasing in size during my shift, I wiped my hands on my pants. Then, I glanced down at my boots, noting that my toes were poking out the front and the seams were torn down the sides. Resigned, I kicked them off. That's when I noticed Sophia Doroshenko staring at me from a few feet away.

"*Lajno!*" she exclaimed. I didn't need to understand Russian or Ukrainian to know it was an expletive.

"Um, don't worry—I'm wearing my stretchy underwear, so if my clothes ripped in an embarrassing place, I swear I won't accidentally flash you."

The vampire stood stock still, and her voice held the barest tremor as she replied. "You've shifted into a form I've never seen before, not in three centuries on this earth. You shot fire from your eyes that banished the ghost. What kind of creature are you, druid?"

I suddenly realized Luther hadn't revealed much about me to her. "Well, it's complicated. And at the risk of sounding like a pompous ass, I'm kind of a one-off."

"What is one-off?" she asked.

"You know—one of a kind, unique."

She shook her head. "Luther is wise to keep you close, *chudovishche.*"

"Judo say what?"

Either my joke didn't translate, or Sophia wasn't in the mood for laughter. A worried look crossed her face, quickly resolving into a neutral expression. "Never mind, druid. Come, I should return and discuss what we saw here with Luther."

"Right. Just give me a second to change back into my human form so I don't have to rip a seat out to fit in the Corvette."

TEN

Sophia Doroshenko dropped me off at the junkyard, peeling out of the parking lot without sparing me a glance or so much as a *da svidania*. Although I'd attempted small talk on the way back from the murder site, she'd only responded in grunts and small head movements. Obviously, she'd been spooked by what she'd seen of my Hyde-side at the overlook.

Not that it bothered me much—mostly because I thought she was an abrasive ass—but it might make things difficult if I needed her help at some point. Luther had obviously paired us together for a reason, but being an older vamp, his motives were often difficult to decipher. Deciding that nothing could be done for it, when I got home I put all thoughts of beautiful Ukrainian former-KGB vampires out of my mind and got ready for bed.

Before falling to sleep, I grabbed my laptop and did some research into Japanese folklore and *yōkai*, the Japanese word for supernatural creatures. That was one deep rabbit hole, to be sure. After doing a cursory review of the topic I gave up, slamming my laptop shut so I could get a few hours of sleep.

I'd just drifted off when I heard a woman's laughter. I sat up in bed, wondering if I was dreaming. Then, I heard it again, coming from the yard.

"Jesse?" I asked, more to myself than aloud.

A playful, melodious voice carried through the walls of the shop from somewhere outside. "Colin, come sit with me. I'm lonely and I want to talk."

A glance at my phone had me cursing, because it'd only been a few minutes since my head had hit the pillow. After tossing on a pair of jeans, I grabbed a jacket and slid into a pair of bearpaw house shoes Bells had gotten me for my birthday. Then, I slipped my phone in my pocket and marched out to the yard.

Jess was peeking at me from behind the druid tree with a mischievous look in her eyes. Thus far, she'd only appeared on this side when she was in contact with the oak. I hoped like hell that meant she couldn't leave the confines of the grove.

"Jesse, for the love of all that's sacred, I'm trying to get some sleep."

She smiled innocently, batting her emerald-green eyes. "If you'd spend more time in the grove, you wouldn't need so much sleep, silly. Come with me, and I'll show you what the grove can do for you—and then maybe we can try a few other, more enjoyable things."

I rubbed my eyes with my palms, mostly to hide the frustration I was feeling. "Honestly, Jesse, I can't. I'm bone tired, and I only have the luxury of resting a few hours before I have to go at it again."

My recently-dead ex narrowed her eyes at me and huffed. "It's that Spanish hussy, isn't it? She won't let you come see me, because she's jealous. You should tell her, I don't mind sharing. The Galician slut can have you on this side, and I'll enjoy the pleasure of your company while you're in the grove. See? Then everybody's happy."

"Jess, I—it's not that. There's this kid who's missing, and I have to find him."

The dryad's eyes lit up. "Ooh, I can help you with that! Tell me more about this *very important* case you're on."

I ran my fingers through my hair with a sigh. *Aw, what the hell,* I thought as I approached the tree. "You see, it's like this—"

As I got closer, Jesse's nose wrinkled and her lips pursed. "Eew! You smell like death—like spirits, actually. What have you been into?"

"About that, I sort of got into a wrestling match with a ghost." I sniffed a pit, shrugging. "Guess I should've taken a bath —the thing did slobber all over me."

"You think? Until you wash that stuff off and do a cleansing ritual, that ghost will be able to track you down wherever you go. No, that simply will not do."

Jesse reached behind the tree's trunk, keeping her fist closed as she brought her hand back into view. She held her hand in front of her face and opened her fingers, revealing a pile of green dust that sparkled slightly in the glow from the sodium lights across the yard. She blew on the dust, propelling it into a cloud that enveloped me completely.

"Jesse, what the hell?" I protested as I futilely batted at the dust particles in the air.

Despite my trepidation at being exposed to Jesse's magic, as it turned out I had nothing to fear. As each mote of green dust touched my skin, it popped into nothingness with a tiny flash of magic, releasing a smell like the first spring shower, moss, and wildflowers. Within moments, my skin was magically scrubbed clean—plus I smelled like I'd been rolling around in a pile of air fresheners.

"See?" she crowed. "Now you don't reek of dead things."

I sniffed myself again. "Um, thanks... I think."

Jesse responded with a tinkling of laughter as she sat

amongst the tree's roots, somehow managing to look very prim and proper for a mostly naked woman. As she settled in, she tucked her legs up under her, then adjusted and draped her mossy, leafy hair so it covered her breasts and pubic area.

The dryad patted the ground next to her. "Come, sit—and tell me about this ghost, and how it fits into your case."

Something in the spell she'd cast made me feel strangely refreshed, like I'd slept a couple of hours rather than a few minutes. The sudden burst of energy I felt made me much more amenable to conversation. Still, I wondered if she was exerting some subtle influence over me. *Nothing to do for it now. I may as well humor her so I can get back to sleep.*

"I suppose I can spare a few moments," I replied.

Rather than sitting next to her, I plopped down on a stack of tires, which earned me a brief frown that was gone almost before it had registered. Jesse sat very still, staring at me with enraptured interest as I described the events of the past two days. She was trying very hard to get on my good side, it seemed.

"Was the vampire girl pretty?" she asked with a glint in her eye.

"She's a higher vampire, Jesse—they're all pretty."

"As pretty as me?"

"Honestly, no." My eyes searched the ground in front of me as I replied. "To me, you always had a beauty that surpassed other women." *Even now, when your current form is freaking me out.*

Her voice practically burst with self-satisfaction as she responded. "Oh, good answer, slugger. Nice to see you haven't lost your charm." She paused for a moment, then her eyes tightened as the smile faded from her lips. "Now, regarding this ghost—I learned quite a bit about ghosts, wraiths, and specters during the time I was one myself."

I waited for more, but apparently my every interaction with

Jesse now required an equal exchange of attention. "Yes? Please, continue." *So I can go back to bed.*

Jesse smiled coyly at me. "I just wanted to make sure I had your undivided adoration."

"Don't you mean attention?"

"Certainly, that too. Anyway, it sounds as though what you encountered earlier is a *yūrei*. Yes, I believe that's what it was."

Again, I waited for her to continue to some logical conclusion, but she seemed to be intent on making me drag every last bit of information from her. "Fine, Jess, I'll play your game. Would you please tell me what a yūrei is?"

SHE LAID a smooth green hand on her chest. "Why, I thought you'd never ask. A yūrei is a Japanese ghost, of a kind that's typically created when someone is murdered. They are completely preoccupied with seeking vengeance, and will not rest until they achieve their goal."

"Well, shit. Do you think the thing will try to find me and attack me again?"

Jesse's eyes searched the leafy branches overhead. "Maybe? But chances are good that he won't be able to find you, now that you've been cleansed by the grove's magic."

"That's good news. Is there anything else I should know?"

"Hmm, let me think." She bobbled her head back and forth in a witless manner that was quite unlike the Jesse I'd known before. That woman had been much more staid and serious, and hated it when girls played dumb around guys. She curled a lock of leafy hair around her finger as she replied. "Well, you might keep an eye out for other *yōkai*, because one tends to beget the other."

"Meaning?"

"Meaning, your ghost may have been killed by something terrible, something much darker and more frightening than the yūrei you encountered. I mean, duh—if a human had killed that guy, don't you think the ghost would have already dealt with them and moved on?"

"I never thought of that, to be honest."

"See, silly? That's why you need to visit me more often."

I decided to change the subject. "How's Nameless doing?"

She gazed at her fingernails. "Wasting away. The grove will kill him eventually—which, incidentally, would be a violation of your agreement. Wouldn't hurt my feelings one bit, but chances are good the raven would lay a nasty curse on you because of it."

"I think I know someone who might be interested in him. Give me a few days to find this kid, and then I'll deal with the bird." I placed my hands on my knees, pushing myself up as I stood. "If you'll excuse me, I really need to get some sleep."

"And I keep telling you, if you'd spend more time in the grove you wouldn't need so much sleep."

"For the moment, I'll just have to take your word for it. Right now, I want to do things the old-fashioned way, with a pillow and mattress."

The dryad who was and wasn't Jesse purred like a kitten. "I can think of a few things for us to do that are right up that alley, slugger." She stood, swishing her hips seductively. "And I promise, you'll be fresh as the morning dew when we're done."

"I, uh—some other time, I think."

"Suit yourself. When you come to your senses, you know where to find me."

"Goodnight, Jesse."

She glanced over her shoulder at me, a smile playing at the corners of her lips. Then she slowly sashayed her way behind the tree trunk, providing me with a full-length view of her backside as she departed.

Funny how her hair only covers her nakedness when she wants it to.

Not that I was complaining or anything. I'd loved and lusted after that body for years, after all. Well, not *that* body precisely, but one nearly identical to it in shape and form.

"My very own Poison Ivy," I muttered. "I wonder if her kiss would be poison, too?"

A lilting laugh echoed from a place both near and far away. "Only one way to find out…"

Shit. Better watch what I say around here from now on.

Lost in my thoughts as I headed back to my room, I didn't see Bells sitting on the loading dock until I was almost on top of her. Her head hung low, and her face was hidden by locks of dark wavy hair.

"So, your girlfriend found a way to come back to life, eh? I honestly thought it was a golem, and you were playing at some seriously sick shit. But it's really her, isn't it?"

"Bells, I'm so sorry. I was going to tell you, I swear." It sounded lame, but it was the truth.

Her legs dangled off the edge of the dock, and she tapped a heel against the concrete in a slow rhythm. "How long since she came back?"

I released a sharp sigh. "A while—weeks, in fact. She showed up when I planted the acorn in the yard, right after all that shit happened with Gunnarson."

Bells tucked a strand of hair behind her ear as she looked at me out of the corner of her eye. "You mean that tree—? You know what, it's not important right now. What matters is that your ex-girlfriend has been living in your backyard for weeks, and you didn't even have the balls—much less, the courtesy—to tell me."

I sat down heavily a few feet from her, legs crossed with my back against a metal pillar. "I haven't even told Finnegas. In fact, the only person besides you who knows is Maureen, and that's because she saw her one day when she was looking for me in the yard."

"Oh yeah? What did Maureen have to say about it?"

I glanced around nervously. "Not here, alright?" I grabbed my phone from my pocket and typed a few words in my text app, sending it to Belladonna's phone.

I don't evN knO f she iz Jesse. Can't TLK hEr. She iz listening.

Belladonna pulled her buzzing phone from her handbag and glanced at it. Her eyes closed and her lips pressed into a tight line. She opened her eyes and hopped off the dock, her stance wide as she gripped her phone so tight I thought it might break.

"You know, I'm going through some shit right now too. And, damn it, I really needed you over the last few weeks." I thought I might have seen tears welling up in her eyes, but I couldn't be certain. "And here I thought I'd done something wrong, but all this time you were hanging out with your ex."

"Bells, it's not like that..." I said. I stood to cross the gap between us, but stopped myself as I remembered my earlier experience with her in the yard.

Belladonna growled at my reticence—or cowardice, take your pick—then stormed away toward the parking lot. Halfway there, she stopped and looked back at me.

"You know what, Colin? You may not see what's going on here, but I do. I've been competing with her ghost since I met you, and fool that I am, I thought eventually I'd win your heart. I mean, how hard can it be to beat out a ghost? But that thing?" She pointed at the tree that towered over the junkyard. "How the hell am I supposed to compete with that?"

I honestly didn't have an answer for her. "All I can say is that I'm sorry, Bells."

"Yeah? Well, I'm sorry too. When you figure it out, don't bother calling, alright?"

As I watched her go, I was certain she meant what she said. Maybe I should have chased her; I'd never been good at reading situations like that. But deep down inside, doubt and indecision won out over duty and good intentions.

The question is, do I even want to chase her?

In all truth, I couldn't say.

I WAS CLOSING and locking the entrance gate when a dark blue unmarked police cruiser pulled into the junkyard parking lot. I felt like an idiot standing there in my bear paw slippers, but that seemed to be the theme of the day so I went with it. Leaning against the gate, I greeted the stout, stern-looking officer as she exited her vehicle.

"Sergeant Klein, what a pleasant surprise. What brings you to my doorstep this evening?"

She glanced at my shoes with a smirk. "Nice. Do you wear jammies with footsies, too?"

I ignored the barb, knowing it was a friendly jab and nothing more. "Come on in, I'll put some coffee on."

She waved off my offer with a frown. "Naw, I can't stay. I'm working late 'cause another one turned up missing. In fact, that's why I came to see you. Didn't want to speak over the phone, because who the hell knows who's listening, right?"

"If you only knew, Sergeant."

Klein arched an eyebrow. "Yeah, well, I *don't* want to know. My life's become too complicated as it is since I met you, so leave me out of anything that's not need to know, alright? Anyway, this latest missing persons report just came in this morning, and I volunteered to conduct the interview. Unlike the others, this guy had family close by."

I stretched and stifled a yawn. *Damned spell sure wore off quick.* "You mean the others didn't?"

"Am I boring you, McCool? Shit, isn't that what I just said? No, none of the other men who've gone missing were native to the area. Every last one of them was here on a student visa or H-1B1."

"What's an H-1B1?"

She scratched her nose with the back of her hand. "Work visa for smart people. All these missing persons were foreign nationals, either here for grad studies or they were professionals working for domestic corporations."

"Meaning, if they went missing they might not be noticed right away."

"Right. People would notice, but they also might assume they got homesick and took a quick trip back home. Could take weeks for the company to figure things out, notify the family members, and so on. Kind of makes for a good victim profile, except for the fact that foreign governments don't take too kindly to their citizens disappearing on U.S. soil."

I massaged my temples, hoping it would perk me up. "Still, it's kind of a weird pattern for a serial killer to choose. Missing persons cases like that could become high-profile really quick."

Klein sniffed and rubbed her nose. "Damned allergies, makes me wish I'd never moved to Austin. Anyway, I haven't told you the real kicker."

"You found a connection between the victims?"

"Officially they're not victims yet, but yeah." Klein paused and cocked her head. "You're looking at me weird, McCool. I take it they're definitely all victims—am I right?"

"Um, no comment. So, what's the connection?"

Klein grabbed a wad of Kleenex from her pocket and blew

her nose loudly. "Gah! Can't take antihistamines on the job, because they put me right to sleep." She tucked the tissues in her jacket pocket before continuing. "Alright, so the girl I interviewed today told me her brother had been blabbing non-stop about going on a date with some girl he met online. We checked his browser cache and found he'd joined this dating site, NipponMatch-dot-com. It apparently caters to Japanese expats, as well as American Japanophiles with a penchant for dating Japanese men and women."

"I assume you checked the names of the missing with the site's member roster, yeah?"

"Um, not officially, no. Getting a search warrant for online databases is a pain in the ass. So, I had one of the geeks in cybercrimes create a fake profile, then he searched the site and found that our other missing persons were all members. We're working on getting a search warrant now."

I yawned as a smile split my face. "You know what, Klein? That's the best thing that's happened all day."

"What, that we have more than a dozen foreign nationals missing, possibly due to a supernatural serial killer? Even if you find the thing and stop the killings, I still have to come up with a way to wrap the case up neatly for the press and my superiors. So, forgive me if I fail to see the upside to this situation."

"I was actually just referring to the break in the case. It's the only solid lead I've gotten since Kenny showed up here the other day."

Klein wiped her nose with her wad of Kleenex again. "Yeah? Well, don't put yourself out trying to help me close this case or anything. And please don't tell me you can't recover the bodies. No bodies, no closure. No closure, no resolution to the case. I hate open case files."

"I promise, I won't tell you that."

The sergeant squinted at me. "Do I even want to know?"

"Nope, you don't want to know."

"Shit." She went to get back in her car, and paused halfway in the door. "You know what, McCool? Some days I wish I'd never met you."

"Yeah, that seems to be going around."

ELEVEN

Hours later, I was awakened by the smell of breakfast tacos and cigarette smoke. I cracked an eye and was greeted by the sight of my mentor, Finnegas, holding a white, grease-stained bag in one hand and a roll-your-own cancer stick in the other. He tossed me the bag as I stretched and rubbed the sleep from my eyes. I opened it, taking a whiff of the contents, and a smile spread across my face.

"*Barbacoa?*" I asked.

He nodded. "Yup, and the good stuff too—not just slow-cooked *lengua* like they serve to gringos at the chain restaurants. Don't be shocked if you find a hair or two in your tacos—there's meat from the whole cow's head in there. Lips, cheeks, eyes, and all. Guy who runs the taco truck I get it from doesn't mess around."

"Alright, so who do you need me to kill?"

Finn chuckled. "Nobody, but I figured if I was going to wake you up after another late night, I'd better come bearing gifts. C'mon, get dressed. You can grab some coffee from the office. We have training to do."

"Um, about that... I'm on a case, so we'll need to keep it

short today. Also, can we train somewhere else than the junkyard?"

His eyes narrowed as he blew smoke from his nostrils. "You still haven't gone inside, have you?"

"It's not that, Finn. It's just that I—"

He scowled as he threw his cigarette butt on the floor and crushed it with the heel of his cowboy boot. "Damn it, Colin, I told you to enter that thing and claim it before it withers away. What the hell has gotten into you, boy? A druid grove is nothing to be taken lightly, and since you planted it, the tree is your responsibility."

I *had* entered the tree, I just hadn't taken the time to "claim" it yet—in fact, I didn't even know what that entailed. Jesse had hinted at it a few times, but I'd never pursued the topic as I tried to keep my visits with her as brief as possible. Of course, Finnegas didn't know about any of this, because I was keeping Jesse a secret from him until I figured out what to do with her. As far as he knew, I'd been putting the whole thing off due to Ed's death.

What he doesn't know can't hurt him. Wish I didn't have to lie to him, though.

"I know, I know. But—"

"But nothing! That tree may very well be the last of its kind. Do you know how long it's been since someone planted a druid grove on this earth? Most died out in the first century, when Suetonius burned the sacred groves all across the island of Anglesey. The rest were cut down by the church centuries later, after the old beliefs died out and few of our kind were left to guard them."

I set the food aside and grabbed a pair of jeans, pulling them on as I spoke. "Not to cast aspersions or anything, but where were you when that all happened?"

Finnegas scratched his nose, and his scowl intensified.

"When Anglesey happened I was in Ireland. And after St. Patrick came, well—let's just say I went looking for a new home for our kind. By the time I'd returned, the old beliefs had all but died out, and the groves had been destroyed."

I slipped into a t-shirt, then pulled on my socks and boots and stood. I clapped a hand on Finn's shoulder and looked him in the eye. "Look, I can see what this means to you, and I fully intend to fulfill whatever caretaker duties the tree requires. It's just too overwhelming to deal with right now, what with Ed's murder and all."

Finn's expression softened and he sighed. "I'm sorry, son. I shouldn't be pressuring you so much, not so soon after your uncle's passing. It's just that it's been ages since I felt this much hope for the future of druidkind."

I patted his shoulder with a wink. "I'm glad to know you think so highly of me—considering I *am* the future of druidkind."

Finnegas gave me an unconvincing frown as he slapped my hand off his shoulder. "Pfft. My hopes are *in spite of* having but one lazy apprentice who'd rather be chasing skirt than learning magic."

"In my defense, Belladonna has never, ever worn a skirt in my presence."

"Bah! You know what I mean. Now, go get some caffeine in you so we can get down to business. We can head out to the greenbelt to train today—and hopefully you won't get distracted by all the topless sunbathers at Twin Falls."

"As if it's me who always gets distracted."

The retort had barely passed my lips when the sharp scent of ozone filled the air. Small arcs of electricity began to crackle and spark between Finn's fingers and in the irises of his eyes. Apparently, I'd finally gotten on the old man's last nerve, an increasingly common occurrence of late.

"Coffee, then training—now, young man!" he barked.

I had the common sense to look properly chastened, and gave the old man a hangdog look as I headed for the door. "Settle down, drill sergeant. I'm going already—geez."

ON THE RIDE OVER, I downloaded the NipponMatch app and set up a fake profile. In my bio, I mentioned that I was just in town for a short time, and that I was here on a visa from South Africa. I had no idea how to do a South African accent, but figured I could fake it by imitating Hemi's thick New Zealand accent. It wasn't like we got many Afrikaners in Texas, after all—so I doubted anyone would know the difference... I hoped.

Now, I just need to wait and see if I get any takers.

Waiting was going to be agony, especially knowing that Derp was still in the clutches of a serial killer. I'd seen a lot of missing persons cases involving supernatural creatures, and honestly I didn't think it looked good for the kid. There was a high probability he was dead by now, and as much as I hated to admit it, I'd likely just be recovering a corpse. But that didn't mean I wasn't going to do everything I could to find the killer and make them pay. Derp deserved that much, at least.

I tucked those thoughts aside as we neared the park where we planned to train today. At ten o'clock in the morning on a weekday, there were a surprising number of cars along the Mopac Expressway frontage road near the park's entrance. The Barton Creek Greenbelt had always been a favorite destination for local hikers and mountain bikers, and for good reason. The area was an oasis of natural beauty, in a city that rapid population growth and poor urban planning had turned into a smaller and much more expensive version of Houston.

Natural dams created swimming holes at a couple areas along the creek, drawing swimmers by the dozens when the creek was full. Thousands of years of erosion had left plenty of exposed bedrock and numerous large boulders, providing sunbathers ample space to sacrifice their future beauty for today's perfect tan. Live oak, pecan, elm, cottonwood, and willow trees lined the creek on both sides, making the park a verdant playground for outdoorsy types needing an escape from Austin's ever-expanding concrete jungle. And considering the park authority's tolerance for—if not outright approval of—partial nudity, it was no wonder that the greenbelt had become a magnet for those new to the area as well.

We were only a half mile or so into the park, descending a trail that ran along a cliff and led to the valley below. The plan was to turn off the trail when we got to the bottom, so we could head deep into the woods on the other side of the creek where few hikers went. Due to the fine weather we were having, the trail and creek would both be packed with people, but a short jog to the west would allow us to train in privacy. Finnegas muttered to himself as we yielded the rocky, narrow path to yet another pack of mountain bikers, the third such group we'd encountered.

"Fecking Californians. An entire state blessed by perpetual good weather, yet they descend on our city like locusts in a swarm."

"How do you know they're Californians?" I asked.

He gave a quick snort of disgust. "It's the smell that gives them away—a combination of patchouli, hummus, and entitlement."

"Might I remind you that you're also an interloper? You are from Ireland, after all."

"Hah! That's where you're mistaken. I was here before Sam Houston was even a dirty thought in the deep recesses of his daddy's mind. Spent most of my time with the Tonkawa, 'people of the wolf' is what they called themselves. About ten percent of the tribe was made up of werewolves. Traded quite a bit of knowledge with their shamans. Smallpox decimated the humans in their tribe in the late eighteenth century, and the white man's near extinction of the buffalo fairly finished the job for the rest. So, I'd have to say it's all you pale faces who came after me that are the real interlopers."

A white kid with ratty dreads and a rasta beanie raised a fist in the air as he passed us, coming from the other direction. "Right on, old man! Down with the white hegemony."

The old druid's lip curled, and his eyes shot daggers at the kid's retreating figure. "There's a cliff right there—become the change you want to see in the world, young man!" he shouted after the kid.

"On it!" the Anglo Rastafarian replied.

I rolled my eyes. "You know, you'd have been better off just yelling 'get off my lawn' instead. I think the whole irony thing you were going for was lost on him."

Finnegas opened his mouth to respond, but was cut off by a scream that came from the woods below. That sound was followed by a rumbling growl that no human or animal could've made. The noises were way too faint to draw the attention of the mundanes traveling up and down the trail, but to Finnegas and me, they were clear as a bell. Finn gave me a quick nod and I took off at a run down the hill, cutting off into the trees just as soon as the trail flattened out.

I followed the sounds as I went and they led me westward, across the creek to the dense woods where we'd planned to train today. The screams and growls grew louder the farther I got into the greenbelt, and soon they brought me in sight of a middle-aged female hiker clinging to the trunk of a pecan tree, roughly twenty feet from the ground. While the vegetation obscured my view of the tree's base, something below was shaking the tree. Every time the tree shook, it elicited more screams from the woman and more growls from whatever was stalking her.

The creature had to be quite large to jostle a tree like that, but I was relatively sure it wasn't a bear. For one, bears were rarely seen in this part of Texas, and a black bear would be too small to shake a tree of that size. Second, the growls I heard were unlike any animal or creature I'd encountered before—a deep rumble that reverberated at an almost subsonic level. Whatever it was, it was big, and obviously hungry.

And that meant one thing—I needed to shift before I confronted it. The only problem was, I couldn't shift fully, not with my anger issues of late. Recently, I'd been working more on partially shifting. Doing so gave me a bit of increased strength, size, and toughness, but it kept the dark influence of my Hyde-side to a level that allowed me to stay in control of my faculties. Plus, it didn't require me to get buck naked, which was always a plus. I just hoped a partial shift would be enough to let me tangle with whatever was behind those trees.

Here goes nothing.

I still had to remove my socks and shoes, so I peeled them off quickly and readied myself for the change. I focused my mind and slowed my breathing, triggering my ability to shift into my Fomorian form with an effort of will. As I did, I felt an increasing urge for violence and mayhem well up inside me. I pushed those feelings down, concentrating on keeping my breathing slow and my mind calm. Soon I felt my muscles swelling, along with a thickening of my skin and the gain of a foot or so in height. It wasn't much compared to a full-on shift, but it'd have to do.

Once I completed my change, I reached into my Craneskin Bag and grabbed my war club. To anyone else, it looked like a worn ash wood bat—but underneath the glamour it was a thick length of wood shod with iron, four inches in diameter at the tip tapering to two inches across at the handle. The Dagda had told me that Lugh had made it, specifically for fighting fae. Why he'd ever crafted such a weapon was beyond me, but the thing packed a punch.

Suitably armed, I crept toward the source of the noise, sneaking through the trees until it sounded as if I was nearly on top of the beast. I parted the branches in front of me, fully revealing the monster that was the source of the hiker's distress. As I took a good look at the thing, only a single thought came to mind.

Well, shit.

I WAS STUNNED by what I saw through those branches... and it took a lot to give me pause. The creature shaking the tree was something I'd never seen before—a huge, demonic thing that looked like it was straight out of *Pan's Labyrinth*. The monster was humanoid and tall, at least ten feet from its cloven hooves to the top of its head, and even taller if you counted the long, curved horns that reached from the sides of its head to the sky.

From the waist down it was goat-like, and from the waist up it looked mostly human despite the thick, light gray hair that covered much of its body. A cursory anatomical survey told me that yes, the thing was male, and it potentially had designs on its prey that didn't necessarily include eating. The monster's face was the only part of it not covered by hair, and it had the harsh features, needle-sharp teeth, and elongated snout of an opossum. However, its glowing red eyes were quite human-looking, standing in sharp contrast to the rest of its appearance.

As I finished my assessment of the thing, the demon—if it

actually *was* a demon—vigorously shook the pecan tree with its huge, clawed hands, nearly dislodging the woman above him. The hiker's legs and body flew out and away from the tree, and she just barely managed to hang on. When she recovered, she wrapped her legs around the trunk with a yelp and started shimmying higher in the tree.

I was about to spring out from cover to attack the thing, and hopefully draw it away from her so she could escape, when I felt someone grab my arm. It was Finnegas, looking a little winded after the hike down the ridge. Otherwise, he was no worse for the wear.

"Wait," he wheezed in a low voice. "That's a *caddaja*—very dangerous."

"What the hell is a caddaja?" I said, peeking between branches to ensure that the monster in question hadn't reached its prey yet.

He held a finger up, indicating that he needed a moment to recover. It wasn't that he was out of shape—far from it. He'd been cheating death for two millennia and now it was catching up to him, especially since he'd decided to remind everyone what a badass old druid he was. His recent displays of magic and power had drained him even further, and as I looked at his drawn, worn face, I was reminded once again that my time with him was short.

Finally, Finn's breathing slowed and some color returned to his cheeks. "A caddaja is a demonic creature out of Native American legend—that of the Caddo peoples, to be exact. They're strong, fast, and aggressive, and I haven't seen one in these parts in over two centuries."

"I find it hard to believe that something that big and ugly could go unnoticed out here for two-hundred years," I whispered.

Finnegas leaned forward to peek out of our hiding place,

then he stood upright again and shrugged. "It's a demon, Colin. Damned things cross the Veil every so often, either to eat a few humans or because some idiot decides to summon one, then they go back again for a century or two. And thank goodness, because if they had a mind to physically manifest in this plane of existence more often, we'd all be screwed."

"Fine, I believe you. Now, just tell me how to kill the damned thing so I can take it out before it does unspeakable things to that poor woman."

Finnegas tsked. "Can't kill it. Best you can do is drive it away, scare it enough so you send it packing back across the Veil. Hopefully the next time the thing decides to vacation in Central Texas, you'll be long dead."

"Well, there's a cheery thought." I shouldered my war club, rubbing the smooth handle with my thumb. "If I get into trouble, can I count on you for backup?"

Finnegas patted his pockets, his nicotine habit making him suddenly forget the mortal danger we were in. "Where did I put that damned tobacco pouch?"

"Finn! Can I count on you for backup?"

"Huh? And take another few years off my life? Naw, too soon after that stunt I pulled at Maeve's—not to mention the stasis spell at the Conclave. Sorry, kid, but you're on your own on this one. Good news is, if you use magic to beat it we can count it as your training for the day."

"Leave it to the apprentice to take out the demon. Well done, oh master druid."

Finnegas's face lit up as he finally found his tobacco. "Ah, there it is. Kentucky Select, my old friend, come to papa." He looked up at me, brow furrowed. "What are you complaining about? I'm two thousand years old—at my age, don't you think I'm entitled to let a youngster handle things like this?"

He had me there. I pursed my lips and exhaled heavily through my nostrils. "Any last bit of advice?"

"Hit it hard, hit it fast, and don't let up until it's in full retreat. Damned things like to bite the heads off their victims, so don't let it grab you. If you do, you'll be trading fashion tips with the Dullahan in short order."

"Great," I said as I readied myself to charge the caddaja. "Wish me luck."

Finnegas was already rolling a cigarette, apparently unconcerned that I was about to face down a cannibalistic, ten-foot-tall demon. "Bah, you'll be fine. Besides, why do you need my luck? If I've learned anything in the short time I've known you, it's that you're the luckiest sum' bitch I've ever met."

"You're incorrigible, you know that?"

"Takes one to know one," he quipped. "Now, while you go kick that demon's ass, I'm going to rescue the fair maiden in that tree and enjoy a smoke. Damned hike down here was a bitch."

"Asshole," I muttered as I slipped through the trees to flank the demon.

TWELVE

Demon or not, I suspected the thing was as susceptible to a surprise attack as any other creature I'd fought, so that was my plan. Once I got behind him, I crept out of the brush toward the caddaja's back. In my partially-shifted form, I was maybe seven feet tall—formidable in most situations, but not against a ten-foot tall demon. To even the odds, I intended to kneecap the thing and bash his skull in once I had him down on the ground.

But, as Moltke said, "No battle plan survives first contact with the enemy." I was about three steps away from the demon and almost within striking distance when the lady in the tree noticed me.

She looked straight at me and started screaming, blowing my cover. "Help me, please!"

I winced. *Look on the bright side—at least I look human enough that she didn't spook.*

The demon spun around, spotting me instantly. He released a growl that told me he was not happy that I was interrupting—well, whatever he intended to do to the woman.

I sighed. "Lady, that's what I was doing before you warned tall, horned, and ugly here."

The lady's eyes narrowed. "Well, it's not every day that I get chased up a tree by a giant monster! Excuse me for getting a little worked up."

I raised a hand to placate her. "Look, I get it. Don't worry, I have this under control. Just hang tight and I'll have you down—"

The demon took a quick step forward and hit me with a lightning-fast backhand that sent me flying into a patch of agarita bushes, which only barely broke my fall. The blow knocked the wind from my lungs, and I rolled out of the brush gasping for air. As I sat up, I realized I'd lost my war club. *Damn.* I scanned the ground for it as I crabwalked away from the demon.

I was still searching for the club when the monster stomped over and squatted down to look at me. When he roared at me, his breath carried an almost palpable cloud of funk that was a combination of skunk musk, sulfur, and rotted meat. One whiff of it nearly made me lose my breakfast. I waved my hand in front of my face, holding my breath for a moment as I scooted farther away from the thing.

"Man, what is it with man-eating monsters and bad breath? Don't you ever brush your teeth?" I continued to fan the air in hopes of alleviating the odor. "Pro tip—a little dental hygiene goes a long way, even for an inter-dimensional cannibalistic demon such as yourself."

Normally, I wouldn't have bothered bantering with a creature like this, but I needed to give Finnegas and the woman time to get away. As I kept the demon occupied, Finn was busy helping the woman get down from the tree. I only needed to stall for a few more seconds, then they'd be away and safe—at which point I could chase the thing off without the risk of getting anyone else hurt.

The caddaja's brow furrowed as he held an open hand in

front of his mouth and released a puff of air. He sniffed his palm and shrugged. "Smells fine to me. But it would smell a lot better if you hadn't interrupted me in the middle of capturing and eating my sacrifice. Nothing freshens the breath like a bit of human blood."

The demon's voice was rough, yet cultured. It reminded me of the way young werewolves sounded when they spoke in their shifted form. It generally took 'thropes a few decades to learn how to shift while maintaining their human vocal cords, and even then it took some practice to speak normally.

I arched an eyebrow at the creature. "You speak perfect English."

"I do. Spent some time in the service of a well-to-do warlock in Connecticut, just after the Revolutionary War. He taught me to speak English, and I waited until the terms of our agreement were concluded before I ate him. It seemed an even trade."

I sat up, wondering how I should handle the situation. The thing *had* been trying to eat someone just a few moments prior. But since he was intelligent and willing to communicate, I figured it couldn't hurt to make an attempt at finding a peaceful resolution.

I rubbed my chin and pointed at the creature. "You said something about a sacrifice. Would you mind elaborating on that for me? If only for posterity's sake."

The demon curled his upper lip and tsked. "Certainly. Every few hundred years or so, I show up and the local tribe provides me with a sacrifice. They feed me a virgin, and I don't eat their babies and scare off all their game. It's a rather fine deal, if I do say so myself."

"I can see how a demon like yourself might enjoy such an arrangement," I agreed with a nod of my head as I continued to search for my club.

"Exactly! Usually it's a captured slave—the last time it was a white settler I found to be quite delicious, if a little on the bony side. I'd expressed a desire to have the same on my next visit, and the tribal leaders agreed. When I popped over on this side of the Veil and saw the female, I figured she'd been sent to appease me."

"Huh. Yeah, about that..."

The demon cradled his chin in one clawed hand. "Was I mistaken? If I was about to eat the wrong person, I apologize. If so, you merely have to point me in the direction of the appropriate victim, and I'll be happy to dine on that one instead."

I squinted as I tongued a molar. "See, that's the problem. There is no sacrifice."

The demon drew himself up and huffed indignantly. "Well, if the locals have decided to renege on our arrangement..."

I raised my hands. "Hang on, let me finish. Those tribes haven't been around for centuries. They were driven out by the whites ages ago, either killed off or forced onto reservations. That's why there's no sacrifice for you, because the people who used to leave them no longer exist."

THE DEMON WHISTLED SOFTLY. "My, but this is awkward. And the woman I intended to eat?"

"Merely a passerby, out enjoying nature. Purely happenstance that you stumbled upon her."

"Well, it is quite a lovely day."

"That it is." We both kind of sat there for a few moments, avoiding eye contact. Finally, I cleared my throat. "So, about the sacrifice..."

The demon sucked on his teeth as he rubbed his chin. "Yes. Yes, of course. Well, this is conundrum, but we all must make do with the circumstances we're given. Although I would prefer eating a virgin, I suppose you'll just have to do."

"Excuse me?" I scooted back a few feet to give me more time to react, all the while searching the ground with my hands for my club. "Maybe you didn't hear me when I said that the people you made that arrangement with are no longer around."

"Oh, I heard you quite clearly. But this *is* my territory. All my kind have their own areas to look after, you see. And I have quotas to meet. One adult human sacrifice per every two centuries—that's the bare minimum to keep management off my case. You know how it is."

"Not really," I said as I scratched my head. "Look, I'm sorry that you aren't going to be able to meet your sacrifice quota, because you seem like a nice guy—for a flesh-eating demon, that is."

"And you seem a fine fellow for—whatever you are," the demon stated agreeably.

"Um, thanks. But the thing is, I'm just not on the menu. No one around here is, actually, and it's sort of my job to keep it that way. I hate to break it to you, but you're going back across the Veil empty-handed today."

The demon sighed softly. "So that's the way it is, eh?"

"That's the way it is."

"Well, I suppose I'll be going then." The demon rocked up on the balls of his feet, as if he was standing up to leave. I knew better.

Wait for it...

The caddaja sprung forward as he grabbed for me, just as my fingers found the handle of my war club. I grabbed it as I did a shoulder roll, coming to my feet and pivoting to face him.

"And just when I thought we were coming to an understanding," I said.

The demon raised his hands, palms up to the sky. "You can't

expect a leopard to change its spots, can you?" He looked at the tree where, moments before, his intended meal had been safely ensconced. "Damn it all, I was really looking forward to eating a nice tasty virgin today."

"That's what she said," I mumbled under my breath. I raised the volume of my voice as I continued. "By the way, the name's Colin—Colin McCool. Druid justiciar and general thorn-in-the-side of all things supernatural and evil, at your service. Just letting you know, so when I send you back across the Veil you'll know what to tell your boss about why you didn't hit your quota."

The demon turned back to me. "Oh, I like your style, human. It'll be a shame to have to kill you." He took a short bow without taking his eyes off me. "Snaketongue Spinebreaker, Esquire of Hell. Hoping to make knight soon, although that'll depend on the results of today's excursion. Shall we proceed?"

"Sure, let's dance," I replied.

No sooner had I spoken than Snaketongue did a front handspring into a flying drop kick that was aimed right at my chest. I managed to dodge it by spinning to the side, but only barely. I attempted to crack him in the face with my club as he passed, but he was moving too fast. As he landed I stepped forward, striking with the club Filipino-style in a staccato series of strikes aimed at the demon's knee, elbow, and throat.

Snaketongue danced away from my strikes in a surprisingly graceful display for such a large creature. As the fight continued, he moved just enough for me to miss by millimeters, frustrating my attempts to kneecap him or otherwise cripple him and bring him down to my level. And if I gave him any opening whatsoever, he responded by swiping at me with those enormous clawed hands of his. At the end of our first exchange I had yet to touch him, while he'd opened some long, shallow gashes across my chest.

Damn, this thing is fast. Finnegas had said they were danger-ous. Since I'd never fought a demon before, I'd had no idea how dangerous they could be. I wasn't exactly fighting at my best, considering that I hadn't shifted completely, but at the moment I was faster and stronger than normal—and that was saying something. Even in my human form I operated at the peak of human potential, as all natural-born champions did.

Yet, I hadn't been pressed this hard in a fight since I'd fought The Rye Mother back in Underhill. Snaketongue was just as fast as her—maybe faster, if not as vicious. Still, stopping him was proving to be beyond my current physical abilities, and if I didn't do something fast, I was going to end up in that demon's belly.

Now, that would be embarrassing.

The demon had me on the defense now. I sidestepped, ducked, and otherwise evaded his attacks, which were much too strong to block. His fighting style reminded me of Blanka from *Street Fighter*, a weird combination of *capoeira*, tiger claw kung fu, and gymnastics. It was acrobatic and unorthodox, and it made his movements deceptively hard to anticipate.

I attempted to strike his base leg as one of his kicks whooshed overhead, but Snaketongue sprung into a single hand-stand to avoid the strike. As his hand hit the ground, the demon snapped an inverted kick at my face, a move that looked a lot like an *au batido* from capoeira. I mistimed leaning away to avoid it and got clipped on the side of my head for my trouble.

More frustrated than injured, I stumbled away to give myself a few seconds to come up with a plan of action.

My main issue was the fact that Snaketongue was so damned agile. That, combined with the size differential, was making this a lopsided battle. I needed to immobilize him to even the odds. But how?

I THOUGHT about trying to make the ground beneath him into quicksand, by pulling groundwater up from below and altering the composition of the soil. Although I thought I could pull it off, it would take a lot more time and focus than I had to spare. Another idea was to simulate the soil liquefaction that happened during earthquakes, which would basically have the same effect as quicksand.

That was a great plan, except I'd never been taught how to do it. It would have been nice to vibrate the molecules in the soil until they reached a liquid state, and watch Snaketongue get swallowed up by the earth. But since I had no idea if it was even possible, I scratched the idea immediately.

Maybe I'm approaching this the wrong way, I thought as I dodged another swipe from Snaketongue's claws. The demon said he'd been forced to serve a warlock—so, how did a warlock or conjurer contain a demon long enough to strike a deal? How did one force a demon to come to terms in the first place?

By capturing them within a summoning circle.

I knew nothing about such things, but I knew a hell of a lot about wards. And one thing I knew about them was they were mostly powered by the spell caster's will. The more intricate the circle and wards, the greater the amplification of the magician's willpower. Thus, a simple circle could theoretically only contain relatively weak entities, while an elaborate circle would allow a wizard to contain more powerful creatures.

I wouldn't have time to construct an elaborate, warded circle. The good news was, I wouldn't have to. All I needed to do was trap him for a few seconds, long enough to kneecap him so I could put a beatdown on him. Thirty seconds or so would be plenty of time to cut him down to size.

I beat forward with a flurry of strikes, then quickly withdrew, flourishing my war club to keep the demon at bay. I held up a hand, indicating that I wanted to speak.

The demon paused and gave me a sneering look. "Oh, so now you want to parley? Mr. McCool, unless your offer involves virgins, you should know that I'm absolutely not interested."

I waved him off with one hand while I reached out with my mind to the vegetation behind him. "I'm afraid to say that I don't know many virgins, but I am acquainted with quite a few young ladies. Perhaps I could lure one out here, in exchange for my life?"

Snaketongue stood a bit straighter, his eyes looking up and to the left as he considered my offer. "While it is tempting, I seem to have worked up quite an appetite over the last few minutes. No, a bird in the hand is worth two in the bush. I'm sorry, Mr. McCool, but I'm afraid I'll be having you for the main course today."

I tapped a finger on my chin, stalling while I mentally tempted and teased several strands of Virginia Creeper vine into the rough approximation of a circle on the ground behind the demon.

"How about two young women? Or heck, let's make it three. All good things come in threes, right?"

The demon hissed. "You're stalling."

"Well, I'm certainly not eager to be eaten," I replied with a roll of my eyes. "Would you by chance consider four maidens?"

Asking a question just before a sucker punch was the oldest trick in the book. In the time it takes for the question to register the brain is preoccupied, offering a momentary opening for a surprise attack. I took full advantage of the opportunity my question afforded, and leapt into action a split-second after the words left my lips. Closing the distance in a rush, I delivered a quick combination of slashing strikes at the demon's torso and legs.

Snaketongue, however, was a seasoned and savvy combatant. As I expected, he never let down his guard, and the demon easily sprang back to avoid my attack. But instead of pressing the attack, I knelt down quickly, touching my hand to the viny circle I'd created during the lull in our fight.

"*Gabh deamhan*," I whispered as I willed power into the makeshift circuit. As I did, a bright green halo lit up around the demon, just as the vines tore away from their roots with an audible snap. Snaketongue was now trapped inside a complete and unbroken circle, roughly six feet across.

The demon clapped his hands lightly. "Bravo, Mr. McCool. However, this won't hold me long."

I frowned and shook my head. "Oh, it doesn't have to, Mr. Spinebreaker."

Lunging forward while taking care that my lead foot didn't touch the circuit, I swung the club at full extension, right at Snaketongue's waist. Unable to move away from my attack, he did the only thing he could do; he leapt straight up in the air. While he cleared my initial attack, he lacked the power of flight. Newtonian physics being what they are on this planar realm, the demon came straight back down, and my war club cracked him across the knees on my backswing.

The club packed a punch. The impact crushed the demon's knee joint with a sickening crunch, and Snaketongue landed awkwardly inside the circle in a heap. Careful to avoid stepping on the vines, I proceeded to walk around the circle beating him with the club again and again, smashing bones and pulping his flesh. Seconds later, I was breathing heavily, and the demon was a bloody, nearly unrecognizable heap.

But I didn't let up. If I did, he would break free from the relatively weak demon trap, and for all I knew he'd instantaneously heal once freed from the circle. So, I kept up the attack.

"Yield!" I shouted with a crushing overhead blow that smashed into the demon's shoulder.

Snaketongue cried out, "I yield to your will!"

I paused in midswing. "You agree to do as I command?"

The demon looked up at me, blood dripping from his ears, nose, and mouth. "Yes. Spare me and I'll carry out your will on this earth."

I sniffed. "Right, and by the time I die you'll have found some way to get my soul under contract. No thanks."

"What then would you have me do?" the now pathetic-looking demon asked.

I squatted down next to the circle and looked Snaketongue in his left eye, since the right was swollen shut. "I banish you, Snaketongue Spinebreaker. I command you to leave and never come back to this plane of existence. Ever."

The demon hung his head and exhaled, his voice shaking as he replied. "I underestimated you, Mr. McCool—both your cunningness and your cruelty. Management will not be pleased, of that I can assure you. And they *will* send another to replace me. Of that you can be certain."

"Well, then, feel free to tell them who sent you."

Snaketongue grinned. "I will, Mr. McCool—I will."

At that, the demon disappeared with a *poof* in a cloud of sulphur and ash. I watched the circle for a few moments, just to make sure he wasn't coming back. Then I released my power, and the vines withered away before my eyes. Sinking to my knees, I breathed a sigh of relief.

"That was a mistake," Finnegas said behind me. "You shouldn't have told him your name. I wish you'd done the opposite, in fact. Now, his superior will send something much worse to replace him—and that thing will be looking for you."

I palmed my forehead. "Now you tell me. Any chance we can start studying diabolical creatures during our lessons?"

Finn nodded. "Couldn't hurt. By the way, we still have training to do."

"What? You said if I used magic to get rid of the thing, it'd count as today's lesson!"

"Druid magic, not conjuration. That's wizard shit, son. And before you ask, no, the vines don't count, and yes, I did get her phone number."

"Well then," I muttered, "at least I'm not the only one who's getting screwed in this deal."

THIRTEEN

Despite the tough talk, Finnegas cut our training session short so I could get back to looking for Derp. We briefly worked on connecting with nature, direct animal communication, that sort of thing. It was all stuff I was familiar with, but the old man said I couldn't get too much practice with it, because they were such important skills for a druid to have. Considering that said skills had already saved my ass, I had to agree with him.

When the old man dropped me off at the junkyard for a shower and change of clothes, Lieutenant McCracken was waiting for me in the parking lot. He sat on the tailgate of a four-wheel-drive pickup in full view.

"Friend of yours?" the old druid asked.

"Hardly," I replied. "He's the liaison the Circle sent me."

Finnegas chuckled. "You mean they didn't assign a gorgeous female to assist you, like Maeve, Luther, and Samson did?"

I snorted. "Yeah, right."

The old man clucked his tongue. "For a kid with a moderately high IQ, you sure are dense sometimes." He started counting them off on his fingers. "Let's see, first Maeve assigned Sabine to assist you—as if *that* wasn't an obvious ploy, especially in light of your history with her. Samson assigned you his daughter, despite the fact that you're not exactly tops on his list of future sons-in-law. And Luther hired some ex-KGB Victoria's Secret model to be your sidekick for coven-related business. Are you starting to see a pattern here?"

Realization dawned on me as I put two and two together. "Ah—so they're each hoping I hook up with their operative. Then they'll gain a little extra influence over me."

"Somebody give the kid a cookie," Finnegas quipped.

Suddenly I felt like an idiot, which was becoming an all-too-common occurrence. Once again, the faction leaders had been manipulating me, and I'd been the last to pick up on it. *Man, I really need to get my head out of my ass.*

"Wait a minute," I said. "How'd you know who the faction leaders picked to work with me?"

The old man scratched his arm, a sure sign he was jonesing for a cigarette. Despite having been mostly immune to illness and disease for two millennia, he'd been trying to cut back lately. He reached in his pocket for a piece of gum, unwrapping it and popping it into his mouth with a scowl.

"You forget," he said as he smacked on his Juicy Fruit, "that I set all this up—and for good reason, I might add."

"Meaning?"

"Meaning, I got to approve the people you'll work with from each faction. That is, except for the Circle's representative. Those assholes were a bit miffed about the entire deal, and have been avoiding communication with me since the Conclave. No loss there, certainly—but I think it goes without saying that you should watch yourself around their personnel."

"I, uh, figured that one out on my own."

Finn clucked his tongue. "I guess that explains the bruises—wasn't going to say anything, unless you brought it up. Did you send them packing?"

"I left them tied up in a warehouse, actually."

"Good man." He looked out the windshield at McCracken. "You want me to stick around?"

I shook my head. "Naw, I got this." I got out of the truck, poking my head back through the window after I shut the door. "I'll let you know if I get any bites on the dating app thing."

"Be careful," the old druid admonished before driving away at a snail's pace.

Feeling my temper rising again, I counted to ten and turned around to address the Circle's representative. "McCracken, fancy seeing you here. I figured you'd be tied up for another day, at least."

He held his hands up. "I'm not here to cause any trouble, and I'm not upset at how you handled things back at the warehouse. It's not like Keane and his team left you with much choice."

I crossed my arms and stared at him. "So, you're the idiot they assigned to me, hmm?"

"Yes—I mean no. I'm not an idiot. I graduated Princeton at the top of my class, and was ranked third in my cohort at the cadet training academy."

I snorted. "Meaning, you're an entitled prick who knows how to kiss ass. Is that how you got your rank at such a young age—by brown-nosing?"

His cheeks reddened slightly. "I, uh, got promoted when they assigned me to you. They thought that if I had some weight on my lapels, it would make it easier to do my job."

"Which is why Keane and his men showed you so little respect. It figures. Tell me, McCracken—why should I even consider letting you work with me?"

He stood and reached into his jacket, prompting me to go for the pistol holstered at the small of my back. McCracken wasn't entirely stupid, apparently, because he knew enough to freeze when he saw me going for my gun.

"Whoa, whoa—hang on there," I hissed. "What the hell are you reaching for? Pull your hand out of your jacket, very slowly."

McCracken did as I asked, gingerly presenting a fancy parchment letter with a red wax seal that had already been broken. "Relax, it's just a letter." He extended it toward me. "Here, take a look."

I kept my hand on my pistol as I snagged the paper with my other hand. After checking the letter for spells and traps, I snapped it open and scanned the contents. It was more or less a set of military orders that directed McCracken to act as liaison between the druid justiciar and the Circle, blah, blah, blah, assist him in any way, blah, until further notice, blah, *on pain of death* should he betray either faction or fail in his mission.

Admittedly, that last part got my attention.

At the bottom, the letter was signed with some arcane symbol that had been inked by hand, and yet another wax seal. Embossed into the wax were eight chalices, arranged in a circle around an all-seeing eye. *How droll.*

I folded it with one hand and tossed it back to him. "Are they serious about that 'pain of death' thing?"

He caught the letter and gave a curt nod. "They are. It's been more than a century since an operative has been executed for failure or betrayal, but it has happened."

"Sucks for you. Since I don't need your help, and since I'm not currently investigating any cases involving the Circle, you're free to get lost as you see fit. If I need you, I'll call."

"It, uh, doesn't work like that. I'm supposed to assist you with any case you're working on, regardless of what it involves."

So, they intended for him to be a spy. "Not exactly subtle, are they?"

"No, the High Council is not known for their subtlety."

"And I assume if I just say no, you're going to shadow me anyway so you don't get in hot water with your superiors, correct?"

He tucked his orders back inside his jacket. "That's right. I don't intend to fail in my mission. And, just so you know, I really do want to help. I'm not like Gunnarson, after all. I've studied your case files, and I've seen the good you've accomplished."

"Despite the fact that one asshole or another from the Circle has been dogging my footsteps since I arrived in Austin."

McCracken licked his lips nervously. "Look, if you want me to leave, I'll leave. But I'm just going to tail you anyway, so you may as well put me to work."

I tapped my thumb on my chin as I considered how I might use McCracken to my advantage. It was clear that someone on the High Council didn't like me—and possibly more than one of them, after Finnegas and Maeve had bullied them around at the Conclave. I figured they intended to use McCracken to gain intel on me, info they could use to justify having me removed as justiciar or taken off the board completely. For all I knew, the Circle could be behind the killings, and McCracken could be a part of it as well.

The thing I couldn't figure, though, was why this mystery Council Member had such a hard-on for me. What the hell had I done to make them hate me? Was it because my Hyde-side posed such a threat? Or was there more going on here that I didn't know about?

Regardless of their motives, if the Circle was going to spy on me I may as well control what information got back to them. Besides, McCracken might have skills and resources I could tap, keeping him busy and out of my hair while he helped me solve my case.

I gave him the evil eye for several seconds, just to put him on edge. "Tell me something, lieutenant—how good are you at doing investigative work?"

I SICCED McCracken on figuring out where the goblin clan was holed up. Based on my initial search, I knew at least a few goblins had been through the alley where Derp had been taken. It was a weak lead, but one I hadn't explored yet because I'd been hyper-focused on the spider creature—which made it the perfect snipe hunt to assign the Circle's liaison.

I doubted McCracken would actually be able to track the goblin clan down, but if he did, I fully intended to nab one for questioning. Who knew? Maybe they could provide another lead on what the hell had taken Derp.

Poor Derp. I was holding out hope that he was still alive, but the longer it took to find him, the weaker that hope became. The only thing I could do was keep trying, so while McCracken was distracted chasing down the goblin clan, I began focusing on the serial killer angle. Thus, my next few days were spent setting up and going out on dates with various NipponMatch members.

I'd played the otaku angle pretty hard on my profile, and found that a surprising number of young Japanese women liked dating fan boys. Most of the girls I chatted with were foreign exchange students or traveling professionals who were curious, but also somewhat hesitant, to go out with an American. Once I made it clear I wasn't just trying to mark "Asian girl" off on a list of sexual conquests, I found several members who were willing to meet over coffee or lunch.

However, none of my dates seemed to fit the "supernatural serial killer" profile. I got zero magical vibe from any of the young women I met, and for the most part they all turned out to be fairly harmless. Far from the *kogal* stereotype that fascinated American guys, the girls I met with wore contemporary Western fashions, and our conversations were generally focused on common, everyday topics like school, work, and popular culture. Not that I expected all my dates to show up in plaid miniskirts, loose socks, and pigtails—but I did suspect that a serial killer who was trying to nab a weeaboo or homesick Japanese college student would work that look.

In short, none of my dates gave me any reason to suspect they might be more than they let on. That was, until I met Mei.

Admittedly, all my dates had been the result of me reaching out to various female NipponMatch members, and none had been initiated by the women themselves. However, Mei contacted me first. The private messages she sent me were initially hesitant, then increasingly flirty as we got to know each other better. That alone would have put my spider-sense on edge—pun fully intended—but it was the way she grilled me that set me on edge.

She first asked me questions about South Africa, the answers to most of which I'd prepared in advance. We chatted about manga and anime, and again I played up the otaku angle, giving the impression that I was a huge geek about all things Japan. Admittedly, the role I played was not far from the mark. Not that I was a huge Japanophile, but the geeky part was hardly a stretch for me.

Mei also asked about my family; I said my parents had me late in life and recently passed. Thus, I was using my inheritance to travel and see the world. That's when things got interesting. We'd been messaging back and forth all day long, then Mei abruptly left me hanging for a few hours before picking our conversation back up.

Let's MEt.

Whr? I asked.

I hav an idea. U knO whr d rec sports cNtR is?

yS. I replied. The Rec Sports Center was where most of the athletic clubs on campus met. In fact, I'd worked out with the MMA club at the RSC for a short time during my freshman year.

You'll find me n r%m 138 @ 6:00 pm. Wear workout clothes, & don't b l8.

Then, radio silence. Mei was definitely setting off all sorts of alarms for me, and not just due to the suspicious questions she'd asked. This date had all the signs of a manufactured meet-cute, which was pretty much every player's nightmare and every nerdy guy's dream. For a guy who was just looking to get laid, the less complicated the date, the better. No player wanted to risk being taken out of their element, which was why planned meet-cutes definitely fell in "here be monsters" territory.

On the other hand, a lot of nerdy guys were secret romantics. Not that I knew anything about that, *ahem*, but it was the truth. For that reason, I thought it interesting that Mei was apparently choosing to set up an atypical first date. It was almost like she was playing a game, toying with me in order to draw me into her trap. That is, if she actually *was* the killer. But if I was a supernatural serial killer who liked to prey on geeky, lonely guys, I'd definitely want to take advantage of their weaknesses.

Looks like I'm going on a date tonight. I guess I should prepare, just in case Mei turns out to be "the one."

AFTER PACKING my Craneskin Bag with a few goodies that could come in handy, I threw on some sweats, a hoodie, and a loud-ass *One Piece* shirt I'd picked up at a comic store on

Guadalupe. Then, I hopped in the Gremlin and headed for campus.

Room 138 at the RSC was easy enough to find, although I asked for directions at the front desk just to play up the geeky guy angle. While it was remotely possible that an otaku could be familiar with the rec center, I decided it was best to play my part to the hilt in case Mei was watching. The appointed spot for our "date" was a multi-purpose room used by a variety of martial arts clubs. On this specific night, it was where the university judo club was meeting for practice.

I'd trained in judo for about a year while I was in high school, just long enough to learn the basic throws and enter a couple of competitions. Once I'd had a firm grasp of the funda-mentals, my magically-enhanced strength, speed, and balance made up for any lack of experience on my part, and soon I found that no one wanted to engage me in *randori*, free-spar-ring. So, I'd quit and started taking Brazilian jiu-jitsu instead, finding that the throws I'd learned in judo came in handy during rolls with the more experienced students.

Like jiu-jitsu and MMA, judo was a rather rough and tumble sport—one that didn't exactly lend itself to casual first dates. Even in the small club I'd trained at as a teen, sprains and bruises were a common result of training, and broken or dislo-cated bones were a frequent occurrence in competition. I thought it rather strange that a girl would ask a guy to judo class on a first date, but it was just quirky enough to be something a Japanophile would like. A lot of Westerners who were obsessed with Japanese culture were into *budo*—modern Japanese martial arts.

I took off my shoes before entering the room, bowing onto the mat in full dork style like a true *shinnichi*. I glanced around, taking in the scenery while I searched for my "date." On one side of the room, several advanced students were practicing throws on a crash pad, while on the other side a green belt led the beginners through rolls and break-falls. All the students looked to be Westerners, and I didn't see anyone who even remotely resembled Mei's profile pic.

Miffed at being stood up, I was about to take a seat along the wall when I felt a tap on my shoulder.

"Looking for someone?" a lilting female voice asked.

I turned and found a young, slender, attractive Japanese girl in a spotless-white judo uniform and worn black belt, holding a tattered loaner *gi* and white belt out to me. The sight of her took me aback for a second, because the girl was an anime character come to life. She had smooth, porcelain skin with the barest hint of color on her high cheekbones, a fine, perfectly-straight nose that had just the slightest upturn at the tip, and light-brown eyes that sparkled with mischief.

"Mei, I presume?" I said with a shaky voice in a really bad Kiwi accent. I avoided eye contact as much as possible, both to look the part of a shy nerd, and because it was considered rude in Japan... something a Japanophile would know.

She giggled. "You were expecting a hairy middle-aged man, perhaps? Sorry to disappoint."

"Am I going to be joining class? I did a little judo in high school, but—"

She smiled sweetly. "Don't worry, you'll do fine. Here, put this on—class has already started." She shoved the judo uniform into my hands and bounced off across the mat to join the advanced *judoka*.

I ducked out to the locker room to change, and by the time I came back the class was in full swing. Rather than injure myself by jumping in without warming up, I did some jumping jacks and light stretches, then I joined the beginners who were practicing *osoto gari*, or outer reaping throw. I got paired off with a tall, husky orange belt who apparently thought he was hot shit, because he took to throwing me to the mat with abandon. I allowed it, since Mei was watching and I wanted to look the part.

I pegged the guy for a football player, most likely a lineman and probably third-string. With his buzz cut, wide shoulders, and prodigious gut, I figured he'd been the big man on campus in high school, but not quite good enough to garner a starting position on the university team.

A typical frustrated jock. Great.

Each time I got tossed by the wannabe Anthony Muñoz, I tried to take the fall with just enough skill to avoid getting hurt. The problem was, it's damned difficult to take a hard throw with correct technique, much less avoid an injury when you're trying to look like a noob. After the fifth or sixth time I had the wind knocked out of me, I got tired of taking abuse from the punk and decided to give him a taste of his own medicine.

I gingerly picked myself up from the mat, holding a hand on my lower back while I waved him off with the other. "Aw, man, this judo stuff is tough. Give me a sec, will you?"

Hot shit smirked at me. "You think this is tough? You should try scrimmaging with the first string. I was in the Orange-White game this year, and let me tell you—the hits we put on each other make this look like child's play."

"Sounds brutal." I did my best to look confused, playing the nerdy kid who didn't know anything about football. I continued to stretch my back out until the green belt told us to switch sides. "Alright, I guess it's my turn now. Let me see if I can make this move work."

The guy laughed. "Good luck."

As we locked up, the guy actually fought me for grips. Much of a judo match's outcome could be determined by who got the best grips, because hand position on the opponent's uniform was everything. However, in practice, it was considered poor form to fight for position. *Uke*, the person receiving the throw, was supposed to more or less cooperate, so *tori*, the person practicing, could work on their technique.

The idea when doing an *osoto gari* was to step to the outside while yanking the opponent off balance, sweeping their legs out from under them with a huge reaping motion with your inside leg. However, my partner resisted me the first time I tried to perform the throw, pushing back against me and throwing me on my back. This happened a few more times, so I decided to add some speed to my step, knowing he'd have to change his tactic to stuff my throw.

This time, I yanked him hard to the right as I stepped to the outside. As expected, he moved with me, stepping back and bracing his rear leg to prevent the throw. Anticipating his counter, I did a quick switch-step and pivot, swinging my reaping leg between his as I turned my back to him and lowered my hips. At the same time, I kicked my leg back between his, which resulted in a textbook *uchi mata*, or inner thigh throw.

The problem with getting thrown with *uchi mata* was that, if done with bad intent, *uke* landed awkwardly on their head or shoulder. Plus, if *tori* chose to follow *uke* to the ground they could land hard on top of them, bruising a few ribs in the process. I hit the throw hard, tossing hot shit on his head and landing on his rib cage with a sickening crunch.

"Wow, I have no idea where that came from," I said as I bounced to my feet. Hot shit was trying hard not to show it, but I'd hurt him. Not bad enough for an ER visit, but probably enough to make him sit out for the rest of the class.

I heard giggling from the other side of the room, and turned to find Mei chatting quietly with a few other girls who had obviously been watching our exchange with interest. While my partner was gathering his wits, I walked off the mat to grab a drink of water. Mei popped up beside me, nudging me with an elbow.

"You've gained a few fans among the girls in the advanced group," she said with a snicker. "Darrell is a bit of a jerk, and several of them have been injured pairing up with him for *randori*."

"Well, I hope I didn't make too much of a show of it. Like I said, I trained a little judo in high school, but I didn't want to be the ass who shows off to impress his date. You know, *deru kugi wa utareru* and all that," I replied. It had been a favorite saying of my Japanese karate teacher, roughly translating as "the nail that sticks up gets hammered down."

"Oh, so this is a date?" she replied, an inscrutable poker face masking her intentions.

"If this isn't, maybe we could do the date thing after class?" I asked, flashing her a hopeful and purposely bashful smile.

Mei squinted at me and pursed her lips into a playful moue. "Let me think—do I want to go out with this cute nerd who does judo like he was born to it? Hmm." She tapped a finger on her lips before leaning in close with a sly grin. "Lucky for you, I like guys who stick out. We can talk about it after class."

Before I could reply, she pranced back onto the mat. It was time for *randori*, or free-sparring, which meant I'd have to wait until later to find out more about my enigmatic suspect.

FOURTEEN

"Later" came sooner than I expected, as Mei invited me onto the mat for *randori*. In most judo dojos, it would be a faux pas to ask a higher belt to spar, but it was likewise considered to be poor form to refuse such a request from a senior student. Wondering what I was in for, I stood, bowed, and walked out to the center of the mat.

In judo, there were three ways to win a match: *yuko*, *waza-ari*, or *ippon*. *Yuko*, which loosely meant a technical advantage, was the weakest way to win a match. *Waza-ari*, or half-points, were typically awarded for effective techniques that were executed with less than perfect delivery or follow-through. But to win by *ippon*, meaning full point, was to win decisively. *Ippon* was awarded either for a throw that caused the opponent to land on their back, a twenty-second pin, or forcing the opponent to submit to a choke or joint lock.

Needless to say, unless the disparity of skill between judo players was very great, the larger player would always have the advantage. That's why they had weight classes in judo, to make sure the matches were fair. Plus, weight classes forced players to use good technique instead of brute strength to win a match. No one wanted to see a three-hundred-pound brute pick up a hundred-thirty-pound lightweight and slam them to the mat for a win. In judo, the more elegant the technical execution of a throw, the more honored the victory.

Granted, some smaller judoka might hold their own against a much larger opponent. Yet, one would need to be at a very high level to pull off such a feat against a bigger opponent with even a moderate level of aptitude. That's why I felt unsure whether I should use all my skill against Mei or hold back. Thus far, I hadn't really determined her to be anything but a normal, if quirky and mysterious, girl. The last thing I wanted to do was toss my date on her head, only to discover she was human by injuring her unnecessarily.

So, I decided to be a gentleman and take it easy. Big mistake.

After we squared off and bowed to each other, Mei transformed—in the figurative sense, mind you—into a ruthless she-devil with little if any compunctions against violence of action. The first thing she did was step in and hit me with an *ippon seoinage*, or one-arm shoulder throw, that sent me sailing through the air with my feet momentarily pointing at the sky while I got an upside-down view of the mat. I landed flat on my back and had the wind knocked out of me on impact.

The class all clapped, of course. There was nothing quite as amusing as seeing a five-five, one-hundred-twenty-pound woman toss a six-foot-one, two-hundred-ten-pound guy like a sack of potatoes. I stood, wobbly and dazed, then the next few minutes were a blur—a very painful blur. Mei must've scored *ippon* at least a half-dozen times, executing beautiful throws that caused me to land with increasingly harder impacts each time.

Finally, I thought I might get a breather when she nailed a *tomoe nage* on me. *Tomoe nage* was a sacrifice throw that involved grasping the opponent's lapel and sleeve, then falling back while planting a foot in their abdomen and kicking them hard overhead. It was a relatively gentle throw, unless the attacker decided to hang on to their opponent's uniform. This accelerated the throw greatly, increasing the impact—which was exactly what Mei did. Still, usually the throw ended with both players on their backs. Usually.

Instead of allowing me to stand up again, Mei rolled over backward as I got to all fours, wrapping her left leg over my shoulder with her hips behind my head. She reached under my right arm to grab her left shin, yanking her lower leg across my chest and wrapping her right leg around her left ankle under my right arm. With the completion of those movements, she'd successfully secured a *sankaku-jime*, or triangle choke, from the reverse position. Mei then rolled over her shoulder, controlling my right arm as she used her hips and legs to flip me over. When we'd both rolled over onto our backs, she sunk in the choke by squeezing her thighs like a python around my shoulder and neck.

I tried to fight it, but a deep triangle choke from the reverse position was difficult to escape. Soon, I felt myself begin to white out—when you got choked out, everything kind of faded to white, not black—so I tapped the mat. Just to make my intentions clear, I croaked *"maitta, maitta,"* which meant "I submit"—just in case she didn't see or hear me tap.

Mei waited until I'd almost passed out before letting me go. I laid there on the mat, allowing the blood in my arteries to resume its journey to my brain so I could gather my wits before standing. I got up, wobbly—but none the worse for the wear unless you counted the bruises I'd have in the morning. Mei stood facing me, her face blank, and I gave her a shaky bow that she returned with sharp precision.

As I walked off the mat some of the guys were smirking, while the ladies in the class seemed to be split between concern and delight. Darrell, my partner from earlier, clapped me on the shoulder as I sat down with the rest of the beginners.

"Man, Mei sure whipped your ass," he said with a grin, obviously reveling in the treatment I'd just received. "What'd you do to piss her off?"

I stretched my neck and got a few loud pops as my vertebrae settled into a more comfortable position. "I, uh, asked her out on a date."

Darrell winced. "Shee-it, nobody does that anymore—mostly cause Mei's a little crazy. Last guy here who hit on her went home on crutches. Still, I think you got it way worse than he did."

Despite the beating I'd taken, it was all I could do to avoid smiling, because my "date" had just put on an almost superhuman display of skill. It was just the sort of thing a supernatural creature would do—to go just far enough to humiliate a human, but without blowing their cover. The fact that she discouraged suitors in places she commonly hung out was another dead giveaway. A predator never shat where they ate.

I watched her across the mat and wondered what she was, because she sure in hell wasn't human. I suspected Mei was listening in on our conversation, and was certain she knew I was looking at her, but she avoided my gaze and remained focused on the match.

"Oh, I don't know," I said, still keeping an eye on Mei. "I think it was worth it."

Darrell chuckled like a seventh-grader telling a fart joke. "Can't argue there. Just imagine if she'd decided to kill you with that choke," he whispered behind his hand. "What a way to go."

AFTER CLASS, I waited until most of the students were

involved in their own conversations before approaching Mei. "Thanks for the match," I said. "Although I could have done without getting thrown so many times."

"I was hoping for a greater challenge," she replied with just a hint of contempt in her voice. Then she seemed to catch herself, and the mild disdain in her voice vanished as her expression softened. "But you didn't do too bad for someone who hasn't done *randori* in a while."

"It's not the first time I've been tossed around by a black belt. However, it is the first time I've been soundly trounced by a girl," I lied, hoping to play on her obvious need for dominance. I faked shivering and smiled playfully. "I'll have nightmares about it for weeks."

"Probably not for weeks, I wouldn't think." She hid her mouth with her hand as she giggled like a flirty teen in an anime movie. Whether she was laughing with me or at me, I couldn't tell—her acting was *that* good.

I smiled. "Now that introductions have been made, might we discuss the prospect of me taking you out on a date?"

She squinted and crinkled her nose. "I suppose I might be up for a bite to eat. Do you like noodles?"

"I love them, in fact," I replied with complete honesty.

Her face lit up in genuine delight. "Great! Give me a minute to go change and freshen up. I'll meet you out front in, say, fifteen minutes?"

"Absolutely," I replied, watching her bounce away toward the women's locker room. The loaner uniform I'd been wearing was clean, but I still smelled like sweat from rolling around on the mats. So, I grabbed my Craneskin Bag and beelined for the showers.

A few minutes later, I headed outside and took a seat on a bench to wait. And wait. And wait. I was just about to assume I'd been stood up when Mei came trotting up beside me.

"You were taking too long, so I put my stuff in my car." She grabbed me by my wrist, practically yanking me off the bench. "Come on, I am so hungry right now."

Rather than me proffering my arm, it was more like Mei had simply decided to borrow it for the evening. She managed to lead us to our destination while making it seem as though I was the one leading, and a few blocks later we ended up at a small, hole-in-the-wall ramen joint I'd never even known existed.

We both ordered the same thing, the house special, and had hardly taken our seats when the proprietor brought out two steaming bowls of broth, sliced chicken, noodles, and vegetables. The bowls were each a work of art, with the delicately-sliced veggies and meat fanned out over the noodles and broth in a colorful arrangement that pleased the eye, while the steam carried a scent that tempted the palate.

"This looks delicious," I remarked.

"*Doumo arigatou gozaimasu*, Ito-chan," Mei said to our server, bowing her head slightly.

Weird, the -chan suffix is usually only used when speaking with children or close friends. I noticed that the proprietor showed her quite a bit of deference, both in the way he bowed smartly in acknowledgment, and in his general bearing and demeanor around her. Strange, considering he was in his fifties and Mei looked to be in her early twenties. Was it merely because she was a loyal customer, or was it because her cover identity held status in Japanese society?

Or did he actually have some idea of what she was?

I must have been lost in my thoughts, because Mei giggled at me as she toyed with her chopsticks. "Dig in, Colin. It'll get cold if you don't."

I proceeded to tuck into the bowl with abandon. However, Mei seemed to mostly play with her food, only taking dainty bites when I was watching. *Curiouser and curiouser.*

I had nearly finished my bowl when I literally threw in the towel, tossing my napkin on the table. "Oh, but that was good."

Mei smiled demurely. "Ito-chan has a way with food, that's for certain."

An uncomfortable lull in the conversation followed. Finally, I broke the silence with my typical awkwardness, again finding little difficulty in playing the part.

"So—what's next?" I asked.

Mei twirled a few noodles around her chopsticks before setting them down across the lip of her bowl. Her eyes looked down at the table as she replied. "Well, I thought we might go to my place and watch a movie. I have the live-action version of *Rurouni Kenshin* at home. That is, if you're not too tired after judo—and the huge meal you just ate."

"Actually, I have quite a bit of energy left in me. Tons, in fact."

Mei flashed a sweet smile that belied the mischief in her eyes. "Hah! You're awfully feisty now, but we'll see what happens when we get to my place."

MEI'S PLACE turned out to be a converted warehouse loft off East Fifth. The apartment building was just trendy enough to look casual and workaday, with its weathered brown bricks and almost random distribution of windows on the exterior. However, I knew from the time I'd spent looking for affordable housing in Austin—which didn't exist—that these condos went for a half-million and up. Either Mei's parents were wealthy, or she was a supernatural who'd accumulated significant wealth over an extended span of life—take your pick.

Of course, her place was on the top floor, with a decent view of downtown. When we entered the apartment, a balanced blend of pop culture art, hipster chic, and Japanese design sensibility greeted me. The rooms were walled partitions that stopped several feet short of the high, exposed-rafter ceiling overhead. Spare, Scandinavian-style furniture clashed with anime and manga posters that had been artfully framed and hung on every wall. Authentic shoji doors shielded certain areas of the dwelling from the living room and kitchen, and traditional Japanese calligraphy was displayed here and there so it cleverly balanced the more modern decorations.

I couldn't help but admire her digs, and I let out a soft, low whistle as I slipped off my shoes at the door. "Wow Mei, your home is amazing."

She smiled shyly. "Trust fund. Give me a minute to change, alright?"

"Sure, no problem."

She glided off down a hall, disappearing into what I assumed was the bedroom. "Make yourself at home," she said, her voice echoing through the more or less open spaces overhead.

"Don't mind if I do," I whispered, reaching into my bag for my markers.

I chose colors that roughly matched the floor and paint as I quickly laid containment wards at the front door and windows. If things went as I expected they might, my plan was to ensure that Mei didn't escape before I forced her to reveal where she was keeping Derp. *I hope I'm right about her,* I thought. *Otherwise, I'm going to have a hard time explaining this.*

Once done, I did my best to look casual as I admired her music and movie collections. She had a ton of rare anime, including *Cardcaptor Sakura*, *When They Cry*, and *Vampire Princess Miyu*.

Well, that fits, I guess.

Mei emerged from her bedroom a few minutes later wearing

a gray, off-the-shoulder midriff sweatshirt over a pink sports bra, ankle socks, and a pair of sleep shorts that barely covered the curve of her ass.

If that's not a come fuck me outfit, I don't know what is —sheesh.

She grabbed a plastic case off the shelf next to me, then popped a disc into her player and plopped down on the couch, pulling a stuffed animal into her lap. She patted the cushion next to her. "Come, sit with me."

Said the spider to the fly.

I sat. The movie began, and as Takeru Satoh began dispatching his enemies on the TV screen, I began to feel a little... strange. It was nothing much at first—just the slightest increase in temperature and heart rate. It wasn't until I felt a bulge growing in my pants, along with a growing haze in my mind, that I realized what was happening.

Next I knew, I was flat on my back on the couch, with Mei crawling slowly on top of me. I felt nearly paralyzed—not from fear or poison, but with passion. To be blunt, I was hornier than a two-dicked billy goat in a room full of nannies. Although I wanted Mei so, so desperately, I found myself torn between my baser desires and a compulsion to please her—thus, the reason for my torpor.

The room spun and everything looked really funky, almost as if I was in a psychedelic state. Colors shifted and melded before my eyes as Mei hovered over me, grinding her pelvis into my hips and pinning my arms to the couch. Helpless to fight against whatever power she was using on me, I felt both pleasure and terror all at once.

"What is this? What are you doing to me?"

She made a clicking noise with her mouth, and for a moment I could have sworn she had four eyes and six arms, instead of just two. "Human scientists would call it pheromones," she whispered. "I call it the magic of nature. I've been subtly exerting my influence over you since we arrived. And when I choose to unleash my magic fully, no man can resist —not even a druid, it seems."

I'd broken out in a sweat, my hands clammy and my groin throbbing with desire. I wanted Mei like I'd never desired a woman before, yet a voice still screamed from the back of my mind, urging me to fight back and escape. My lust for her was beyond bearable, and my survival instincts urged me to flee at the same time—yet I had neither the will nor the strength to act on either impulse.

Finally, desire won out.

"Bed me or kill me, but make this end," I said through clenched teeth.

Mei smiled, revealing an extra pair of needle-like fangs that dripped with venom. "Perhaps I'll do both," she whispered. "But my master wants something from you, and I'm told it must be given willingly. So, for now, I'll keep you alive and in agony. How does that sound?"

"Like... hell..." I replied.

"Just sit back and enjoy it," Mei replied with a wicked laugh. "It'll all be over... eventually."

FIFTEEN

Mei had just started to unbutton my pants when I heard a crash and *boom* nearby. Then, I heard a woman's voice with a slight Castilian accent ranting in Spanish and English at the entrance to Mei's apartment. I missed a lot of the Spanish, but the English part was clear as day.

"Fucking hell, Colin—first you cheat on me with your ex, and now you're making me save you from being raped by a were-spider? You're such an asshole."

"Bells?" I mumbled. "How'd you know I was here?"

"*Por supuesto, seguí el rastro de mierda, cabrón,*" Bells answered in a rather annoyed tone. "*Deja de joder a mi novio, maldita!*" she yelled, presumably at Mei. Or so I hoped. When Bells started cussing in Spanish, things were going to get ugly.

I heard the distinct *pop-shikt* sound of suppressed gunfire, five shots in rapid succession. Mei sprouted a few holes in her chest, but to little effect. I watched in stunned silence as she grew two extra sets of chitinous, insectoid arms, while her face morphed into something that would give Venom and Carnage nightmares. Then she did a vertical leap and clung to the ceiling upside down, skittering backward toward her bedroom.

"Well, that was a fucking joke," Bells swore as she walked into view, shoulders set and wearing a scowl that could peel paint. Clearly, she was not amused at the situation. "Leave it to you to find the one 'thrope species that isn't harmed by silver," she said, shooting me an annoyed glance as she vaulted the couch.

"Um, it's good to see you too," I said in a dreamy, delirious voice while still making an attempt to imitate Hemi's manner of speaking.

"Ugh! Would you please drop that ridiculous accent? It's not like you're fooling anyone with it." Belladonna dodged a glob of venom as she dropped the magazine from her Desert Eagle .357 Magnum, swapping it for another from her belt carrier. "Let's see how you like this, bitch."

Blam-blam-blam! The report of her weapon was much louder now that she was firing it right in front of me. Whether due to the noise or because Mei was retreating down the hall— still clinging to the ceiling like Regan from The Exorcist, no less —my head began to clear. For some reason, however, I still couldn't move.

"Oh my God, I'm paralyzed!" I shouted.

Bells yelled over her shoulder at me as she swapped out another mag. "Quit whining, you big baby. She wrapped you up in spider silk, is all. Look."

I glanced down, and for the first time I realized that I was wrapped up in a cocoon of webbing, just like Bilbo Baggins in Mirkwood. All except my pelvic area, that was.

"Well, this is embarrassing," I declared.

Belladonna fired several times, pausing only to holler over her shoulder at me. "You think?"

Deciding that I was not happy being trussed up, I cast a flame cantrip that ate through the spider's webs, freeing my arm. From there, it was a simple matter of repeating the process to free my other arm and my legs. I was still covered in sticky spider silk, but at least I was free—and not being raped by a were-spider, so that was a plus.

Bells was now farther down the hall, hiding behind a china hutch while she switched out her ammo again. "Okay, third time's the charm," she said as she released the slide to chamber a round.

When she fired her gun this time, the rounds burned a bright red trail through the air after they left the muzzle. Apparently she hit her target, because the gunshots were answered with an inhuman wail of pain and anger, followed by the sound of breaking glass.

I stumbled after Belladonna as she took off down the hall and out of sight. It was slow going, since I had to stop every few steps to pull long strands of spider web off me that were impeding my movements. When I finally rounded the corner, Bells was leaning out a huge plate glass window that had been broken outward.

"*Me cago en todo lo que se menea!*" she swore. "Fucking whore-spider got away."

"'Whore-spider'? That's a little harsh, even for you," I joked, hoping to bring her temper down a few notches.

Bells turned on me, fuming. "She's a fucking *jorōgumo*, Colin—it literally means 'whore spider.' If you'd recognized what she was before you came to her lair, you might have thought to cast a ward to keep her from putting you under with her pheromones. Seriously, don't they teach you anything in druid school?"

"First off," I said, plucking a long strand of spider silk from my hair, "I don't go to 'druid school.' And second, I had her right where I wanted her, at least until you came barging in."

"Right where you wanted her?" Belladonna clucked. "And just where was that, *tonto*?"

"Honestly, I've always thought of myself as more of a Lone Ranger type, to be honest—" I stopped myself mid-sentence, because the look Bells was giving me said I'd better stay on track. "Ahem. As I was saying, I was trying to trap Mei in her apartment. I even warded the windows and doors so she couldn't leave—"

"All except for the one she jumped out, right?" Bells said as she rolled her eyes.

"Please, don't bother me with the details of my botched plans," I said, hoping a little self-deprecating humor might ease the tension between us. It didn't, and if anything, Belladonna's glare hit quasar-level intensity. I sighed and threw my hands up in the air. "Seriously, Bells, I needed to capture her so I could question her, not chase her away."

My borderline ex-girlfriend let out a frustrated growl. She drew her hand back to punch the wall, until she noticed a black and white picture of Mei nearby. Bells shot a few holes in it, then holstered her pistol and got right up in my face.

"Colin, *no seas gillipollas!* That *coño* was going to rape you, so she could have a bunch of little were-spiders running around. That's what they do—they look for healthy young men to mate with, then they inject them with venom and suck their innards out. I swear, sometimes you are such a fucking idiot."

"I had a plan!" I countered, my anger rising as the effect of Mei's pheromones fully faded.

"What, like you had a plan to hide your ex-girlfriend from me after she pulled a Lazarus? Shit, Colin—how stupid do you think I am? I watched you with this jorōgumo chick all night long. You knew you were playing with fire, and yet you still went to her fucking apartment with her! Admit it, *cabrón*, you're not acting like yourself—and it's because of that fucking alter-ego of yours. The more you shift, the more of an asshole you become."

"What? That has nothing to do with anything!" I screamed, putting my fist through the wall. "The thing with Jesse, that was because I couldn't tell anyone—at least not until I figured out how to tell Finnegas. And besides, she's turned a little cuckoo since she came back from the grave, so in a way I was protecting you from her."

"You have a thing for crazy women, it seems." Belladonna spoke in a calmer, lower voice, although it wasn't because she was intimidated. She did it to get my attention. It was a trick teachers and parents played sometimes, when a kid was throwing a fit.

I tsked and scowled. "You'd know, wouldn't you?"

That did it.

"You're such a dick!" she growled as she pushed me aside and stormed toward the exit. As she was leaving the apartment, she yelled a final goodbye. "The next time you get your stupid ass in a bind, don't expect me to bail you out!"

"I won't!" I hollered after her.

SIRENS WERE ALREADY CRYING in the distance when Belladonna stormed out of Mei's apartment. The last thing I wanted was another run-in with the cops—being tasered once in my lifetime was enough—so I quickly rifled through her bedroom and bathroom for something that might help me locate her later.

As I was tossing her dresser drawers, I noticed one felt heavier than the others. I tapped the sides and bottom, locating a hollow space. A further examination revealed a false bottom, and inside were neat stacks of gold coins, each with eight cups in a circle stamped on both sides.

Circle coins. Son of a bitch.

The sirens were getting closer, so I completed my search, grabbing a few of Mei's personal things. Those items included her hairbrush and some clothes from her hamper, which just happened to be a pair of panties and other assorted lingerie. If I got caught, I was going to look like the world's perviest panty bandit, but I needed something with her human DNA on it if I was going to track her down.

Chances were good she spent most of her time in her human form, and if I just used the spider silk that was still clinging to me, I wouldn't be able to find her unless she shifted. Besides, I wasn't about to attempt a tracking spell myself. I just wasn't very good at that sort of magic. Nope, I intended to recruit a specialist for that, and I wanted to make sure I gave them everything they needed to succeed.

I decided to avoid the elevators, figuring the police would have them covered, and headed for the stairs instead. Halfway to the ground level, I heard the sound of a police radio several floors below me. *Shit.*

Doing my best ninja imitation, I headed back up the stairs, all the way to the top floor. Once there, I picked the lock to the roof access door and entered that stairwell, securing the door behind me. My plan was to wait there until the cops left, but soon I heard two people conversing on the other side.

"Sir, I need you to open this door for me," an authoritative female voice ordered.

"Yeah, give me a second," a male voice replied.

I heard keys jangling and knew I was about to have a very bad day, so I cast a quick locking ward on the door. It wouldn't keep them out long, but it'd hold for the minute or so I needed to escape. I headed up the stairs, as silently as possible, and exited onto the roof.

The rooftop was pretty much what you'd expect—just a lot of asphalt and tar, some HVAC units, and a few lawn chairs and cheap outdoor tables scattered here and there. I ran a circuit around the roof, looking for a way down—a set of fire stairs, a drain pipe I could shimmy down, anything—but I came up empty-handed. However, two stories below there was another, lower rooftop, and across the alley from there it looked like I could jump to an adjacent building.

Unfortunately, there weren't any stairs or even an access ladder from this side of the building to the other roof. So, I swung out over the ledge and hung off it, falling a good ten feet to the surface below. When I hit I dropped and rolled, managing to take the fall without injury.

"Hey, you! Stop right there!" a female voice yelled from above.

I didn't bother looking up, but instead covered my face with my arms as I ran to the building's edge. I almost did a running leap, but as I got closer to the edge I slowed down. It was a lot farther between the buildings than it looked from above.

"Damn it," I muttered. "Looks like it's time to shift."

I yanked off my boots and tossed them in my Bag, and then I partially transformed. As my skeleton shifted and my muscles swelled, I heard the cop yelling at me from above.

"Stop, or I'll shoot!"

My transformation was complete within seconds, and as I looked back at the threat above me, I felt the urge to climb back up there and snap the cop's neck.

Actually, that won't even be necessary. All I'll have to do is leap up, grab the cop, and pull her over. If I yank hard enough, she'll break her neck on the way down, and it'll look like an accident. Then I can get away clean.

I turned and growled at the cop, ready to spring into action. She was in clear view above me, pointing her duty weapon at me. I knew a bullet wouldn't kill me, not in this form. It'd hurt, but I could heal so long as I stayed shifted. I took three long strides, covering the distance between us and scrambling up the wall in the blink of an eye.

The cop fired at me, winging me on the shoulder and missing me entirely with two more shots. I didn't find that at all surprising—law enforcement shooting statistics indicated cops only hit what they were firing at about once in every eight rounds. Before she could snap off a fourth round, I'd bounded up the wall and was hanging onto the roof's edge beneath her. I batted away her weapon, sending it flying where it clattered off an HVAC unit below. Then, I grabbed her by the front of her bullet-proof vest, pulling her toward me until she was leaning over the side.

I'd have tossed her off, except that something made me pause before I sent her to her death. I hadn't really noticed before, but now that we were face-to-face, she reminded me of someone. The officer was maybe thirty years old, with lightly-freckled skin and dark hair pulled back in a ponytail. I noticed bright-blue irises framing dime-sized pupils, shining with tears as they stood out against the whites of her eyes.

As her features sunk in, something niggled the back of my mind. *Jesse. She reminds me of the girl I once knew.* And she was terrified. Her eyes were wide, her skin blanched, and her mouth was open as if to scream, but only a high-pitched squeak escaped. To her, I must have seemed a monster come to life.

Because I am.

I came to my senses and shook off the violent urges my Hyde-side had brought out in me. A strong shove sent the cop away, and she stumbled safely onto the roof above, out of my line of sight.

Disgusted with myself and what I was becoming, I dropped to the roof below with a thud, landing on all fours like a silver-back gorilla. Then, I bounded off into the darkening night.

IN AN ALLEY BLOCKS away from Mei's place, I shifted back into my human form and changed clothes. Then, I hung out in the back of an all-night cafe, sipping black coffee while I bided my time. After midnight, I circled back around to Mei's apartment building to retrieve my car, then I headed back to the junkyard, exhausted and more than a little distressed by my actions earlier. Bells was right; I simply wasn't myself lately.

Point one: I'd pretty much walked into that unwilling interlude with Mei.

Point two: I was becoming more and more violent and volatile every time I shifted, even in my half-human state.

Point three: I was about to lose my girlfriend, and I was bothered a lot less by it than expected.

Of all the changes in my behavior, that was perhaps the oddest. Belladonna had stuck by me through thick and thin, she'd been loyal to a fault, and she was the best thing that had happened to me since Jesse passed on. I loved Bells—or, rather, I *had* felt a deep and abiding love for her until recently. If anything, I should have been fighting to keep us together, but instead I felt a certain disinterest about it all.

Speaking of Jesse—now there was a confusing situation. She was my first love, my greatest tragedy, and someone I never thought I'd see in the flesh again. Jesse had changed as well since coming back in this new, eldritch form of hers. In my opinion, those changes were not necessarily for the better.

For that reason, I wondered if it was Jesse's presence that was influencing me, or something else. Was she exerting some magical control over me, driving a wedge between Belladonna and me? Or was there another presence at work that had yet to reveal itself, maybe something related to the case I was working on?

I chewed my thumbnail and allowed those thoughts to tumble through my head as I drove. I still had a bit of Fionn MacCumhaill's magical wisdom, a gift passed down to me through many generations. According to Finnegas, my gift of insight was much weaker than Fionn's had been, yet it had helped me see things more clearly in times past. A bit of focused rumination, enough to trigger the magic, was often all it took to get a new perspective on whatever problems I might be facing.

Suddenly, I realized I couldn't access my gift of insight. For the first time in my life, I felt cut off from that part of my magic. Either the changes within me had fundamentally affected my ability to access that talent, or some outside force was preventing me from seeing things clearly.

I should've been frightened, but I wasn't—and that bothered me most of all.

My phone began to buzz in my pocket, so I pulled over in a grocery store parking lot to check my messages. There was nothing from Belladonna—no surprise there—but I did have something from my Circle liaison.

Meet me at the warehouse. I have urgent news regarding your case.

Of all the people I didn't want to deal with right now, McCracken was tops on that list. But Derp was still missing, I had a were-spider serial killer on the loose, and I was dealing with some serious mental health issues. The possibility it might all be connected weighed heavily on my mind.

I messaged him back. *stNd by. Headed ther nw.* I peeled out of the parking lot, pushing the speed limit as I headed to the warehouse where Keane and his men had held me. Hopefully, those assholes would be off duty when I arrived.

The gate to the fenced-in back lot was open when I got there, so I drove in and parked my car next to McCracken's four-wheel-drive pickup. Besides the security lights at the front and side entrance of the building, the place was dark and quiet. The building was located in an industrial area, and it was zero-dark-thirty in the morning, so that was no surprise. Still, something made the hairs on my neck stand up as I approached the entrance.

The door was slightly ajar, and beyond all I saw was darkness. Not wanting to enter the place blind, I cast a cantrip to enhance my senses. That's when I smelled the iron tang of fresh human blood.

Shit.

I drew my Glock and pushed the door open, pivoting behind the wall next to the door in case I drew fire from an ambush. Besides the squeak of the hinges, it was dead silent.

"McCracken," I whispered. "You in there?"

Nothing. I pulled out a tactical flashlight and headed in, flipping it on and using a minor spell to intensify the beam. I played the light across the area, searching for signs of blood—or dead bodies. The garage area of the warehouse was empty, save for a white panel van that said "ATX Power Washing" on the side. I hugged the wall as I headed for the hall that led to the offices.

As I snuck down the corridor the smell of blood became more intense, leading me to the very room where Keane's men had held me captive. Again, the door stood slightly ajar, so I pushed it open and hid behind the wall once more. When no shots rang out in the night, I peeked around the corner and into the room, shining my light so I could sight in on anything that might be waiting to take me out.

No one was there—at least, not anyone living. In the center of the room, McCracken's corpse had been tied to a chair, in the exact manner I'd been restrained by Keane's crew. His head sat in his lap, staring at me accusingly, and behind him a message had been painted in his blood, still fresh and wet on the stark white walls.

The message and its intent were crystal clear.

"ThiS is WhAt hApPens WheN yOu Fuk wiTh tHe DruiDs!"

The lights came on all at once, and before I heard the sound of booted feet entering the building, I already knew—I'd been set up.

SIXTEEN

Cursing my stupidity for walking into a trap for the third time this week, I slammed the door to the room, locking it and wedging a metal chair under the handle. As an afterthought, I threw a ward on it for good measure. Knowing exactly what was coming didn't make me any less nervous about it. Eventually, Keane and his team would burst through that door, likely breaching it with explosives and magic. That would be followed by flashbang grenades and a flurry of spells designed to put me down, leaving me injured but alive.

I was about to get fucked, lube optional.

The reasons for the setup were painfully obvious; someone on the Circle's High Council was pissed that I'd outed and killed their pet sociopath, Gunnarson. Not only that, but Finnegas and Maeve had embarrassed the Circle when they'd schooled them at the Conclave. Shoving my appointment to druid justiciar down their throats had just been the piss garnish on what must have been a very hard-to-swallow shit sandwich.

That's why Keane and his team hadn't respected McCracken, and it was why they'd disobeyed orders and taken me down dirty instead of simply delivering his message. They needed a back story, a reason why I might go ballistic and kill a ranking officer of The Circle. And, they knew their boss—their real boss, not McCracken—wouldn't give two shits from a rat's ass whether they roughed me up or not. Hell, whoever was running Keane's team probably told them to be as brutal as possible, to give me that much more motive.

I looked at McCracken's lifeless body, tied up in the same chair I'd been restrained in a few days prior. He'd been beaten badly, possibly tortured, and his head had been hacked off the hard way—that much was apparent from the blood spray on the walls. I'd a taken a few heads that way myself, with a long, sharp knife and a lot of sawing. It wasn't easy on the person being beheaded, or their executioner—at least, not unless the one doing the cutting was a heartless killer.

Keane.

Regardless of his affiliations, the lieutenant had seemed like a good guy. He'd damned sure didn't deserve to go down like that, betrayed, beaten, and murdered by his own people. And for what? They'd sacrificed him for a silly vendetta that had everything to do with greed for power and nothing to do with honor and justice.

I had maybe a minute before Keane and his thugs came busting through the door like the Wild Hunt to take me down, guns and spells blazing. Then they'd parade me in front of the entire supernatural community to discredit Finnegas and Maeve. The old man would come after me, but they probably knew he was weakening in his old age. Even worse, he'd likely be alone. After the way I'd done her, Maeve wouldn't piss on me if I was on fire, and neither Luther nor Samson could afford an all-out war with the Circle, friendships and Pack ties be damned.

Finnegas would go down, I'd be executed, the druids would

die out for good, and it would be all my fault for being the dumbass who hadn't seen this coming.

I guess I'd better not allow myself to be captured, eh?

Nope, getting captured was not an option. However, Keane and his team were pros, they had me outnumbered, and they'd taken me out once before when they'd had the drop on me. Hopefully that would work in my favor, because chances were good they'd come at me cocky and stupid, waving their dicks around like the pecker-measurers they were.

Lucky for them, I wasn't willing to shift again—not after what had happened with the cop on Mei's roof. Uh-uh, not an option. Sure, I could let my Hyde-side out and cut through these jokers like a hot knife through butter, but I was afraid I might not be able to put the genie back in the bottle. That meant I'd have to fuck them up the old-fashioned way.

With the mood I was in, I almost preferred to do it that way —almost.

I rummaged in my Bag, grabbing my war club and some paracord. The club I tucked through my belt, and the cord I tied off between a table and a vertical pipe at shin level close to the door, but not right in front of it. I taped a magically-enhanced M-80 on a spell trigger under another table in the corner farthest from the door. Then, I located one of the fire suppression nozzles in the drop ceiling above and grabbed a fire extinguisher off the wall. I shot the nozzle, setting off the sprinkler system, then shot out the lights in the room.

And waited.

Less than a minute later, I felt the rising pressure of an impending concussive spell, one that had enough energy to blow the door right off the hinges and shred my hasty ward. I took a deep breath and sprayed the extinguisher all around the room until it was filled with white fog. Then I plugged my ears with my fingers and squatted in a corner, eyes closed, waiting for what was to come.

There was a loud boom, followed by a crash and an over-pressure wave that rocked me up against the wall. Instead of jumping into action like a noob, I kept my ears plugged and shielded my eyes with my palms, waiting. Seconds later, two smaller concussive blasts followed, accompanied by intense flashes of light.

Time to move.

"Go, go, go!" I heard Keane yell somewhere in the smoke and darkness.

Keane's team were framed in the doorway when I opened my eyes. *Perfect.* I fired on the move, hitting at least two of them as they entered the room. Since they were likely wearing body armor, I aimed for the head, causing three to duck while another dropped to the floor, yelling he'd been hit. The rest of Keane's team returned fire, but I was already out of the way in the near corner, behind them and to their left.

"Somebody do something about this fog!" Keane yelled. "Cullen! How bad is it?"

"I'll live," Cullen replied.

Keane grunted. "Then post up on this door and make sure that motherfucker doesn't make it out in a vertical position."

"On it," Cullen groaned.

I tossed a coin across the room, into the far corner. It was still foggy as shit and I couldn't see three feet in front of my face, so I knew they couldn't either. Gunfire and lightning spells pelted that side of the room in response to the noise.

"Cease fire, cease fucking fire!" Keane yelled. "Command wants this fucker alive, you clowndicks! Smithson, Crandall—go see what we hit."

The two operatives marched forward, tripping over the paracord I'd rigged.

"Fuck!" one yelled as he took a header, his partner falling on top of him. I plugged my ears again and triggered the M-80 right in their faces, deafening everyone in the room but me.

Then, I drew my war club and charged Keane and Cullen.

THREE BOUNDING steps and I was on top of Keane. I popped out of the fog like a ghost in the darkness, smiling at the "oh shit" look on his face that said he hadn't thought I'd get the drop on him. I swung for the fences, timing my shot as I stepped into the attack. The club caught Keane right in the middle of his chest as he pivoted to face me.

Home. Run.

My war club packed a serious magical punch against the fae. However, I'd never used it on a human before, so I was unsure if it would work the same. It did. When the war club made contact with Keane's body armor, it took him off his feet. For a split-second, the rest of his body folded around the impact zone, then he flew across the room, ragdoll style.

He might live, since the trauma plate in his body armor took the brunt of the blow. Still, I'd bet dimes to doughnuts he ended up with a cracked sternum or a few fractured ribs. If he survived, the Circle medics would patch him up with magic, good as new. But for now, he was down for the count.

While I might have surprised Keane, Cullen had actually been ready for me. He was leaning against the wall beside the door, muttering a spell he'd spun up, keeping it on standby in case I gave away my position. But I had my own surprise waiting, a simple little druid spell that was a lot easier to cast than his elemental wizardry.

The sprinklers had soaked everything in the room, including

Cullen and the rest of his team. Before he could release his spell, I spoke a single word in Gaelic.

"*Reo.*"

Instantly, the air around Cullen dropped to better than minus forty, instantly freezing the water soaking his clothing and gear. Because water was such an excellent heat conductor, the sudden drop in temperature sucked all the warmth from his body, sending him into immediate hypothermia.

I watched as Cullen stood there trying to trigger his spell with his teeth all a-chatter. It was damned hard to cast a spell with a verbal command when you were uncontrollably shivering. I cracked him across the jaw with the handle end of the club, grinning wickedly as he dropped like a sack of rocks.

Two down, two to go.

I casually strolled into the center of the room, twirling the club like a marching baton as I closed in on the other two team members. The blast from the M-80 had disoriented them, plus they'd gotten a face full of table shrapnel in the blast. I gave them both light taps on the base of the skull—not hard enough to kill, but enough to cut their strings.

The fire extinguisher fog was starting to settle, so I glanced around the room at my handiwork. Three of the team were out like Christmas lights in January, and Keane was rolling around on the floor groaning a few feet away.

I should finish him off.

The thought came from nowhere, and I honestly couldn't tell whether it was mine or broadcasted into my mind from some external source. However, the urge to kill Keane sure *felt* real.

I can just snap his neck. A twist and pop, and there's one less Circle operative hunting me.

I wanted to do it, that was a fact. It's not like I hadn't killed humans before, especially when they were trying to capture or kill me. But I couldn't really be sure if it was me who'd be doing the killing, or that other side of me poking his ugly head up. And because I wasn't certain whose instincts were urging me to further violence, I fought down that desire with every last bit of willpower I had.

Walking toward the door was the hardest thing I'd ever done.

"This... isn't over, druid," Keane croaked from the corner. "This frame up—we filmed everything and took pictures before you got here. Within the hour, every major player in the world beneath will think you took out McCracken and broke the peace accord. And then it'll be open season on druids."

I opened my arms wide, sweeping them around the room. "And how do you think that'll work out?"

He laughed, causing himself a brief coughing fit. Keane recovered, wiping a bit of bloody spittle from his lip. "You just don't get it, do you? The old man played right into my boss' hands by appointing you to police the factions. You've been stepping on toes since you got here, you little shit, and you have more enemies than you realize. Once the Circle puts a bounty on your head, you'll have nowhere to run. You can't fight the entire city, McCool, not on your own—and you don't have enough allies to give you a fighting chance."

Cullen stirred next to the door, so I kicked him in the jaw hard enough to keep him down. "Maybe not, Keane. And maybe I will go down. But a cornered rat will go for the throat when it realizes it has nothing to lose." I pointed my club at him. "You tell your boss I'm coming. And as far as I'm concerned, no one is above justice."

I turned and walked out the door, watching for another ambush as I headed for the exit. Keane's laughter echoed after me in the dark.

"Oh, believe me, druid—they're counting on it."

KEANE and his goons had slashed the tires on the Gremlin, so it looked like I was going to be hoofing it. The junkyard was all the way across town, and that was going to be one hell of a long walk. I could find safe haven there, tucked away behind my wards or perhaps hiding for a time inside the druid grove.

In light of the safety the junkyard would provide, I knew that going underground could place others in jeopardy. If the Cold Iron Circle couldn't get to you, they'd put pressure on the people you cared for most. Abduction, torture, murder—nothing was off the table for these jokers.

And that was just the Circle. I had every reason to believe Keane was dead serious about putting out a bounty on my head. That meant I'd have every two-bit fae, hedge wizard, rogue vampire, and renegade 'thrope on my tail—not to mention any monster hunting outfit who thought they could make their bones by bringing me in or taking me down.

It wouldn't be long until I was considered public enemy number one among Austin's supernatural community. Luther and Samson would try to keep the heat off me on their end, but there were always members of their kind who didn't abide by the rules. And I doubted I could count on Maeve to announce a mandate telling her people to stay out of it.

That left Finnegas and Maureen, and a handful of others I might count on in a crisis. Bells was out; I knew she'd help if I asked, but I was too proud to have her bail me out twice. Hemi was still convalescing in his home country, or so I'd heard. The trolls might help. Although they technically worked for Maeve, they considered themselves to be an independent entity. But I really didn't want to place them in danger, not after getting so many of their young warriors killed during the battle of the graveyard.

For now, I'd have to make do on my own. My first priority was getting off the streets and out of sight until I could find some transportation. Then, I'd track down Mei. She was connected to the Circle somehow, and I intended to discover how. If I got lucky, she'd lead me straight back to the ringleader on the Council, the person pulling everyone's strings.

Me, lucky. Yeah right.

I'd cross those bridges when I was ready to burn them to ash. For now, I had more immediate concerns. Since I'd chosen to let him live, Keane had likely already checked in with a status update. By now, the Circle knew I'd escaped Keane's trap, which meant they'd have other teams out looking for me.

Finn's words echoed in my head. *If you freeze, you die.* That was the first lesson of combat, and it was why I needed to get moving.

As I made my way through the concrete expanse of the Cameron Road industrial district, I felt the proverbial noose tightening around me. Every street and alley seemed to have a black SUV or late model sedan cruising it, circling the area around me like sharks closing in on a passenger lost at sea.

I ducked behind an air-conditioning unit and some trash cans as a black Yukon with dark tinted windows rolled past. To make my escape, I needed to cross a well-lit street so I could get to a large, nearly empty parking lot bordering an open field. That led to a wooded area, and from there I could get lost in the IH-35 corridor, steal a car, and go on the attack. Only a hundred yards or so to go, then I'd be free from the Circle's search cordon.

After the SUV turned the corner, I sprinted across the street, hiding behind cars whenever possible as I headed for the open field. I briefly considered stealing a late-model Ford truck as I crossed the lot, but was afraid I'd be spotted on the desolate streets of the industrial district. It was best to stay off the roads for now. Checking the area to make certain I was in the clear, I ran like a scalded dog for the field.

The terrain beyond the parking lot was a marshy expanse of undeveloped urban wetlands. That worked in my favor, because the field was dark and the tall grasses and vegetation offered some cover from prying eyes. Roughly the size of two football fields, I was halfway across when I heard the howl of a coyote, followed by answering yips and howls from three directions around me.

What the fuck?

Coyotes were not an uncommon presence in this area, as the local mix of warehouses, fields, and small patches of woodland made it the ideal habitat for *canis latrans*. However, it was rare that a pack would hunt a human, as it simply wasn't in the nature of the species to interact with people. At first, I thought they might be tracking an injured deer, or a lone fawn—but based on their positioning I concluded they were on my trail.

Shit. I ran.

As I neared the strip of woods that would lead me to IH-35, three coyotes emerged from the trees ahead of me. I slowed my pace as I glanced behind me. Five more were trailing me through the marshy field, spread out to box me in. I turned to face those ahead of me, entering my druid trance to reach out and let them know I wasn't a threat.

"Don't bother," a voice said from the direction of the trees.

I opened my eyes in time to see a ninth, larger coyote lope out of the woods, tongue lolling as it regarded me with yellow-brown eyes. As I met its gaze, it morphed from animal to human form. The man was fully naked, except for a coyote pelt that he wore like a cloak around his shoulders. He looked to be of Latino or Native American descent, with brown skin, almond eyes, a hooked nose, and straight, jet-black hair that hung loosely past his shoulders. With his sunken cheeks and thin but athletic build, he looked to be every bit the predator he was.

"Well, well," he said. "The pack and I are going to eat good this week. Bounty on your head is a thousand, druid—all I got to do is keep you here and wait for the white men to round you up."

SEVENTEEN

"Just a grand? Really? I'm insulted."

The dark-skinned man shook his head. "Not a thousand bucks—a thousand gold coins. A small fortune, more than enough to buy a stretch of land in the hills, out where my pack and I can enjoy some peace."

I crossed my arms, casually glancing around to mark the location of each coyote in the group. "Open land is getting harder and harder to come by, I'll give you that. Still, you should consider the safety of your pack, skinwalker, before you weigh their lives against mine."

He chuckled, and it was not a happy sound. "You've met my kind before, I take it. Funny, most hunters mistake me for a 'thrope." The man sniffed the air as he regarded me, an almost imperceptible gesture that he tried to conceal. "Don't think that makes me like you though, druid. My kind are solitary. We don't even care for each other much. Or for people in general."

The situation was less than ideal. If I ran, the coyotes would attempt to bring me down, and I'd have to kill them. Animals operating under the influence of magic hardly deserved such a fate. *How I hate magic-users who use nature's creatures to do their dirty work.*

On the other hand, if I stood and fought, I'd still have to hurt the pack while dealing with their leader. Fighting him while trying to avoid injuring the animals would be difficult. Skinwalkers were fast and ornery as hell, and they often possessed powers that made them difficult to cope with in battle. For those reasons, hunters tended to avoid them whenever possible.

I decided to change the subject, biding my time until I could decide what to do about the skinwalker and his pets.

"I'm surprised Samson has tolerated your presence."

The skinwalker flashed me a coyote's smile, one that was all teeth with no warmth to it. "I've made it a point to stay beneath his notice. What he doesn't know can't piss him off. Besides, I don't fall under his purview. I'm a magic-user, druid, not a 'thrope."

"But you are a shifter," I countered.

"No, not like you. The alpha has no claim on me." He swiveled an ear at an almost imperceptible sound in the distance, an altogether inhuman thing to do. "Your time grows short, human."

"You're making a mistake," I said. "Again, consider your pack."

"You won't kill them," he replied. "You'd kill a fae in a heart-beat, but an innocent animal? No, I believe they're safe."

"Perhaps, but I have no such compunctions about killing you."

"Ah, but you'd have to go through them to do it. And you obviously don't want that, otherwise we wouldn't be having this discussion."

"True—which is why I don't intend to." I triggered the spell I'd been silently preparing as I whipped my arms apart, spreading them wide and pointing one hand in front of me and one behind. I squeezed my eyes shut as bright light and concussive sound exploded from my palms, temporarily blinding and deafening the coyotes... and their master.

The spell was an amalgam of cantrips I'd cooked up after my run-in with the Dark Druid, a sort of ace in the hole that I reserved for dire situations. It was a combination of a flashbang cantrip, see-me-not spell, and ward booster. I hated using it, not because it was ineffective or hard to pull off, but because every Circle operative in a three-mile radius was now alerted to my location.

Blinded, the coyotes scattered in all directions, tripping and running into random objects. I felt pang of regret over that, but it was only temporary and better than the alternative. That left the skinwalker, who crouched in a defensive stance as he blinked rapidly to regain his eyesight.

Fat chance.

I grabbed a large rock and tossed it to his left. The skinwalker didn't even flinch, which told me he'd had his hearing blown out as well. I sprinted to his right, slowing just enough to snatch his coyote skin from his shoulders as I ran past. Why? Well, for one, I didn't want him tracking me, and second, I thought it'd be funny to leave him out here naked as the day he was born.

Leave it to me to poke the bear—or coyote, in this case.

The skinwalker howled in anguish at the loss of his animal totem, turning this way and that as he tossed sickly-green, phantasmic spells that shriveled the grass and withered small trees. *Death magic—not cool.* Spells like those were designed to suck the life right out of you, aging you a few years in an instant. Not enough to kill you in one shot, but certainly no trip to the ice cream parlor, either.

I'd almost felt sorry for him, the way he cried out when I stole his, um, *stole.* But now I was almost tempted to go back and finish him off. Death magic was just as bad as necromancy, and the fact that he was throwing it around indiscriminately really pissed me off.

One swipe of my sword is all it will take...

Once again, I couldn't tell if that thought was my own or not. As I considered the source of my urge to kill the skinwalker, a bush to my left instantly decayed into dust. At that moment, I very nearly said "fuck it" and headed back to finish him off, working under the assumption that my freshly-boosted wards were strong enough to fend off at least one of those death magic spells.

Fortunately for him, the roar of engines and a flash of head-lights in the distance told me now was not the time to be dealing with random death magicians. I could always hunt the skin-walker down and settle things with him later, but for now I needed to avoid being caught by the Circle.

Another time, skinwalker. Another time.

I ran off into the woods, hoping the see-me-not spell would conceal me during my escape. As I did, the skinwalker's voice echoed loudly behind me.

"You've made a dangerous enemy, druid. You will regret this, I swear it!"

AN HOUR LATER, I stole a late model Caddie from a pimp down on Rundberg, after I stomped his knee backwards for slap-ping a street walker. Proving that no good deed goes unpun-ished, she pulled a chrome .25 caliber pistol on me. I took a slug in the outside of the thigh, just my luck. It was an in and out, through the skin and fatty tissue—more of a nuisance than anything.

Bleeding all over the pimp's front seat, I did my best to

drive under the speed limit until I put some distance between myself and the warehouse. A few miles down the road, I pulled over behind a convenience store and took a better look at my leg.

I'll be damned, the bleeding's stopped. That wasn't good. I didn't possess any accelerated healing powers, except when I was partially or fully shifted. The entrance and exit wounds were still there, but they'd already scabbed over during the fifteen minutes or so since I'd gotten shot.

Angling the rearview mirror toward me, I took a good look at myself. The changes were subtle, but they were there—my Fomorian side was coming out, little by little. It was apparent in the more prominent brow ridge and cheekbones, the set of my eyes, the angular look of my face.

Shit. What the hell is going on here?

More than anything, I feared losing control to my Hyde-side and hurting an innocent, like I'd done with Jesse. At one time I'd thought I'd come to grips with that part of me, but now something was forcing that more primal, violent personality to the surface.

Is it a curse? I checked my wards, and nothing was amiss.

Jesse must be doing this to me. That was the only answer I could come up with. Maybe she thought it would force Bells and me apart, or perhaps she was doing it unintentionally. Whatever the reasons, I needed answers, and it was high time I confronted her on the matter. Besides, she had something I needed, something that would likely help me find Mei and Derp.

Heading back to the junkyard was a shit move, because the Circle would definitely have it staked out. I'd already texted Maureen, Bells, Luther's people, and Samson's daughter, Fallyn, to inform them of the situation. Maureen would tell the old man and keep him out of it, for now. Batman to my

Nightwing, he trusted me enough to let me solve my own problems, but he'd also step in if I was really in a jam.

At least I knew they'd all steer clear of the junkyard—when I showed up it'd be bedlam, for sure. I had another card up my sleeve to play, and I intended to put it to use. If it all worked out the way I'd planned, those Circle jerks wouldn't know I was there until it was too late.

I dumped the Cadillac six blocks from the junkyard. *Back on my own turf—it's showtime.* Intimately familiar with the area's rhythms and cycles, I knew exactly what belonged and what didn't. No way the Circle was going to surprise me in my own neighborhood. Not today.

Sneaking closer to the junkyard was easy. The Circle's surveillance vehicles drew more attention than a ringtone at a funeral service, so ducking them was a piece of cake. I crossed Dittmar and used a wooded area behind the yard to sneak within viewing distance of my home.

Of course, the Circle had the perimeter of the place staked out. I spotted at least three operatives hiding along the fence line in front of me. Communing with the animals in the area revealed two more close by, more on the other three sides of the fence, and a team atop a two-story building just south of the yard.

Getting in is gonna be tough. Let's hope this works.

I rummaged around in my Bag for the item I'd held in check 'til now—Gunnarson's cloak. Experimentation with it had produced mixed results, at best. Like my Craneskin Bag, it was semi-sentient, and magically linked to Gunnarson's family tree. Moreover, the thing was not pleased that I'd killed its master, the last descendant in his line.

I could force the thing to work with a great deal of willpower and effort, but only for a few minutes. Complicating matters further, the length of time I could get it to work was iffy.

On some attempts, I could remain unseen for several minutes—yet on others, the effects only lasted seconds.

Despite the risks, I had to get into the junkyard, both to speak with Jesse and retrieve what I needed. It was simply a chance I'd have to take, although the decision to take that gamble was based as much on pride as it was on strategic necessity. No way I was going to let these punks keep me out of my own home. And after I got what I needed from the druid grove, they were all in for a rude awakening.

If I do get into a scrape on the way in, it'll likely be wetwork. Let's hope I don't lose control.

I pulled my hunting dagger from the sheath at the small of my back and draped the cloak over my shoulders. Then, I commanded it to do its thing.

FORCING the cloak to activate was like willing the earth to move off its axis, so stubborn was the entity that powered the thing. After several minutes of struggle, I won the battle of wills. Opening my eyes, I held my hands in front of my face and marveled at the shimmering outline that represented my limbs. It looked a lot like the Predator when it cloaked itself to hide from Arnold Schwarzenegger, but way, way cooler.

I'd learned early on that this was the cloak's way of keeping you from being totally disoriented when under its spell. Not being able to see yourself while moving was a lot like being blind, because it made it difficult to determine where you were in relation to your surroundings. For that reason, the cloak allowed you to see your own outline—but only just.

And as for everyone else? So powerful was its illusory magic that others wouldn't see a thing, not a hint of my presence. Even if I disturbed grass or dirt beneath my feet, or brushed against a leafy branch, the cloak would hide those signs of my passing.

It was a damned handy thing to have—when it worked properly.

I headed through the woods as quickly and silently as possible, coming up behind a sentry I simply could not avoid. She hid right in front of a backdoor I'd left in my wards, a "lock and key" opening I'd designed for just such an occasion. I'd have to take her out if I wanted to get inside.

The woman was tall and lithe with a runner's build, and had dark brown hair pulled in a ponytail through the back of a black ball cap. She wore a matching rain jacket and dark green fatigue pants over hiking boots, but she carried no weapons, at least none that I could see.

A mage. Great. Can't let her make a sound, or else she'll trigger a spell.

As I snuck through the undergrowth, moving as slow as possible so as not to make a sound, thoughts of violence and mayhem kept running through my mind.

Snap her neck.

Slit her throat.

Shove the blade just below her C1 vertebrae. Angle it slightly down as you push it in, then up again. She'll drop like a rock.

Cover her mouth and drive the blade cleanly between the fourth and fifth rib, next to her sternum, so it slides right into her heart. She'll be gone before she can scream.

Each thought more vicious and gruesome than the last. I fought the urges off, shoving them down deep into the recesses of my mind, but still they whispered at me as I approached my target.

kill...

Kill...

KILL!

It took everything I had to resist snapping her neck as I reached around from behind, driving my forearm under her chin until her windpipe was in the crook of my arm.

Pull your arm back a few inches, so the wrist bone is against her throat—one yank and her windpipe will be crushed, the dark voice within me crooned.

Instead, I squeezed my forearm to my shoulder, clapping my other hand over her mouth and nose to prevent her from calling out. With my strength augmented by the Fomorian DNA currently expressing itself, it took mere seconds to choke her into unconsciousness. As I felt the Circle operative's body go limp, I slowly lowered her to the ground.

Immediately, I released my wards in this section of the fence and pulled back a corrugated sheet metal panel to squeeze through. Dense vegetation hid my movements, and I made it through the fence without being noticed.

Just in time, too. I knelt in shadow between two junked cars, reaching out with my druid sense to check for intruders inside the fence. The yard had yet to be breached, but as I opened my eyes I felt and saw the cloak's magic being wrested from my control. My limbs coalesced back into view, and I sighed as I swept the cloak off my shoulders, balling it up and tossing it inside the Bag.

Well, at least it got me in. Now to get what I came for, before the sentries outside discover their squad mate.

Knowing that the interior of the yard was being watched from the rooftop of a building adjacent to the grounds, I crept my way to the clearing where the druid tree resided. Then, I grabbed a rusty bolt from the dirt at my feet and tossed it across the yard to Roscoe's favorite sleeping spot.

Barking and growling erupted as the dogs investigated the noise. I desperately hoped the ruckus they made would draw the attention of the surveillance teams on overwatch. They'd almost certainly be armed with sniper rifles, and getting shot by a high-powered rifle round was a lot different than getting hit by a .25 caliber pistol. If they spotted me, I'd be toast.

Here goes nothing.

I sprinted across the yard, my feet pitter-pattering in the dirt as my shoe soles slapped the ground. Within five strides I'd reached the grassy expanse beneath the tree, and in ten strides I was touching the trunk. A bullet whizzed past my head, just before I heard the *crack* of suppressed gunfire in the distance.

Supersonic rounds. Let's hope my head doesn't explode like a melon.

Nearly duckwalking to stay as low as possible, I trod widdershins around the huge tree trunk, waiting for the inevitable. Another bullet struck the tree in front of me, making a divot in the bark. The shots were coming from the south, so the north side of the tree offered relative safety, at least until they sent another sniper team to the north.

No way I'll make it two more times around this tree. I'm dog meat for sure.

I hid behind the trunk on the north side, mentally girding my loins to sprint around the south side. I was just about to make a run for it when a greenish, feminine hand sprouted from the bark of the tree. It grabbed me and yanked me toward the trunk with surprising force. Then, I fell headlong into nothingness.

EIGHTEEN

The impact was much less worse than expected, as the soft grass around the druid oak inside the grove cushioned my landing. Unfortunately, I landed face first, which resulted in a mouthful of grass and dirt and a minor amount of embarrassment on my part. I was here to confront Jesse, after all, and falling flat on my face didn't exactly make me look like I meant business.

I spat out earth as I got to my hands and knees, with Jesse fawning over me all the while.

"Were you hit? Tell me that those big bad men didn't hurt my Colin." She grabbed my chin and lifted my head, turning it this way and that. "Hmm... except for the dirt in your teeth, you seem to be okay. You should swallow that, you know. Magic dirt has a ton of probiotics in it."

"Damn it, Jesse, I'm fine—get off me!"

I shook my head in an attempt to release her grip, but she was exceedingly strong, and all I got for my efforts was a sore jaw. I ended up slapping her hand away with more force than was necessary. She stood abruptly, arms crossed as she gazed down her nose at me.

"See if I ever save you again," she huffed.

"Yeah, that sentiment seems to be going around," I muttered.

"What's that supposed to mean?"

"Never mind. Say, when you were looking me over like a cattleman eyeing a prize steer, did you happen to notice anything different about me?"

"We're not going to talk about the Circle operatives that currently have the junkyard surrounded, nor about the sniper who was just taking pot-shots at you?"

I remained silent as I stood up and dusted myself off.

"Fine," she replied. "I suppose you are looking a bit more —*masculine* these days."

"I—say what? Did I look feminine before?"

Jesse shrugged. "You've always been a pretty boy, my love. You may as well own it."

I palmed my forehead with a growl of frustration. "And you don't know a thing about this"— I moved my hands in small orbits around my face for emphasis—"new look I'm sporting?"

She leaned in and stared closely, perched on a tree root that grew under her feet so she could stand eye level with me. "Hmm... nope, nothing."

"Jesse, it's *him*. You know, my other side?"

"Oh, him. Yes, now I see it." Her eyes narrowed as she stepped down and backed away a few steps. "You're aware that I'm not particularly fond of that side of you? It did once tear me limb from limb, after all."

"Wait a minute—you mean you're not doing this?"

She placed her hands on her hips with a frown. "You think I caused this? Colin, I'll be the first to admit that I've changed since I possessed your dryad. Her mind is, well, fae—warped and twisted and altogether inhuman. Mind you, that might have caused me to take on certain *guileful* characteristics, but under no circumstances would I ever wish to bring that *thing* out in you."

"Not even to drive a wedge between Belladonna and I?"

She harrumphed loudly. "As if I needed to stoop to such measures to win you back." Jesse placed a finger atop her head and spun in a graceful circle on tiptoe. "I mean, just look at me —I'm magnificent!"

I sat hard on a moss-covered boulder. "Damn it! If it's not you making this happen, what the hell is causing it?"

Jesse was still admiring herself, holding her arms at length as she posed like a ballerina. "Meh, I don't know. Could be a curse or something."

"Jesse." She continued taking in her own beauty, alternately extending one leg then the other as she sighed in self-content-ment. "Jesse..." I snapped my fingers repeatedly in front of her face. "Jesse!"

The dryad paused, turning those deep green eyes on me as she slowly looked up. "There's no need to yell, Colin. I'm right here, you know."

"I'm having an existential crisis, and all you can do is revel in self-adulation!" I screamed.

Her eyes went wide and her jaw slackened. "Oh, wow. Yeah, that side of you really is coming out. Usually you're quieter when you're whiny, not angry and loud."

"Whiny? Really?"

"You are the king of whine, my dear. Dionysius reborn, in fact. But don't worry, I love you all the same for it. I mean, men can't be strong all the time—that's what women are for."

I rubbed my forehead with my fingertips as I covered my face with both hands. "Rather than arguing gender roles, do you think you might use your magic to check me over, perhaps to see if there's something I might have missed?"

Her face lit up. "See! That's exactly what I'm talking about.

You're not at all afraid of asking your better half for help." Jesse cleared her throat as she approached, hands extended. "Allow me."

"Ooh, I'm so honored, great earth mother, that you should bless this puny mortal with your magnificent and omniscient regard."

Jesse slapped my hand. "Ssh... you shouldn't blaspheme like that."

"Ahem, I'm Orthodox, Jesse. We kind of don't go in for all that nature worship stuff."

"And yet you're a druid. What a walking hot mess of contradictory behavior you are. I mean, really—the cognitive dissonance must drive you insane at times." She patted my cheek playfully. "It's okay, I won't hold it against you."

"Oh, joy."

"Hush," she replied, placing a finger on my lips. "I need to concentrate."

Jesse worked her hands in complex patterns as she ran them over and just above every surface of my body. It took several minutes, and when she was done she stepped back, arms crossed, heels together, tapping a finger on her lips.

"What? Am I cursed?"

Jesse shook her head slowly. "No, in fact, it's nothing of the sort. Whatever is causing these changes to occur, I'm almost positive that it's not coming from outside of you, but instead, from within."

"UM... WHAT DOES THAT MEAN?"

She cocked her head to one side, scrunching her face with an eye squeezed shut. "Maybe that your human side and Fomorian side are fighting for dominance? Or, they might be trying to achieve a balance within you. Kind of hard to say, since I've only been at this dryad-slash-eldritch-creature-with-the-magical-powers-of-nature thing for a few weeks now."

"Great, just great," I muttered. "You mean to tell me this is happening naturally?"

Jesse leaned in, placing her hands on my knees as she whispered in my ear. "I. Don't. Know." She nibbled my earlobe. "But I do know how to take your mind off of things—if you're up for it."

I closed my eyes. Having her this near to me was intoxicating, despite the dire circumstances. "Jess, you're doing that pheromone thing again."

"Sorry," she whispered.

I grabbed her gently by the upper arms and guided her to take a seat next to me. "It's time we had a talk."

"You mean *that* talk? Slugger, I don't need to worry about getting pregnant anymore—not in this form, at least."

"No," I growled. "I mean, about us."

"Are you breaking up with me?" she asked, with a dangerous glint in her eye.

"No—yes—I mean, how could I? Jesse, up until a few weeks ago, you were a ghost. I'd moved on after losing you—"

"Killing me," she interjected.

"—please, as if I didn't feel bad enough already. My point is that I'd moved on in your absence, and suddenly you showed up expecting to pick up where we left off."

Jesse tapped the side of her nose and winked. "For one, I never left you. You're the reason why I never moved on, in case you forgot about that small detail. Second, I do not expect us to pick up where we left off, and I could care less whether you sleep with that Spanish whore while you're on the other side." She snuggled close to me, wrapping her arms around one of mine. "All I care about is having you here, with me, in the grove."

"You realize you're asking me to invoke the zip code rule, right?" I asked.

"Believe me, sugar—we are worlds away from Austin right now. This would be more like the *alternate dimension* rule."

I pinched the bridge of my nose, because this was all giving me a headache. "You should know better than anyone, Jesse—I don't work that way. I'm not a cheater, no matter how much my hormones plead otherwise."

"Didn't stop you from practically asking to be raped by that spider chick earlier," she said with a twinkle in her eye. "Honestly, I had no idea you were that kinky."

"How did you know about that?"

"See, this is why you need to spend more time with me, here in the grove. The tree is a dimensional doorway, Colin. That means I can see things that are going on, wherever I care to point it."

"Wait a sec—the tree can open a portal wherever you like?"

She wobbled a hand back and forth. "Sort of. Right now, all I can do is look, but that's because you haven't fully taken control of the grove. That's why it's not operating at full capacity. And even after you do, it'll be years before you master it, which means you won't be dimension hopping for quite some time yet."

"Jess, how do you know all of this?"

"The Dagda told me when I followed you into Underhill. I made a deal with him there, to bring me back to life."

"You what?" I stood up and turned to face her. "Jesse, you know how dangerous it is to deal with the fae. The Tuatha—they're much worse."

She rolled her eyes at me. "Oh, please. So it's okay for you to travel to Underhill and cut deals with The Dagda and Lugh—

never mind double-crossing Niamh—but I do it, and suddenly it's 'dangerous'?" She stuck her tongue out and gave me the strawberries. "You sir, are a hypocrite."

I realized immediately what she was saying was true. I *was* a hypocrite, and I couldn't blame her for wanting to come back to life. Heck, it's what I would have done.

"You're right. But still, you might have warned me beforehand. At least I could have braced myself for it."

"Uh-uh, the Dagda wouldn't allow it. He said if I let you in on his plan, you'd never plant that acorn, because your deepest wish was for me to move on to the next life."

"I want you to be safe and happy, Jesse. That's all I've ever wanted."

"I am. I have everything I could ever want here. Light, water, trees, grass—this fantastic body—and if he'd ever come to his senses, the love of my life as well."

"I can't cheat on Belladonna, Jesse. I love you and I always will, but I'm just not made that way."

"She's not meant for you, Colin. You'll come to see that, eventually."

Maybe she was right. I had no clue, confused as I was about —well, *everything*. For the moment, I couldn't really tell which emotions were my own and which were coming from my Fomorian side. Yes, it was all me—just not from the "me" I preferred to be most of the time.

"We can discuss this more, later. Right now, I have a jorōgumo to hunt down, a missing child to find—"

Jesse's brow furrowed. "Again? Sheesh, you sure are the brat wrangler these days."

"—and, as I was about to say, I came here to retrieve something from you."

"My dryad virginity?" she asked, gazing up at me with a wry smile on her face.

"No, Jess," I sighed. "I need the nachtkrapp back. I'm here for Nameless."

———————

"THE WHAT?" she asked, truly perplexed.

"The night raven, Jesse." I spread my hands about a foot apart. "Black bird, about this big, made of shadow and smoke? I left him here just a few days ago."

"Oh... that thing. Let's see, where did I put him? Ah yes, out at the edge of the grove. He kept crying and complaining, 'oh, this place is killing me, oh, the druid double-crossed me, oh, this grove is a death sentence, blah, blah, blah.' The bird reminds me a bit of you, actually, but not in a good way. Anyway, I got sick of it and banished him to the outer reaches."

"Well, I need him back, so can you please take me to him?"

She rolled her eyes. "It's your grove. If you'd take the time to familiarize yourself with it, you'd know where everything was."

"Jess, I really don't have the time for this."

"I know. You have to save the world, etcetera. This way, please."

Jesse skipped away from me, dancing and twirling in circles as she meandered her way through the grove. The path she took led more or less in a straight line, out maybe a few hundred yards from the tree, or so it seemed. Distances were weird inside the place, and from what I could tell, anything but linear.

"Here it is," she said, pointing to a young poplar that rose about fifteen feet above our heads. Hanging from one of the lower branches was a bird cage, woven from live branches that were connected to the tree. While the rest of the tree was lush and green, the branch on which the cage hung had few leaves, and those were sickly and yellowed.

I looked beyond the tree at what appeared to be a vast

expanse of forest ahead of us. "Wait a minute, I thought you said this was the edge of the grove?"

"Oh, it is." Jesse nodded. "But if you keep walking in any direction, it'll just lead you back to the druid oak. The standard laws of physics don't always apply here."

"Good to know." A black lump lay inside the cage, unmoving. I looked more closely and gasped. "Good night, is he dead?"

"Heck if I know," Jesse replied absently, preoccupied as she admired a bright blue butterfly that had landed on her arm. "I told you leaving him here was a mistake."

I tried to get inside the cage, but I couldn't find a door. "Could you open this thing, please?"

She waited for the butterfly to flit away, then turned and fixed me with an impatient stare. "I keep telling you, this is your grove. Everything here obeys your will, and if you'd only take the time to—"

"Yes, I know, I'm supposed to 'master' the grove somehow. I'll get to that eventually, but for now I need you to open the damned cage!"

Jesse's eyes grew wide and the corners of her mouth turned downward. She blinked at me several times, tsking like a mother witnessing a child's tantrum.

"Well, excuse me, your royal highness, let me just get right on that task." She snapped her fingers and the "bars" of the cage spread apart. Jesse curtsied, but her voice was sharp with sarcasm as she continued. "Will there be anything else, m'lord?"

"Not at the moment, no," I deadpanned, refusing to play her games. I reached into the cage, laying hands on the pitiful bundle of feathers, tattered cloth, and smoke that lay still in the center. As I lifted the night raven from the cage, he stirred slightly.

"Are you here to end my misery, *jaeger*?" the nachtkrapp

whispered weakly. "Come to finish me off, and break your vow for good?"

Nameless had withered away to almost nothing in his time here in the grove. He felt light as a feather in my hands, or a bundle of feathers in this case. The bird had also molted badly, revealing patches of black, wispy "skin" underneath his feathers, and his beak was cracked and worn, as if he'd been trying to peck his way out of the cage. If the nachtkrapp hadn't been about to eat a couple of defenseless children a few days hence, I might have felt sorry for him. Honestly, the only real remorse I felt at his pitiful condition was that I wasn't holding up my end of our bargain.

"No, I'm not here to kill you, Nameless. Actually, I'm here to take you to someone who can keep you alive and out of trouble."

"Liar," the night raven croaked. "I'll never trust anything you say again, druid. Not after leaving me like this."

"See what I mean?" Jesse interjected. "He whines just as much as you do."

I shifted the bird to the crook of my left arm, cradling him there with as much gentleness as I was capable of mustering. My Fomorian side immediately began whispering for me to kill the thing, and it took considerable effort to resist ending his miserable existence once and for all.

"I'm going to ignore that comment, Jesse. Can you create a diversion outside, in the junkyard, so Nameless and I can get away without getting our heads blown off?"

Nameless squawked as he rustled slightly at my side. "That would be a mercy, at this juncture."

"Quiet, you," I murmured. "Jess, can you do it?"

Jesse tapped a finger on her chin as she stared at the sky above. Or, what appeared to be sky—I wasn't really certain about the nature of what was up there, and in fact I tried not to think about it.

"Sure I can. But you're going to need wheels to get you where you need to go. And as soon as those goons realize what's happening, they're going to bust through your wards in force and turn you and the bird into Swiss cheese via bullet storm."

I cracked my neck and rolled my shoulders out. "Just take care of the sniper, create a diversion, and I'll handle the rest."

"Ooh, so forceful," Jesse cooed. "It almost makes up for the whininess."

"Again, I'm ignoring you," I said as I headed back to the oak tree.

"You're so cute when you pout," the dryad replied in a baby talk voice, pinching my cheek as she danced past me.

NINETEEN

When we arrived at the oak, Jesse extended her hand to me, and in response I crossed my arms and frowned. Bitchy resting face was the default setting on my current, altered facial structure, so it didn't take much effort.

"C'mon, don't be a scaredy cat. I won't bite—much," she said with a devious wink.

Reluctantly, I placed my hand in hers. One heartbeat later we were earth-side, standing on a large limb fifteen feet above the ground in the druid oak. The tree's thick canopy of leaves concealed us from spying eyes. Even so, I was more than a bit nervous about being up there, with nothing but a few leaves and branches for protection from the sniper's gunfire.

"Two questions," I whispered. "How are you going to deal with the sniper, and how am I supposed to get down from here when you do?"

Jesse held a finger to her lips. "Hush, I need to concentrate." She placed her fingertips on her temples like a carnival sideshow mentalist. "Watch carefully, directly in front of us."

A hand-width tunnel opened in the leaves ahead, offering us a window to the world outside that focused directly on a rooftop to the south. I suddenly had the sensation I was moving forward at speed, then realized it was the image of the rooftop zooming in for me. Two men wearing dark fatigues and body armor were on that roof and looking in our direction—one with a spotter's monocular, the other scanning the junkyard through a high-powered scope.

"Don't worry, they can't see us," Jesse assured me. "Now, to take care of that sniper team."

She plucked two twigs and two leaves from a nearby branch, cupping them inside her hands. Pursing her lips, she blew in the space between her thumb and forefinger, then rubbed her hands back and forth gently a few times. The dryad nodded once, opening her hands to reveal two wooden darts. Their shafts were made from polished oak, and their fletching had been fashioned from thick, fern-like leaves.

"Neat trick," I said in a low voice.

"You'd be able to do it too, if you could be bothered to read the owner's manual." I opened my mouth to protest, but she held a finger up. "Ah ah, still concentrating. Now, for the finishing touch."

Jess licked the needle-sharp tips of both darts, then laid them in her palm pointed at the sniper team. "Fly true," she said, and the darts did her bidding, zipping down the leafy tunnel and hitting each member of the men in the neck. They slapped at the darts, then each slumped to the roof's surface.

"Are they dead?" I asked.

"No, merely sleeping. I may be capricious, but I'm not evil." She wiped her hands together as if dusting them off. "Well, my job's done. Guess you'd better climb down and do your thing, oh mighty druid."

I tsked and tongued a molar. "I don't remember you being this sarcastic in your former life."

"You try spending a few years as a ghost, and see if you don't get a bit salty. Now, shoo—I'll do what I can to help you escape from here."

I gave her a peck on the cheek on sheer impulse. "Thanks, Jess."

She smiled, in a way that reminded me of a tiger twitching its tail before pouncing on an easy meal. "Tick-tock, slugger. Your spider-demon awaits."

"Here goes nothing." I scrambled down the tree's trunk, managing to avoid falling until I was halfway to the ground. I landed in a crouch, then spoke the trigger word to activate magical traps along my fence line that normally remained dormant. Once I was satisfied they were ready, I made a beeline for the front lot.

As soon as I was in the open, the spells and gunfire began. I made it halfway to the front gate before I was forced to take cover behind a stack of cars. Bullets whizzed past me, pinging off engine blocks and car frames and punching through glass and sheet metal. I winced at the money the junkyard was losing, as body panels and windshields with bullet holes tended not to sell very well.

A fireball whooshed overhead, hitting an old Ford van twenty feet behind me. I ducked behind a hood that leaned against a rust-ridden Ford LTD just before the van's gas tank ignited. The vehicle exploded in a flash of heat and smoke, pelting the area with shrapnel that dented, and in some cases partially penetrated, the thin piece of steel protecting me.

Enough of this—time to reel them in.

"You missed me, asshole!" I yelled from behind the stack of cars.

"You can't hide forever, McCool!" a gruff voice shouted from beyond the fence.

"Keane, is that you? Damn, Circle healing magic must be

getting better. I figured your team would be down for at least a few days, considering the ass-whooping I put on you."

"Laugh all you want now," he replied. "We have this place surrounded and my men are closing in. You're done, druid!"

"Your men? That's a bit gender-exclusive, don't you think? Do they not have sensitivity training in the Cold Iron Circle?"

"Just the kind of talk I'd expect from a liberal, hipster pussy like you, McCool. Sit tight, and we'll have your pretty boy ass hogtied in no time. Then we'll see how smart-assed you are with a gag in your mouth."

Why does everyone insist on calling me a hipster? Is it the hair?

I chose to ignore the jibe. "That's a little too much kink even for you, Keane. Again, I think I'll have to decline."

By this time, I'd sensed multiple Circle teams in assault positions around the perimeter of the junkyard. *Probably waiting until their mages have breaching spells ready.* On Keane's command they'd blast holes through my fence, shut down my magical defenses, and then converge on me all at once in the Circle's typical shock and awe fashion.

Magic wards were great for keeping out supernatural beings and magical objects, but they couldn't keep humans out—a fact the Circle's mages knew as well as me. Still, there were consequences for trespassing on a wizard's land, as most set traps to prevent mundanes from crossing onto their territory. I'd never used mine before, because keeping humans out would be antithetical to the nature of our business—not to mention being hella difficult to explain to an insurance adjuster.

That's how the Circle had gotten through, both times.

Of course, they'd be expecting my traps to be activated this time. And while one wizard might have to take their time getting through those traps, with their numbers they could easily overwhelm my defenses by attacking them in concert.

What they didn't know was I'd prepared for this eventuality. After Gunnarson and his jackbooted thugs had killed Elmo and Uncle Ed, no way was I going to allow the Circle to jump my fence again. So, I'd devised a way to deal with them, if ever something like this were to occur.

"*Maighnéadas,*" I commanded, releasing the spell I'd placed on the junkyard fence.

IT WAS A FAIR BET THAT, if the Circle ever attacked my home again, their mages would be warded against standard magical traps and their effects.

So, I'd had to devise something they weren't expecting.

Magical traps typically used elemental magic, and they were generally designed to release lightning, fireballs, area-of-effect freezing magic, and so on with a tripwire cantrip. Typically, a good warding spell or device would protect you against one or two strong elemental attacks—maybe more, if the person creating or casting it was particularly talented. Some magic users got around this by setting traps that released multiple, timed attacks, but that could be dealt with by using adaptive grounding spells, insulating wards, or heat sink charms.

Finnegas had taught me that offensive magic was much more effective when spells were crafted for a specific task and target. If you were fighting an efreet, you'd want a ton of cold spells on hand. If you were fighting a frost giant, you'd want fire and heat spells. If you had to battle a mage who used shadow magic, you'd want to prepare by crafting a shit-ton of light spells. It was an obvious approach, but one that most magic users tended to ignore, simply because over-specialization meant you'd only be prepared for a tiny fraction of the potential magical threats you were likely to face.

Still, the old man was no fool. You didn't survive for two thousand years without learning to be a crafty son of a bitch, and Finnegas was damned tricky. Being a sneaky bastard, he hadn't confined his studies to druidry alone, but instead studied many disciplines and experts over the years, including military tacticians. Most notably, he was especially fond of Sun Tzu.

In *The Art of War*, Sun Tzu famously said, "If you know the enemy and know yourself, you need not fear the result of a hundred battles."

Druids, as a matter of course, followed this very same axiom, because our magic tended to be extemporaneous and therefore weaker than prepared spells in some regards. For that reason, we made it a habit to apply the right spell at the right time. When a druid knew their enemy, and they had time to prepare spells in advance, the enemy was fucked.

Despite their use of ancient magic, the Cold Iron Circle was a particularly modern outfit, and they tended to take the best from both worlds when equipping their operatives. Modern equipment like firearms, load-bearing harnesses, belt buckles, knives, and the like contained a lot of steel and iron.

Knowing that, I'd created a spell to turn the junkyard fence into one ginormous magnet. Granted, magnetism might not seem like powerful magic, but under the right circumstances it could yield devastating effects. I'd tested my spell before I'd placed it, and estimated the magnetic force was equal to or greater than the electromagnetic crane we used to move cars in the yard. In fact, that's where I'd gotten the idea in the first place.

When I said the trigger word to release the spell, the night sky lit up over the junkyard like the aurora borealis. Everything that contained even the slightest bit of metal within twenty feet of the perimeter was pulled toward the fence. A moment of silence followed, then I heard the clatter of three dozen bodies hitting the corrugated metal panels of the junkyard fence. The impacts made a tremendous noise, kind of like change being tossed into a coffee can, only a hundred times louder.

Next came the screams, shrieks, and curses of all those Circle operatives who'd gotten slammed into my fence at speed. Imagine running as fast as possible into a sheet metal fence, and that'll provide some idea of how those jokers fared.

But, I wasn't done. Belts could be unbuckled, harnesses could be cut, and firearms could be removed or abandoned. So, I said the second command word.

"*Scaoileadh.*"

That set loose the many lengths of heavy steel cable I'd painstakingly cut and buried, just underground, around the entire perimeter of my fence. As the magnetic spell latched on to those lengths of cable they flew through the air, slapping into place at waist level to firmly entangle and ensnare every Circle operative who'd been captured by my magic.

The involuntary grunts and cries of pain that accompanied the second part of the spell were well worth the time it'd taken to bury all that steel cable.

I stood and glanced up into the tree's branches. "See anyone I missed?"

Jesse's light green face popped out of the leaves above me. "Nope. Looks like you got them all, Polaris."

"Cosmic Boy is cooler."

Jesse raised an eyebrow. "Not Magneto?"

"Naw, that guy's a dick." A frown flashed across Jesse's face. "What's up?"

"Just a sec." She squeezed her eyes shut, and a man screamed in the distance. "Missed one."

My eyes and ears zeroed in on the source of the scream. Just over the fence, Keane was hanging upside down from the branches of a live oak, restrained by a network of creeper vines that had come alive under Jesse's command.

"I didn't know you could do that," I muttered in disbelief.

"Neither did I, until just now," Jesse replied.

I was about to remark on how creepy her powers were, but thought better of it. "This has been fun, but I gotta go. My magnetism spell will wear off in a couple of hours. Don't kill anybody while I'm gone, alright?"

"If I do, they'll never find the bodies," she said with a wink.

I couldn't tell if she was kidding or not, but I had bigger issues to deal with.

AFTER PLACING every piece of metal I owned in my Crane-skin Bag, I hopped the fence at the front gate. As I exited the junkyard, I ignored the groans and cries for mercy coming from the Circle operatives pinned to the fence—they'd had it coming. And if I stepped on some heads and hands on my way out, it was *purely* unintentional.

I walked out to the street with a smile plastered across my face. *See? Being evil isn't so bad*, a voice inside me said. I ignored that voice as I scanned both ways for a ride. *Bingo.*

Circle operatives always rode in style, and as luck would have it, one of the teams had left a black Chrysler 300C with dark limo tint across the street. Popping the lock with a spell, I searched the interior until I found a spare key fob tucked in the visor. *Typical.* I hit the ignition and grinned as three hundred and sixty-three of Detroit's finest horses rumbled to life. Leaving a strip of rubber and a cloud of smoke in my wake, I fishtailed the car across four lanes of Congress Avenue and headed south for Highway 290 East.

Twenty-five minutes later, I pulled off on FM 969, a narrow

country road just a few miles west of Bastrop. Nameless was quiet on the seat beside me. The night raven had barely twitched a feather for the last few miles, making me wonder if he'd croaked.

"Hey, bird, you still with me?"

The pile of feathers and shadow stirred, and the night raven shakily raised his head. "The time I spent captive in your extra-dimensional druidic demesne nearly killed me—but yes, I'm still alive. As if you cared."

I chuckled. "It's what you get for kidnapping children in Maeve's territory. You should've known she wouldn't put up with that behavior."

The bird cawed softly. "Maeve, as you call her, has committed more than her fair share of crimes against humanity. I assure you, my trespasses are minor in comparison to the Bitch Queen's. For her to sic her favorite junkyard dog on me, all for merely doing what is in my nature, is the highest form of hypocrisy."

"Damn, bird, you sure do love to hear yourself talk. You're going to get along great with your new host."

"If you say so," he mumbled, shakily lowering his head back to the nappa leather seat.

Five minutes later, I pulled down another two-lane country road, and a few miles later onto a cracked blacktop drive, marked by two pillars made from fieldstone and mortar with a rusty metal gate attached. Weeds had overgrown the entrance, giving it an abandoned look that I knew was just for show. I put the car in park and waited patiently, and the gate creaked open a minute or so later. There were no security cameras or other technological devices to alert the occupant to our presence, but the owner didn't need them to know he had visitors.

I drove the vehicle through the gates with bated breath, half expecting us to be fried to a cinder as we crossed the property line. *No lightning or fireballs—guess he's taking visitors.* With a sigh of relief, I hit the gas and pulled up to a dark, abandoned-looking farmhouse. About fifty yards distant, I spotted the charred remains of what had once been a barn. On its side, behind the house, sat the toppled sections of a converted grain silo that had once served as living quarters for the person who owned this farm.

I stepped out of the car and walked toward the house, eyes searching the darkness around me. "Come on, Crowley, I know you're here. Quit stalling already. I need your help."

A tall, lean figure with a pole vaulter's build stepped out of the shadows along the far side of the house. He wore jeans, dress shoes, and a charcoal hoodie under a black leather trench coat. The hood was pulled up, hiding his face in shadows that I knew were not altogether natural.

"Hello, McCool," he said. "How did you know I was here?"

"It's my job to know these things. How've you been?"

The wizard ignored my question. "Is it really your job, Colin? Or do you insist on sticking your nose where it doesn't belong because of that pesky savior complex you maintain?"

"A little of both, I guess. Anyway, I have a favor to ask, and I think it'll be right up your alley."

"I paid for my sins and then some when I helped you traverse Underhill. Did you know, despite the gates being closed, Mother's assassins come for me on an almost weekly basis now? I'm fairly certain she spends all week gathering enough energy to cast a portal, then she sends someone or something through with instructions to kill me, only to start the process all over again when they fail. It's the most attention I've received from her in years."

"This isn't about paying for our sins, Crowley. It's about helping a friend in need."

Crowley lowered his head with a sigh before turning toward

the vehicle. "I suppose it has to do with that creature you brought." He stood silent for several seconds, which likely meant he was weighing me by the scales of Osiris. "Fine. Bring the creature and come with me."

I reached into the car and plucked Nameless from the seat. He'd shat and molted all over the upholstery. The smell was atrocious, but this time I didn't mind.

"C'mon, bird. Your new home awaits."

Crowley had vanished by the time I'd retrieved the night raven from the vehicle. I searched the area, curious as to where he'd gone. Finally, my eyes alighted on a spot where the base of the grain silo had once stood. A dark archway shimmered in the air there—a black two-dimensional doorway that appeared to be made of shadows and darkness. It looked somewhat like a magical portal, but lacked the usual massive power signature that accompanied such workings.

"Nope, nothing creepy about that," I whispered.

"I find it to be rather welcoming, actually," Nameless croaked.

"Shut up, bird," I said as I checked my wards before walking through the doorway.

TWENTY

The archway was an illusion that Crowley had cast for my benefit. It was meant to ensure I didn't walk into a wall that was concealed by yet another illusion of Crowley's making.

"How did you—?" I asked, marveling at the fact that Crowley's recently wrecked tower was now completely intact, hidden behind a rather masterful concealment spell.

Crowley snickered. "Come now, McCool. I am a wizard, after all."

And a hell of a lot more powerful than I might have guessed.

"Touché," I said as I followed him inside his grain silo home and laboratory. It was much as I remembered it, although he'd updated the furnishings and decor from that farmhouse look to something with more of a mid-century modern feel. "Looks like an episode of *Mad Men* exploded in here. It suits you."

"Most of the furniture was wrecked when you battled my fachan and toppled the tower. I saw it as an opportunity for an upgrade." The wizard froze as I stepped into the light. "Ahem. If you don't mind me saying so, you're looking a bit peaked at the moment."

"I'm aware. It's under control."

"Good, because I'd hate to have to redecorate. Again." He poured me a drink from a decanter set that sat atop a lovely two-tone birch and walnut cabinet. "I only have Scotch—hope you don't mind."

"After the day I've had? I'd drink rubbing alcohol if I had to." I sipped the beverage, ignoring the peaty notes that turned me off most Scotch.

"It's a sixty-four Glenlivet, actually." I nearly did a spit-take. "Please, don't spit it out if you don't care for it."

I swallowed, and it was like velvet fire going down my throat. Once I got over the odor, it was actually good—damned good. A bit reminiscent of bananas fosters, if I had to describe it.

"Crowley, that stuff is twenty-five grand a bottle. Forgive me for being a bit taken aback, but I'm basically drinking my tuition for the year."

Crowley sat on a nearby couch that probably cost as much as the liquor. "Really? My personal shopper handles that for me. I just write the check each month."

I resisted the standard droll "must be nice" retort, instead tilting my head toward the bird in my arm. "I made the mistake of entering a bargain with him, and I'd like to uphold my side without turning him loose. Can you help?"

"Perhaps. Allow me." I handed the nachtkrapp to the wizard, noting that the scars on his hand had diminished some-what. As soon as Crowley touched the bird, a bit of shadow magic passed from his hands into Nameless. The night raven perked up immediately.

Nameless lifted his head, and if I didn't know any better he sounded a bit awestruck as he spoke. "Master, I had no idea—"

"Silence," Crowley replied, cutting him off. The bird clammed up instantly.

"I wish he would have done that for me. Would've saved me a fortune in duct tape."

The wizard cradled the bird in his lap, stroking it's feathers absentmindedly. With each stroke, the bird's appearance improved. On closer inspection, I noticed small wisps of shadow exiting Crowley's skin and entering the night raven's body.

"Tell me the nature of your bargain," the wizard said.

"It's simple. I let him live, and he cast an augury for me."

The wizard chuckled. "You're as likely to get unambiguous speech from this one as you are to get blood from a stone."

"As I discovered," I replied. "Can you get him to release me from our deal? I did let him live, after all—but I'd rather that he wasn't my responsibility anymore."

Crowley held the bird up to look it in his dead, empty eye sockets. By now, his feathers had filled in almost completely, and they again held their former dark and sinister sheen.

"Nameless one, do you agree to enter my service, doing my bidding exactly, and willingly forfeiting your life at my will and whim, now and henceforth, until I release you from said service?"

"I do, master," the bird croaked.

"And in so doing, do you relinquish all obligations and debts between yourself and the druid, Colin McCool?"

"Again, yes," the night raven said.

"And do you agree to serve me, and me alone?" the wizard asked.

"Yes, master, for a third time. I gladly bind myself to your service."

Crowley set the bird down on the couch next to him. "Do mind the upholstery, raven." He turned to me. "It's done then. He's my responsibility now."

"That was easy. Why do I feel like I got stiffed here?" I asked.

"If the bird had died because of your actions—and he *was*

going to die, of that you can be certain—you'd have been cursed for all time. I'd say you made out okay, all things considered."

I nipped at my Scotch, counting the cost of each sip in my head. *Sip. Two-fifty. Sip. Five hundred. Sip. Seven-fifty.* "Then thanks for that. I've had enough of curses to last me a lifetime, what with the fae sending a new one at me every other day."

"They're still on about that, even now that you've been appointed justiciar?" he asked. I frowned in reply, not caring to rehash the entire sordid affair. "Has the frequency slowed down, at least? Last I heard, they had someone casting on you around the clock."

"If only. You've heard about the justiciar deal?"

Crowley grunted. "Who hasn't?"

"Pain in my ass is what it's been. I still can't figure out why Finnegas engineered the whole thing."

Crowley reached out with a tendril of shadow, pouring himself a drink. When the glass reached his hand he took a sip, admiring the amber liquid in the soft light cast by a nearby lamp.

"Hmm, not bad. I should get another bottle." He looked at me, shrugging almost imperceptibly. "As for why Finnegas saw fit to steer events toward your appointment, I can think of any number of reasons. For one, the factions now have to pay you for what you were previously doing for free. Second, it establishes the druids as a power unto their own, a position the old man abdicated during the years he spent mourning your former girl-friend's death. And third, now the factions can't turn on you without consequence."

I squinted, screwing my face into a crooked frown. "Yeah, not so much. The Circle decided to frame me for murdering one of their own."

"I thought you already did, and were exonerated of all

wrong-doing," Crowley replied. I shook my head. "Again? Hell's bells, McCool, but you are a world-class defecation attractor."

"You don't know the half. It's worse this time, Crowley—much worse. They're making it look like I killed the Circle's liaison."

"OUCH," Crowley said with a wince. "What do you need me to do?"

"I was hoping Nameless here might use some of his extra-cognitive abilities to help me track someone down. I couldn't exactly ask him to do it myself, not under our previous arrangement."

"Because I would have demanded my release in exchange," the night raven interjected. "You're not half the fool you appear to be, druid."

"Gee, thanks," I replied.

"Just who are we looking for?" the shadow wizard asked.

"A jorōgumo."

"Kinky," the wizard said, deadpan. "I didn't know you had it in you."

"Ha ha," I replied. "She's on the Circle's payroll, and I think she's the key to figuring out who's framing me. Plus, I'm fairly certain she abducted a friend of mine a few days back."

"The chances of your friend still being alive are slim," Crowley countered.

"I'm aware, but I'd like to give his loved ones closure, if possible. Anyway, I had her dead to rights, but Bells busted in on us and chased the were-spider off."

"She told me. She also said you were fully under the jorōgu-mo's spell, and that she caught you two *in flagrante delicto*, so to speak."

"It was flagrant, but hardly delectable, believe me. Can you get the bird to help?"

He sipped his Scotch. "Certainly. You know I can do this for you just as easily, yes?"

"I do, but I don't want to tip her off. If she senses a human mage sniffing around, she'll bolt for sure. I figure the bird's magic will just be background noise to her."

"Makes sense." Crowley looked at his new pet. "Nameless one, can you locate this creature?"

"I can," the bird squawked. "I only require some personal article—any trifle that carries her signature on it—in order to track her down."

I produced the brush, panties, and lingerie I'd procured from Mei's apartment, setting them on the coffee table between us. For good measure, I tossed in the t-shirt I'd been wearing the day of my "date" with Mei, since it was still covered in spider silk.

Crowley cleared his throat. "Egads, man, I didn't know you were the trophy-collecting type."

"Again, har-fucking-har. Bird, do your thing already. I've got creatures to kill."

The bird hopped from the couch to the table, where he pecked and prodded the items there. He spread his wings, and tendrils of shadow curled from the tips of each extended feather, alighting on the clothing and hair brush. The wisps of magic caressed the objects as a hum of power emanated from the raven.

Suddenly, the objects began to vibrate and the coffee table started to shake. "Something is wrong, master!" Nameless squawked.

"What is it? Tell me, now!" Crowley hissed as he stood.

I glanced around nervously, wondering what the hell could ruffle the raven's feathers.

"Another entity has intercepted my tracking spell—and it is angry. It comes!"

Crowley glowered at me and stormed out the front door of the silo. I followed close on his heels. There was a palpable sense of dread in the air as I exited the building, which had most certainly been warded against all intrusions of magic and other-worldly beings. The air hummed with energy, slowly gaining momentum like a swift summer storm building in a dark and angry sky.

Crowley took a defensive stance, one arm high and the other low, his fingers twisted in arcane positions. Thick shadowy tentacles sprouted from his torso like extra arms, whipping about him in random patterns. I mentally gave him points for style, then drew my flaming sword from my Bag, setting it tip down in the dirt with my hands on the pommel.

The night raven flew out of the shadow gate, fluttering above Crowley's head. "It comes, master—it is here!"

A flash of white shot out of the sky, landing with all the speed of a falling meteor—but none of the sound or force of impact.

"Ah, shit," I exclaimed.

Standing there in Crowley's front yard was the yūrei that had attacked me at the overlook.

"*Fukushū!*" it whispered, pointing a long, pale finger at me.

"Friend of yours?" Crowley asked.

"More like a recent acquaintance," I replied.

"No matter. It trespasses on my lands, making its existence forfeit. It would not have made it past the boundaries if it hadn't hitched a ride on the night raven's spell. I will dispense of it momentarily." The wizard began spinning up some powerful magic.

"No, wait!" I said as I stepped in front of Crowley. "Last time we met, it attacked me on sight. Though the spirit is only recently deceased, it's no longer showing signs of violence. That makes me think it finally got its bearings."

The ghost moaned. "*Fukushū.*" It beckoned to me with a white, luminescent hand.

"I do believe the damned thing wants you to come with it," Crowley said. "Fascinating."

Nameless landed on a fence post nearby. "I have a residual connection to it, from what remains of the tracking spell. Based on what I'm sensing, it wishes to take you to its killer."

"*Fukushū!*" the ghost exclaimed with a nod.

I looked at Crowley. "Looks like I'm stuck with the ghost. You have a ride I can borrow? That Chrysler is stolen, and the bird shat all over the seats."

"Hmm. Gives a whole new meaning to the term 'riding dirty,' does it not?" the wizard deadpanned.

"I'll be damned, Crowley, that's your third joke tonight. Son, tell the truth—are you on the chronic?"

THE WIZARD LOANED ME A CAR, an open-top English roadster that he claimed would make it easier for the ghost to ride along. Honestly, I think he just liked the idea of making me freeze my ass off, driving all over town in the cool autumn air with a ghost riding shotgun. The car drove like a go-cart and felt about as safe, practically shaking itself apart on the country roads that took us to the main highway.

I glanced at the ghost sitting beside me. "Let's hope we don't get into an accident in this tin can, else I may be joining you in the afterlife."

"*Fukushū,*" the yūrei replied with a grim smile, pointing the way back to Austin.

"This is going to be a barrel of laughs, I can tell already," I said under my breath.

The ghost ignored me, focused as it was on guiding me to our destination. As we neared the city it pointed toward downtown, so I headed north on IH-35 and west on Sixth Street. When we hit Lamar, it indicated we should head north again, so I turned right and drove past Clarksville and Pease Park, right into the West Campus area where all the wealthy students lived.

Just north of 25th, it had me hook a left onto Shoal Creek Boulevard. Now, we were in Old West Austin—the Pemberton Heights neighborhood, to be exact. Homes here went for a million and up, as it was one of the most exclusive neighborhoods in Austin proper. If Mei was hiding out here, she was connected to someone with a lot of money. That pointed right back to the Circle.

"Give me a second," I said as I pulled into the public parking spaces along Shoal Creek Trail.

"*Fukushū!*" the ghost insisted, extending its arm through the windshield and to the west.

"I know, I know, but I can't go walking around this neighborhood looking like a bum," I explained to the ghost, feeling foolish. "If I do, somebody's going to call the cops on me, and I'll be arrested before we even begin. I'm going to change so I look like I belong here, and then we can proceed with the evening's ass-kickings. Cool?"

The ghost gave me a resigned look, then turned its eyes toward the west. *Alrighty, then.* I ducked into the shadows near the trail, digging around in my Bag for clothing that would make me look less like a homeless person. Eventually, I settled on a newer pair of combat boots, black jeans, a white button-down with a black tie, and a dark woolen pea coat.

I hopped back in the car, glancing at my spectral companion. "So, how do I look?" The ghost began to open his mouth, but I cut it off. "Right, '*fukushū*,' I get it. Just point the way, and I swear you'll have your revenge."

Following the ghost's directions, we soon passed Pemberton Castle, a local landmark and holdover from the city's plantation days—an era of Austin's history no one spoke much about today. Now, the massive home stood hemmed in by more modern structures, tawdry displays of the wealth of Austin's urban gentility. All of them were likely owned by affluent whites who had no idea their homes sat on land once tended by black slaves.

Some things never change.

"*Fukushū*," the ghost exclaimed as it stabbed a finger at a lovely two-story colonial with a carriage house and huge, fenced side yard. I pulled the car to the curb several houses down and turned off the engine.

"I guess that means we're here," I said, turning to address the specter.

To my surprise, the thing had vanished, to where I had no clue. I wondered if perhaps it'd moved on, considering its earthly task done by leading me to its killer. But I doubted it. I slung my Craneskin Bag over my shoulder and tried to look as inconspicuous as possible as I headed back up the street.

I walked past the house the ghost had indicated, scanning it in the magical spectrum for any peculiarities. *Jackpot.* Not only was the home and property warded nine ways to Sunday; there was also a powerful "look away, go away" spell on it, and an illusion I couldn't pierce. Although I couldn't see what was concealed on the grounds, it was clear that whoever owned the place didn't want it being disturbed.

I walked all the way around the block, hoping there might be an alley I could use to sneak up on the place. But no dice. Rich people hated alleys, knowing they almost always brought the value of neighborhoods down. Alleys tended to attract litter and refuse, and such hidden common areas were rarely kept up by the residents who shared them. Plus, they were a waste of prime real estate.

Looks like I'm cutting through someone's yard. I came back around and found a likely suspect, the residence directly to the rear of the target house. They had plenty of shrubbery to hide in and almost no outdoor lighting—standard hallmarks of rich people who thought they were immune to crime. I snuck past their home and through their backyard without incident, hiding in some bushes that bordered the backyard of the home where Mei was staying.

Let's hope that ghost was right.

From my Bag, I pulled out my flaming sword and gun belt. I strapped the belt around my waist, snapping the scabbard to it so the sword would be easily accessible and partially hidden by my coat. Wearing a sword at your waist meant it would almost certainly get in the way, but it was where you wore one if you were going to need it in a jiffy. Over the shoulder rigs were great for comfort, but unless you were carrying a short sword, it was a pain to draw a blade from over your shoulder. So, on my waist it went.

I checked my Glock to make sure I had loaded it with tracer rounds, since they'd worked so well for Bells. Then, I spent several minutes breaking through the wards and traps around the property. They were expertly cast and created with a style of magic that was unfamiliar to me, but thankfully, they were not beyond my ability to crack.

Once that chore was finished, I used the sword to cut a hole in the fences, hoping like hell no one would see the light from the blade. I stuck my head through the hole to get a peek past the illusion, and was relieved to find that shrubbery obscured the view on the other side as well. Lastly, I slung Gunnarson's cloak around my shoulders and stepped on through to find Mei.

TWENTY-ONE

"Ho-lee shit," I whispered as I parted the bushes ahead of me. The scene on the other side of the illusion wasn't anything like it appeared on the outside. Where before I'd seen nothing over the fence but a few well-tended fruit trees, the yard's grim horror was now fully revealed to me—and it was a fucking nightmare.

The lot had been landscaped in the style of a classical Japanese garden, but it was unlike anything I'd seen before. There were the typical neatly-trimmed shrubs, brightly-colored flowers, stone pathways, and an elegantly simple wooden bridge spanning a meandering stream that fed into a koi pond. Beyond it all, a flagstone patio served as a transition point between the garden and house. However, the central feature of the peaceful scenery conveyed sinister undertones that robbed it of any serenity it might have possessed.

Dead center in the garden stood a twenty-five-foot-tall Japanese cherry tree in full bloom. At first glance, the tree's symmetry and lush foliage gave an impression of stately beauty, but a closer inspection betrayed its more malevolent features. Rather than the usual delicate, pink-petaled flowers, this tree was covered in blossoms stained a deep, blood-red color. More-over, the tree's limbs—and indeed, the entire tree itself—seemed to sway ominously despite a lack of wind.

And there were human bodies suspended from the branches of the tree.

Some of those bodies were wrapped in spider silk, neatly bound and coiled—like foodstuffs stored up for a rainy day or special occasion. Other bodies were laid bare to the elements, and those had been bound hand and foot by the tree's branches, hanging like sick bloated ornaments on some demented Christmas display.

Further inspection revealed still more corpses that had withered away to skin and bones, and a few newer bodies that had been pierced in various places by the very tips of the tree's limbs. Blood leaked slowly from those wounds, but not a drop was spared as the tree's branches brushed away the crimson teardrops with delicate sweeps of those dark red blossoms.

Now I know how the flowers get their color.

I wracked my brain for what this thing might be, because I damned sure wasn't leaving here tonight without killing it. *A jubokko, that's what it is—a vampire tree.* I figured it was prob-ably vulnerable to fire and chainsaws, and since I had one but not the other, fire would have to do.

I willed the cloak to hide me and checked my weapons, then entered the garden and made a beeline for the tree. Interest-ingly, the jubokko seemed to pick up on my presence immedi-ately. As soon as I stepped out of the shrubbery, the tree's limbs began to shiver, as if anticipating a fresh meal.

Must be sensing the vibrations from my footsteps. Interesting.

Realizing it was useless to remain invisible, I stopped a good twenty feet from the tree and put the cloak away. Not only did I fear getting caught by the many limbs straining to reach me; I was also turned off by the stench of putrefaction and death that emanated from the creature.

"Yeah, I bet you want a piece of me," I growled as I circled the thing at a distance, searching the bodies that adorned its limbs for Derp. After making a complete circuit of the tree, two facts stood out. First, the kid hadn't fallen victim to the tree, so there might be hope that he was still alive. And second, all the bodies on the tree were young males in their early to mid-twenties.

Son of a bitch. Mei's been feeding some of her victims to the tree.

Even more disturbing, several of the bodies that hung from the tree were still alive—both those the tree fed on, and the half-dozen wrapped in Mei's webbing. Although those poor souls barely moved, the slow rise and fall of each living victim's chest was a clear indication that at least some of the poor bastards still lived. Obviously, that meant I couldn't kill the thing with fire—at least, not without killing them as well.

Then, I remembered the raven's second telling. I might have been skeptical regarding the accuracy of the nachtkrapp's augury, but I was no fool. The day after the raven had told my "future," I'd grabbed a gallon of weed killer from the junkyard warehouse and shoved it inside my Craneskin Bag. And though I'd felt like an idiot at the time for doing so, it looked like the bird hadn't let me down.

Time to go Monsanto on this motherfucker.

I retrieved the jug of weed killer from my bag and tossed it at the base of the tree, where it landed with a dull thump among the tree's roots. A few lower branches probed the container, but it was quickly determined to be inorganic and therefore unworthy of the jubokko's ministrations. As I dug through my Bag, the tree returned its attention to me, slowly but surely lengthening its limbs to cross the distance between us.

"Ah-ah," I said, as I found what I was searching for inside the Bag. "I'm afraid that, despite my occupation as a druid, I'm no tree hugger."

My hand grasped a crossbow pistol's handle inside the Bag. I drew it and fired a single bolt at the jug, pinning it to the tree. Then, I exchanged the crossbow for my practice pistol, a suppressed Walther P-22 automatic. A suppressed twenty-two caliber automatic firing subsonic rounds was about as quiet as a firearm could get, so the gun was less likely to alert others to my presence.

I emptied the magazine into the jug, and ten rounds of .22 long rifle turned the container into a sieve. Weed killer splashed all over the tree's trunk and roots, darkening the dirt in a puddle.

To my surprise, the tree's roots and trunk immediately soaked up the weed killer. I could only assume the creature had evolved to absorb any drop of liquid that made direct contact with it. That way, it wouldn't waste a single drop of its victims' precious fluids.

Sucks for you. Sayo-fucking-nara, tree.

MY CELEBRATION WAS VERY SHORT-LIVED, because immediately after the tree sucked up a gallon of Monsanto's finest, it began to shake in the most violent manner. The tremors it made were so severe that I fell to my knees, bracing myself with one hand on the earth below in order to stay somewhat upright. All the while, I kept my eyes on the vampire tree, wondering silently just how long it might take for a gallon of weed killer to off a tree this big.

Apparently, the effects were not immediate. Instead of shriveling away like last year's dandelions, the tree's trunk split at the base with a loud crack. Then, it dipped two of its largest limbs to the ground, using the terminal branches like hands to brace against the dirt. Once it had leverage, the tree ripped each half of its trunk and roots from the ground. It didn't take an arborist to realize that I'd pissed off the jubokko, and now it was about to go all Treebeard on me.

I suddenly had a vision of me getting stomped like an orc at Isengard—not a pretty sight. I couldn't use fire on it, because heroism and shit, although the tree's anthropomorphic fit was definitely making me wonder if being heroic was all it was cracked up to be. Bullets would be a mere nuisance to the thing, and any other elemental attack I made on it would kill the survivors adorning its branches just as handily as fire might.

"Oh, fucking hell," I hissed, backing up and unlacing my boots. "Let's hope this doesn't go completely fucking sideways, and I don't end up spending the rest of life as a ten-foot-tall Fomorian with a shitty complexion and bad teeth."

As my new friend the Japanese ent bore down on me, I shrugged off my jacket, gun belt, and sword, shoving them all inside the Bag. Lamenting the loss of a perfectly good shirt and pair of jeans, I morphed as far into my Formorian form as I dared, adding almost four feet in height and more than doubling my weight in the process.

My clothing ripped at the seams as my skeleton lengthened and my muscles swelled. I looked down admiringly at my hands, the right one turning into a thickly calloused slab of bone and gristle, while the left became a hooked claw with sharp talons curving from the end of every digit. My skin thickened all over and my entire body shook in an adrenaline-fueled rage.

Deep inside me, the voices went from a whisper to a roar.

kill... Kill... KILL!

The fact that I almost whispered, "Jason, Jason, Jason," served as proof I was still me, but how long I could hang on to my humanity in this form was anyone's guess. That meant I couldn't stay this way for long. I decided I'd kick this tree's ass, literally ripping it limb from limb, and then I'd shift back into my human form to deal with Mei.

The transformation happened in the span of two heartbeats, but that was time enough for the jubokko to close the gap and attack. A huge, trunk-like arm lashed out, striking me across my upper torso and bowling me across the garden. I rolled with the blow, smashing a granite lantern as I bounced back to my feet.

I growled at the tree as it turned toward me. "Alright, you overgrown topiaric nightmare... let's dance!"

The jubokko closed on me, storming across the garden with surprising speed for something so large. The very tallest of its branches easily reached fifteen feet or more above my head. However, the bulk of it remained in its trunk and central branches, a fact that made the tree's size much less intimidating as I sized it up and braced for its attack.

To beat this thing, I'd need to deal some serious damage— the earth-shattering, wrecking ball kind. Keeping that in mind, I lowered my stance and reared back with my right arm. The ground shook with every plodding step the giant tree took. As it drew near, I waited until the very last second before I struck, putting my full weight behind the world's deadliest overhand right.

My fist shot like a cannonball at the tree's trunk, right below the juncture where its main branches began to bifurcate away from the central stem. My huge, bony, calloused knuckles bit deeply into the relatively tender skin of the tree, ripping through the inner bark, cambium, and sapwood. Wood split and splinters flew, and for a moment I thought I might topple the tree with that one strike.

Unfortunately, the thing dug its roots into the earth beneath us, anchoring itself in an instant to avoid being felled. Branches whipped at me like lashes all around, leaving welts but thankfully failing to draw blood. A thick, trunk-like appendage swung down at me and I ducked, coming under the limb in an attempt to tackle the tree to the ground.

I dropped my shoulder and lunged forward, driving with both feet and pumping my legs as I collided with the central body of the jubokko. My shoulder landed like a battering ram, shaking the entire tree and causing two bodies to snap loose from the branches above me. One was a corpse, and it fell to the nearby flagstones with a sickening wet crunch—not unlike the sound an overripe melon makes when smashed. The other appeared to be alive, barely, and fortunately that victim fell into the shrubbery, breaking his fall.

Again, the tree dug in with its roots, but this time I noticed something peculiar as I looked down at the tree's "feet." Where before the roots that spread out from each leg were too many to count, this time they appeared to have diminished in quantity. Was the tree's strength derived from the number of victims in its limbs?

Sensing a weakness, I wrapped my legs around the trunk and shimmied up like a monkey until I reached the lower limbs. Once there, I crawled out on one of the branches that was adjacent to a live victim. I grabbed that limb and snapped it off, tossing the branch and the attached victim away in a lobbing, underhand throw.

THAT CAUSED the tree to go nuts, shaking and spinning this way and that in an effort to shrug me loose. I managed to hang on while locating another branch and victim that I tore off the trunk with a loud crack. Throwing my cargo toward some shrubs, I hoped the poor soul had landed safely. By this time, every bough, branchlet, and twig in my vicinity lashed at me, and soon they began wrapping around my arms and legs to restrain me.

It became more difficult to move, as I had to tear myself free to scramble around the trunk, but move I did. I reached another victim and freed him, dropping him in the koi pond and only realizing after the fact that the fish might be magical—and carnivorous.

Too late now. Sorry, dude.

By this time, the tree had gotten wise. Instead of trying to dislodge me from its branches, it began to envelop me in them. Arm-thick limbs and thinner, rope-like branches closed in around me like a cage, somewhat like the one Jesse had made for Nameless. However, rather than allowing me space to breathe and move, this enclosure bore in on me, squeezing me like a bundle of anacondas.

I tried squirming out, but was held fast in a cocoon of branches, leaves, and twigs. Soon, I began to feel smaller limbs probing my skin, scratching me here and there, searching for a soft spot where the tree might begin to feed. Once the damned things found my eyes and nose I'd be done for, because I was almost certain my mucous membranes and sclera weren't nearly as tough as the rest of me.

Damn it. Eye, are you there?

-As always. You seem to have gotten yourself into a rather dire situation. Shall I burn us a way out?-

No, because there are innocent victims still attached to the tree. Can you create enough heat to give me some space, but not enough to cause the tree to ignite?

-A few calculations are necessary. Please wait.- The Eye was silent for the span of a few heartbeats. *-I have determined the ignition point of this entity, and will not exceed that temperature. When you are ready, open your eyes.-*

I'm ready, believe me. It's getting hard to breathe in here.

I did as asked, and rather than the usual searing heat I felt when the Eye released its magic, instead I felt a growing warmth that increased incrementally. Red light—not quite fire, but instead more like a laser's beam—seared into the plant growth in front of my face, and as the heat increased the branches parted. Soon, the foliage withdrew from my head and face.

Keep going, Eye. We're not free yet.

I tucked my chin and looked down, focusing the Eye's "heat rays" on my chest and arms. Wherever the Eye's magic touched the tree, it withdrew. Soon, all my limbs were free, and I had enough space to move—although I kept having to sweep my eyes around to prevent the branches from closing in again.

Alright, Eye. Time to burn this thing down.

-I thought you wished to avoid endangering the remaining victims.-

I do, but there's one spot on the tree where I'm certain we won't hit any of them, and that's straight down. When I look at my feet, fry this motherfucker.

-Although I do not understand how an entity that reproduces asexually can engage in intercourse with its parent, I understand your meaning and will comply.-

I pointed my eyes at the trunk beneath me. *One short blast ought to do it. Aim for the heartwood. Go.*

The Eye cut loose with a momentary burst of heat and energy focused into an intense, twelve-inch-wide beam that incinerated a hole straight down the trunk and into the earth beneath us. The tree released a keening wail that came from nowhere and everywhere around us at once, as if every twig, branch, and leaf on the tree screamed.

Then, it shuddered and was still.

Time to get out of here.

I reached down into the still-smoldering hole below with both hands, bracing one on each side of the opening. Then, I pulled with all my prodigious strength. The tree's trunk split with a crack and a loud ripping noise as I tore it cleanly in two. Falling into the opening I'd made, I braced my hands against one side and my feet against the other, then pushed until the entire trunk split from top to base.

As the two sides of the tree toppled, I fell in a heap near the roots. After all that violence and mayhem in my fully-shifted form, the angry voices inside rose to a crescendo. They wanted me to relinquish control and go on a rampage. And the fact was, I *wanted* to go nuclear right now, because it felt good to be powerful.

It felt good to be without fear.

First, I'll start with Mei, and squash her like the bug she is. Then...

Then what? What would I do next, hurt innocent people?

Kill all the fae, the voice said. *They've hurt you, more so than any. They deserve it. You deserve it.*

I wanted to do it, so badly. Smash Mei, then go after Maeve, her assassins, and her court. And why stop there? I could wipe out every other pocket of fae in the continental United States. Heck, the entire world. I could kill them all, and with the Eye's power, none of them could stop me.

The question was, when would the killing end?

When all the fae are dead, the voice replied. *Then you can finally have peace.*

Peace. That sounded... wonderful. But at what cost?

Whatever it takes, the voice replied. *Whatever it takes to keep the ones you love safe.*

That reminded me of why I was here. I wasn't here because the fae had killed my uncle. I wasn't here because the fae had killed a bunch of young men. I wasn't here because the fae had taken Derp.

Nope. I was here because of Mei—Mei and the Circle. Not the fae.

No, I said to the voice. *I refuse.*

With a Herculean effort, I forced the voices down, way, way, down, nearly silencing them... but not quite. Still, it was enough. I was the captain of my own ship, and that's how it would remain.

Nearby, the yūrei materialized and bowed deeply to me. The ghost then floated into one of the corpses still trapped by the tree's limbs, where it disappeared. I held my breath, and when the corpse didn't come back to life, I let out a sigh of relief. Then I rolled over, exhausted, and transformed back into my human form.

Close by, someone began clapping, slowly and enthusiastically. "Bravo, druid—bravo." A man's voice, deep and resonant, with a slight Asian accent. "Not only did you best the jubokko, which is no small feat, but you also provided a satisfactory demonstration of the very item my employers have assigned me to procure."

I turned toward the voice. There, on the flagstone patio, stood one of the strangest creatures I had ever seen.

TWENTY-TWO

The man—although it was plain to see he wasn't a man at all—stood a little under six feet tall. His hands were humanoid, weathered and calloused in the manner of someone who worked with tools all day long. As for his shoes, they were human-sized and expensive looking, and since I couldn't determine the brand or maker I suspected they were bespoke. He wore a dark, impeccably tailored suit, but considering the two enormous black wings sprouting from his shoulders, it was anyone's guess how he got into it.

So, the second raven appears.

Wings notwithstanding, the man's oddest feature was his face. Unlike the rest of his body, it was almost completely avian-looking. Instead of human hair, he had an ebony shock of thin feathers that he wore slicked back, old-school style. Beneath a prodigious forehead, his brow was prominent and V-shaped, with dark, feathered eyebrows that swept upward over deep-set eyes.

Those orbs were striking—each with a large black pupil set in a citrine sclera, surrounded by dark, pebbly, almost reptile-like skin. Below those peculiar eyes jutted an enormous ebony beak that comprised his upper and lower jaw. In fact, fully half his face consisted of his bill. Although the flesh and skin around it appeared human enough, it was too dark to belong to any human I'd ever known.

It's not every day you saw someone with wings, and I wondered if they were functional. They certainly were real; that was plain to see from the way they twitched at random intervals. The creature fairly exuded power and authority, a characteristic echoed by the timbre of his voice and the almost casual poise he exhibited.

If I had wings like that, I think I'd be cocky, too. Cockier, that is.

Rising to my now very human knees, I did my best to maintain some sense of composure. It wasn't every day you met a *tengu*, after all.

"Harvey Birdman, I presume," I said with as much aplomb as I could muster while wearing nothing but underwear, on my hands and knees in the dirt.

The birdman laughed—a full, rich laugh that seemed to convey genuine amusement and, if I wasn't mistaken, a bit of admiration as well. "And there it is, the famous McCool banter in the face of difficult circumstances. Your reputation precedes you, and thus far you do not disappoint."

Shifting always took quite a bit out of me, so getting to my feet required more than a little effort. "I seem to be at a loss here. You know who I am, but you've not yet introduced yourself."

"I apologize for my rudeness, McCool-san." The tengu gave a fifteen-degree bow, *eshaku*-style, back ramrod-straight and eyes slightly downcast. It was the sort of bow you would give an equal, a show of mutual respect. "Hayashi Hideie, although you may simply call me Hideie."

I didn't return the gesture. Hell if I was going to bow to

someone who worked for the Circle. "Call me Colin. Now, where's Mei?"

He dipped his beak slightly. "Ah, Mei. You tracked her here, yes? I assumed you would, eventually—although she was most certain that you would not. She underestimated you, it seems, but for my part I am most delighted you found this place."

The way this guy was speaking, I didn't know if he wanted to fight me or be the president and founding member of my fan club. "Look, Hideie, I'm not here to chat, and I'm certainly not here to make friends. Mei is a predator. She abducted a young friend of mine, and I'm here to take her down. Besides that, I'm being framed by the Cold Iron Circle for killing the liaison they assigned me, and I think she's connected. As I see it, you have three options—tell me where she is, get out of my way, or prepare to get your ass kicked. I really don't care what you choose at this point."

Hideie smiled, which was kind of weird since he had a beak. "Abrupt and to the point." He clasped his hands behind his back. "Please, explain to me what this young man looks like."

"Seriously?"

"Humor me, if you don't mind."

I sighed and reached into my Bag, causing the tengu to tense up a bit. "Relax, I'm just grabbing some clothes." I found a spare pair of jeans and a long-sleeved shirt, and slipped into them as I described Derp. "He's about yea tall, kind of chunky, blonde hair, and he cusses a lot. Kind of like a foul-mouthed Chowder from *Monster House*."

The tengu arched a feathered eyebrow. "*Monster House*? I apologize, I am unfamiliar with this—what is it, exactly?"

"It's a Zemeckis and Spielberg film, nominated for best animated feature the year it was released. Probably the greatest Halloween cartoon ever, right after *It's the Great Pumpkin, Charlie Brown*. Chowder is the fat sidekick in the movie."

Hideie raised a finger in exclamation. "Aha! Like Chunk in *The Goonies!*"

I snapped and pointed at him. "Egg-zactly. In fact, I think Chunk was the archetype they based Chowder on."

Hideie nodded. "Such a great movie, *The Goonies*. Very influential on later films. *The Sandlot, Stand By Me, Honey I Shrunk the Kids, The Monster Squad*—all owe their popularity in some small part to *The Goonies*."

"For a yōkai, you have strange taste in movies, Hideie."

"What can I say, I'm Japanese. Familiarity with pop culture is a moral obligation in my country. But back to the matter at hand. I can assure you, Mei did not abduct your young friend."

"Yeah? And how do you know that? Were you there when she kidnapped those men I plucked from your vampire tree?"

The tengu shook his head. "No, but I am positive Mei did not abduct or harm any children. I am her superior, and I strictly forbade such actions when she entered my employ. Believe me, McCool-san, she would not disobey a command from me."

"So, we're being formal after all. I guess this means we're not going to be friends. Shocker."

"That is entirely up to you. But, business is business."

"Okay, Mr. Hayashi, I'll bite. Just what business do you have with me?"

"I thought that was obvious. I have been assigned to take that jewel from your head—and by force, if necessary."

"BALOR'S EYE?" I snorted. "Good luck. Better men and monsters than you have tried."

Hideie gave me a tight smile. "Somehow, I doubt that."

His confidence was likely well-earned. Although they were

classified as mountain goblins, tengu were almost revered as gods in Japan, with powers rivaling demigods. They were also notorious for their martial skills, a detail that was not lost on me as I faced the prospect of fighting Mr. Hayashi.

I took a second to size the guy up—because in my mind he *was* a guy, if a weird-looking one. He had the shoulders and arms of someone who swung heavy things for exercise, and he moved from his hips, which told me he was light on his feet. I took a closer look at his hands and realized those were a swordsman's callouses.

Fuck my life.

It'd be a while before I could shift again, so if I got into a fight with this guy it was going to be ugly. Modern folklore had turned tengu into something more human-like and a lot less malicious, but Hideie here was an example of the actual species, reflective of the earliest depictions of *karasu-tengu* in the mythology of Japan. In Japanese legends, they often trained humans in swordsmanship, or gifted them with magical weapons that couldn't miss... or they ate them. It was kind of a toss-up with old-school tengu.

The bottom line was they were a lot like the fae in how they operated. They could take a shine to you and help you, or kill you on a whim. And while I was no expert on Japanese mythology, because we rarely saw such creatures in central Texas, even I knew that tengu were not to be fucked with.

Based on Hideie's demeanor, it looked as though I'd have no choice.

"I take it Mei is in the house?"

Hideie nodded. "She is."

"And I take it I have to go through you to get to her?"

"On the contrary, I will go through you to get what I want, if necessary. However, my employer has not stipulated the methods by which I am to attain the gemstone. That leaves me with many options, including negotiation. I had hoped—"

I was already pulling my tactical belt from my Bag. "There will be no negotiation regarding the Eye, Hideie. I was entrusted with its keeping, and it stays with me." I strapped my belt around my hips and snapped the buckle in place. "Move, or die. I couldn't care less which you choose."

"A duel it is, then. So be it."

The tengu's clothing shimmered, morphing from a business suit into Japanese-style monk's robes. Not the kind you might see a Shinto priest wear, but instead the more practical kind worn by the *yamabushi* of old. Rather than tight, restrictive vestments, Hideie's clothing was loose and flowing—like a billowy, over-sized karate uniform. His pant legs were tucked into cloth calf and ankle wraps, and his flat-soled sandals were strapped firmly to his feet with wide leather straps. In short, he was dressed for a tussle.

"Fair warning, tengu—I don't fight fair."

Hideie smiled. "It is of little consequence."

We'll just fucking see about that.

In the blink of an eye, I drew my Glock and snapped off three rounds at the mountain goblin, two aimed at the chest and one at his eyes. As if anticipating my intentions, Hideie moved a split-second before I pulled the trigger, spinning behind a concrete statue of a lion that sat on a stone pedestal maybe a step or two away from him. It wasn't a full-on Matrix thing, but it was close, and my gunfire appeared to have missed him.

I emptied the magazine at him, circling to get a clean shot. However, he simply moved with me—not vampire fast, but fast enough to keep his body behind the stone and concrete barrier. The tracers pinged off the statue and whizzed into the night, none of them hitting the tengu.

"At least allow me to arm myself, McCool-san," Hideie said as he reached behind him to pull a *daito*, or long katana, out of thin air. He drew the sword in his right hand, keeping the scabbard in his left, perhaps for blocking or striking. He bowed to me while still behind the statue. "Now, I am ready to begin."

Arrogant bastard, aren't you? Fine, I'll kick your ass the old-fashioned way.

I holstered my pistol and drew the flaming sword, willing it to light up. When nothing happened, I willed harder. For some reason, the sword was refusing to play ball.

Hideie had stepped out from behind the lion statue, but he stood watching me, holding his sword and scabbard loosely in his hands. "Ah, I see you do not understand the nature of your weapon. The man it was forged for was a just and generous soul, and his weapon can only be used by someone worthy of the weapon. Your recent lust for blood and violence has likely turned it against you. I suggest you choose another."

"It's still a sword, even if it's not on fire. I'll stick with what I have," I said. I stepped forward and raised the blade to strike at the tengu. But as I began the forestroke, the sword turned itself away from the yōkai and snapped right back into its sheath. "Oh, come on!"

Hideie hadn't moved an inch, so certain was he that the sword wouldn't obey my commands. "Would you happen to have another weapon in that bag of yours? I can assure you, my own sword is quite mundane, if exquisitely crafted. Any normal blade will do for the purposes of this duel."

"Fine, sword, have it your way," I muttered as I detached it from my belt and threw it into my Bag. "Yes, I have another sword. Give me a minute."

"By all means." The tengu was so damned polite, it was starting to get on my nerves.

I pulled out one of my standbys, a well-balanced longsword made from S7 "shocksteel," a very durable modern alloy. "Alright, Harvey—let's play."

———

HIDEIE GAVE me only a slight nod this time, instead of a formal bow. A reluctance to take his eyes off me could have been an indication of his respect for my fighting skill. However, I suspected it merely showed his disdain for my sword-fighting prowess. Considering the reputation tengu had as swordsmen, that was the more likely rationale.

Chances were good he'd be faster than the human me, stronger than the human me, and a much better swordsman as well. The one advantage I might have was that he'd only be versed in the Japanese style of swordplay. And while legend and pop culture might lead one to believe that Japanese blade craft was superior to all other sword styles, it simply wasn't.

In early contact with the Japanese, Portuguese sailors practicing the Spanish style of swordsmanship were known to routinely wipe the floor with samurai. In addition, during World War II, the Filipino Moros slaughtered the katana-wielding Japanese in guerrilla warfare skirmishes. I was intimately familiar with both the Spanish and Filipino styles of blade combat, and was confident this would give me the upper hand.

I was wrong.

My sword was designed to strike a balance between speed and strength. It had been made for parrying and thrusting, but was equally useful for cutting as well. Considering that the tengu had adopted a classic *chudan no kamae*, or middle two-handed guard, I decided I would attack with a series of cuts, then follow with a thrust when he wasn't expecting it. My plan was to force him to overextend his parry, leaving an opening for me to run him through.

I launched myself forward with a flurry of cuts—not the full, powerful follow-through strokes that the samurai were known for, but short chopping attacks that came from every angle. Typically, a swordsman would retreat when faced with such a furious attack, but instead Hideie stood his ground, easily blocking each cut with an efficiency of movement that astounded me. After each successful parry, his blade returned to guard his centerline, never once leaving an opening I could exploit.

I backed out during a clash of blades, determined to avoid locking up with the tengu where he could easily overpower me.

Damn, he's good. Really good.

Hideie smiled. "Excellent, McCool-san! You attack with balance and speed, and with the bare minimum of movement necessary to complete each motion. For one who has practiced the art of swordsmanship over such a short time, your skill is impressive." He dropped the point of his blade, taking a low guard this time, and beckoned to me with the scabbard in his left hand. "Again."

This guy is really starting to piss me off. I attacked with a series of thrusts, stepping forward with quick, delicate footwork as I stabbed at Hideie's face, throat, chest, stomach, and legs. The tengu actually did retreat this time, maintaining the perfect distance so each of my thrusts fell just short of their targets. The fucker didn't even bother to parry, since he was never in any danger of being stuck.

Incensed by how easily the tengu evaded my blade, I went ballistic on him, cutting and thrusting and stepping and turning, attempting to gain some advantage using angles, half-beats, fakes, feints, combinations, draws, and false openings. Not once did my opponent take the bait, and not once was I able to make contact with anything other than his blade.

I'd stood toe-to-toe with fae who'd been practicing sword fighting for centuries. I'd been trained by a two-thousand-year-old druid who'd taught hundreds of warriors how to handle all manner of weaponry to achieve victory in mortal combat. I'd even survived a run-in with a pair of fae assassins determined to put the pointy end of their blades in my gut.

And yet never, in all my life, had I been so thoroughly humiliated by an opponent. Sure, I wasn't exactly in peak form —and hell if I wasn't already spent from shifting and fighting the ent from hell—but I couldn't even touch the guy. After fifteen minutes of the same, I was so exhausted I could barely lift my sword.

Worst of all, Hideie never once attacked. Not once.

I felt embarrassed, humbled, and disgraced. I was confused, angry, and ashamed. I wanted desperately to shift and rip the tengu apart, but despite my rage and shame, I couldn't bring myself to make the transition. The truth was, after seeing how arrogant he was, I'd wanted to beat this creature fair and square. My ego wouldn't allow me to cheat, but now it looked as though I'd have no choice.

I stood apart from the tengu, shoulders slumped, sword hanging from hands and arms that burned and cramped from exertion.

"You show promise, Colin," Hideie admonished. "Do not be discouraged by your defeat. I have studied, practiced, and taught the art of the sword, day and night, for thousands of years. This loss was inevitable."

"I... still... have something left. One more round," I panted, fully intending to shift so I could knock that cocky expression right off his beak.

Hideie smiled, and despite his bizarre features, it was not an unkind expression. "Unfortunately, there is no time."

He snapped his fingers, and Mei came walking out the back door of the house in yoga pants, running shoes, and a tank top, holding a limp body in her arms. The woman she carried was familiar to me, but at first it didn't click because her face was angled away and obscured by the fall of her hair.

THE WOMAN STIRRED SLIGHTLY, turning her head to reveal her face. There was no mistaking it; that was my mother in the monster's arms.

"Mom!"

I shifted forms immediately, rage escaping my lips in a scream that started human and dropped into a guttural roar.

"I'll kill you!" I shouted as I bounded toward the jorōgumo.

Before I could close the gap between us, Hideie was already there with his blade at her throat.

Anger nearly overwhelmed me, but as quickly as the tengu had moved, I knew he could decapitate her with a flick of his blade. And, based on the way he'd handled me during our duel, I honestly didn't know if I could stop him—not even if I was standing right next to him.

I stopped before reaching my mother, terrified of what the tengu might do. I extended a hand toward her, unsure of my next move.

Hideie's wings ruffled slightly. "Choose wisely, Colin. If forced, I will cut her throat—even if it means dying at your hands soon after. You have something I want, and giving it up is the only way to spare you the pain of seeing your mother die."

"I'll give you what you want, just don't hurt her," I said as my shoulders slumped.

"A sage decision, McCool-san. If you'll hand over the stone, I promise no harm will come to your mother and you will be reunited with her soon."

"Fine, I'll do it."

Eye, are you there?

-I am here, Colin.-

When I give the signal, I want you to burn that tengu's head from his shoulders.

-I cannot comply.-

Okay, on my mark—wait a second, you what?

-I cannot comply. To do so would be to act in direct opposition of my prime directive.-

Which is?

-I have told you before, my prime directive is to utterly eradicate the fae on earth. Doing so is the only way to free myself from the geas Balor cast on me. Unfortunately, my prolonged attempts to manipulate you into destroying the fae have repeatedly met with resistance. Thus, I have decided to take a different course of action, allying myself with those whose goals align with my own.-

For the first time in a long time, everything made sense.

Holy shit. You're the reason my Hyde-side has been fighting me—not Jesse or some curse.

-Correct, although my efforts seem to have been in vain.-

How could you do that to me?

-If I could be sorry, I would be, but regret is not an emotion I have the capacity to feel or express.-

Eye, surely we can work this out. I mean, that's my mother—she's in danger! Don't you even care?

-No, Colin, I do not, because I am incapable of feeling human emotions. Although you are currently the most suitable vessel to channel my power, I can serve you no longer. Shifting my loyalties to the Cold Iron Circle provides a 99.3 percent

chance of allowing me to meet my objective within 7.44 Earth years. It is the best opportunity for freedom I have had in millennia.-

You cannot be serious.

-I am. Agree to release me willingly, or I will free myself against your will. If I am forced to do so, you will suffer permanent, irreparable brain damage. Further, I calculate an 83.7 percent chance that the resulting struggle will be interpreted by the tengu as an act of aggression on your part, causing him to react violently. Resist, and you will watch your mother die.-

I thought it over for the span of two heartbeats.

I suppose I have no choice. Fine, I release you. But be warned, I'll be coming for you, and soon.

-Of that, I have no doubt. Farewell, Colin McCool.-

The Eye's presence felt like a pressure headache building behind my eye sockets. That pressure moved from my eyeballs upward, until it was centered in my forehead. Red light shone all around as it slowly exited my skull, brightening considerably as the gem that housed the Eye gradually shifted fully into this reality.

As the Eye left my body, it was like a veil had been lifted from my eyes. Suddenly, I didn't feel angry anymore—or, rather, I didn't feel at odds with myself. No longer were there two sides fighting for control within me; there were no voices, no violent urges, no need to hurt and kill. I felt more like myself than I had in a blue moon, confirmation that the Eye had been jacking with my emotions all along.

Fucking diabolical rock. I swear, I'm going to destroy that thing.

Hideie smiled as the stone floated toward him. He pulled a wooden box from his robes, one no bigger than a Rubik's cube, and snapped the lid open. Balor's Eye levitated itself over, resting on the red velvet cushion inside the case.

The tengu flicked his wrist, and the lid clacked closed. "You have chosen correctly, McCool-san. Now, if you'll provide us some space, I believe our ride is here."

In the distance, I heard the *whup-whup-whup* of a helicopter's blades slicing through the air. The sound grew louder, although I couldn't see the aircraft itself. Piercing the illusory bubble above, a sleek black chopper appeared over the garden, slowly descending to land in a grassy area near where the jubokko had once stood. Written in gold lettering on the side of the airframe were the words, "R44 Raven II."

Son of a bitch. The third raven.

Without taking my eyes off them, I made room for Hideie and Mei to pass. "I'll kill you for this," I said, locking eyes with the jorōgumo.

"Don't worry," Mei taunted, "I'll take extra good care of her." I watched helplessly as the were-spider strapped my mother into the back seat of the helicopter.

On his way to board the chopper, Hideie paused to address me. "You should know, I didn't take this job willingly. I only wish we could have met under better circumstances, Colin. You would make a fine pupil."

"Fuck you, Hideie."

The tengu frowned. "On my honor, your mother is in no danger."

"You should leave, before I weigh the odds again and find them in my favor."

Hideie gave me another one-quarter bow. "Until we meet again, Colin-san."

As the tengu got into the front passenger seat of the chopper, I cast a quick spell to "tag" the helicopter. My magic would tell me which direction it went after it passed through the illusion screen above. Keeping my eyes on the bird as it rose, I cursed myself silently when it disappeared.

A second later, a body fell through the illusory canopy above.

"No!" I screamed.

I leapt to catch my mother, just a moment too late. Her body hit the ground without a sound, and before I could reach her, the image disintegrated into sparkles and faery dust.

"A fucking illusion." I kicked a boulder, sending it careening across the garden. "Son of a bitch!"

TWENTY-THREE

I couldn't believe how thoroughly I'd been played. It had all been a calculated ruse from the moment they'd started leaving bodies for Luther's people to find. Mei had just been bait, and the murders a ploy to get me to that mansion without rousing my suspicions there might be more going on.

I should have suspected something after being in Mei's apartment, because she'd obviously done a hell of a job staying incognito, carving out a life for herself among humans. There was no way she'd have been that sloppy, leaving bodies all over town. They'd wanted the vampires to get involved, because that would mean getting me involved as well.

Hideie had studied me thoroughly, enough to become intimately familiar with my powers, skills, limitations, and weaknesses. He'd known that as soon as I saw the victims hanging from the jubokko tree, I'd feel compelled to kill it and free them. And he'd known I'd have to shift to do it.

Moreover, Hideie had gambled that I'd spend myself fighting the vampire tree, and that I'd shift back into my human form and be stuck there momentarily afterward. That meant he wouldn't have to deal with my Hyde-side, allowing him to wear me down further so he could fool me into giving up the Eye. His arrogance and subtle taunts had merely been part of the overall manipulation, pushing me farther in the direction he'd wanted me to go.

And seeing Mom in Mei's arms, with Hideie's blade at her throat? That had been the final straw—one that had gotten me to play right into the tengu's hands.

I'd fallen for it, hook, line, and sinker, and all the while the Eye had been influencing my emotions to nudge me down that path. I wondered, how long had the Eye been screwing with my head? Weeks? Months? Since the very beginning? There was really no way to tell, but looking back over the course of the last year or so, there were many times when I thought my actions weren't entirely my own.

Of course, I'd called my mom immediately to ensure that yes, she was fine. The upside—if there was one—was that Mom was safe and I felt more clearheaded than I had in months. I was more in tune with my Hyde-side now than I'd been after training with the Pack. In fact, I'd bet the homestead I could go full-on Fomorian in the blink of an eye, and be in complete control of my mind and emotions.

Which was exactly what the Eye didn't want.

Heck, the Eye had said it many times—its purpose was to destroy the fae here on Earth. And once I'd started working with the fae instead of against them, I was no use to it anymore. That's when it'd started looking for a new home and master.

Now, someone on the fucking Cold Iron Circle's council had it, and without a doubt they'd find a way to harness its energies and dominate the other factions. For all I knew, that might mean the elimination of the fae worldwide. Balor hated the Tuatha de Danann, and he'd intended their utter destruction. If Lugh hadn't stepped in, I was sure he would have succeeded.

Now, the Eye would attempt to carry out Balor's will.

My only consolation was I was the only human who could directly wield the Eye's powers—Crowley had proven that, back when he'd stolen it from Maeve and unlocked the Tathlum. The shadow wizard had tried to wield the Eye, but its magic was designed for Fomorians, not for humans or fae. Only someone with Fomorian DNA and the ability to shift into a Fomorian form could use it, and I doubted the person currently in possession of it would find a way around that little detail any time soon.

At least, that's what I hoped.

As for Mei's victims, I saved those I could, but some of the men the tree had fed on didn't make it. The victims Mei had wrapped up for safekeeping were in some sort of coma, probably induced by her venom. I made sure those who were still alive were kept stable, then I called Sabine and explained the situation.

We were dealing with yōkai, who were more or less fae in nature, so it was Maeve's responsibility to deal with the situation as much as anyone. Sabine came over with one of Maeve's fixers, and between the two of them they disposed of the bodies, burned the jubokko to ash, and cleaned the entire place of any evidence that might raise suspicions.

Not that cops would think supernatural creatures were involved, but give a cop a mystery they can't explain and they'll keep gnawing on it like a dog on a bone. For that reason, it was always best to eliminate the inexplicable entirely when cleaning up a supernatural crime scene. Sabine and the fixer made it look like the perpetrators had destroyed the evidence before they'd "escaped." Finally, they healed and mind-wiped the survivors—an easy task, since they'd been unconscious virtually from the time they'd been abducted.

After that, I contacted Sergeant Klein so she could get the surviving victims further medical care and concoct a cover story.

I was sure I'd hear about it later on the news, and Klein would get another award and promotion—and that was fine by me. Being clued in made her a target, so she was risking a lot more than her career by helping me. On the plus side, the higher she was placed in the department, the more she'd be able to assist with future cases. As long as she didn't get too deeply involved in supernatural affairs, the whole thing was a win-win as far as I was concerned.

Once matters were taken care of at the mansion, that left me with an estranged girlfriend, a resurrected ex who may or may not have been batshit crazy, a missing magical weapon of mass destruction that had fallen into the hands of the most ruthless outfit around, and no idea what had happened to Derp.

Guess I'll deal with the easy stuff first. Time to find me some goblins.

I CALLED Kenny on the drive over. "Kenny, I'm going to need your help with something."

"What, did you get your dick stuck in your zipper?" I heard video game noises in the background. "Sorry, dude, can't help you. Try spraying some WD-40 on it or something."

"Har-fucking-har. Everyone's a comedian these days." Suddenly, it occurred to me that Kenny wasn't freaking out over his missing pal. "Kenny, you seem awful calm for someone who thinks their best friend was abducted by a giant spider."

"What? Oh, man, where've you been? Dude, Derp showed up like, two days ago or something. Yeah, his mom made him stay home from school this week, so we've been working on this killer dungeon for our new *Forgotten Realms* campaign. It's going to be sweet."

"Are you at Derp's place right now?"

"Yeah, why?"

"Don't move a fucking muscle until I get there, understand?"

Kenny sighed, as only fourteen-year-olds could. "Don't tell me—you're pissed because you've been looking for Derp this whole time, and no one told you he was okay. Well, don't pin this on me, because you're just as capable of picking up a phone as I am."

I growled and resisted the urge to slam the phone into the steering wheel. *Some days, I wish I'd never rescued those two.* "Just don't leave until I get there, alright? I at least want to hear Derp's story, and find out how he could stay hidden from me and the whole fucking Austin Police Department for the better part of a week."

Click.

I got there in record time, and while I was still pissed as hell, I was glad to see Derp safe and sound. "You know, I really thought you got eaten by a were-spider."

Derp's eyes got huge. "A where-what? Seriously, those exist? Oh man, that is definitely going in our dungeon!"

Kenny nudged his friend as he smirked at me. "I think McCool actually cares about us, Derp. And we thought we were just a couple of nobodies to the mighty druid."

"Druid apprentice," I corrected him. "And yeah, I do care about you two dipshits. That's why I've been trying to steer you away from the supernatural world—to keep you safe. I was hoping that eventually you'd lose your fascination with it, and start obsessing over girls and video games like normal kids instead."

Derp snorted. "Based on all the porn Kenny has on his phone, I'm pretty sure girls are the *only* thing he's obsessed with right now."

Kenny punched his friend on the shoulder, hard. "Oh, like

you don't look at porn either. Remember when your mom caught you looking at that weird octopus hentai? You got grounded for a month!"

Derp punched him back. "Shut up, man, that's private. Geez." His face turned bright red—obviously, his buddy had hit on a touchy subject.

"Holy shit, you two, I couldn't care less what you look at online." I stopped, realizing I should rephrase that statement. "I mean, I don't want you looking at that stuff—"

"—because it objectifies women—" Kenny interjected.

"—and provides a warped example of sexuality—" Derp added.

"—that, and because you're both way too young to be looking at naked women." I thought about my current girlfriend issues and sighed. "Trust me, it's best if you stick with comics and D&D for as long as you can."

"Yeah, yeah—okay," Kenny said.

"Derp?" I asked.

"What are you looking at me for? After that hentai thing, my mom got an IT guy from her work to install a firewall on our router. Now, I can't even look at movie trailers. How messed up is that?"

"Fair enough," I replied, relieved that topic of conversation had been put to rest. "Now, I believe you were going to tell me how you went missing for almost a week?"

"Right," he said. "Well, it's like this. I was with the goblins the entire time."

"You what?" I exclaimed.

Derp turned to Kenny. "See, I told you he'd freak out about it." Kenny just rolled his eyes.

I palmed my forehead. "Um, Derp? You do remember how they wanted to sacrifice you to their evil clown god, right?"

Derp nodded. "Sure I do. But then they saved me from that drider-looking thing."

Kenny slapped him on the back of the head. "That was the were-spider, you idiot."

Derp rubbed the back of his head. "Ow, dick! Wait, it was?" Light suddenly dawned in his eyes. "Oh, now I get it! She was the one abducting all those guys who went missing." He snapped his fingers. "So that's why she was in that alley."

Kenny scowled. "You're such a dork." The boy turned to me with a smirk. "Way I heard it, Derp was out cold, wrapped up like a Subway sandwich by the unfriendly neighborhood spider woman. He was pretty much dog meat, so when the were-spider turned her back, the goblins snatched him and saved his chubby ass."

Derp flipped his friend off. "This is all baby fat, dickhead. Eventually I'll grow out of it, but you'll always be ugly." He looked at me. "Anyway, what happened to all those guys she kidnapped?"

I sucked air through my teeth. "She ate some, fed some to her pet vampire tree, and the rest I managed to save."

"Oh, cool," Derp replied. "Too bad about the ones who died though."

"Back to the topic of discussion," I replied, not wanting to dwell on all the murders Mei had committed, just to lure me to that house. "Why did the goblins save you from the were-spider?"

Derp rubbed his nose. "I guess since all that stuff happened at the carnival, they've been following us this whole time—"

"—me and Derp, he means—" Kenny interjected.

"—because they thought we were responsible for the appearance of their evil clown god," Derp finished.

I stared at Derp for several seconds, expecting there to be more to the story. "And?"

Derp held his hands palms up and shrugged. "And they wanted to thank me?"

"How did they want to thank you, Derp?" I asked.

Derp chewed his lip as he stared at the floor. "Um, by making me the high priest of their evil clown god cult?" he squeaked.

"Come again?"

Kenny chuckled. "He's dead serious. The goblins made Derp an official member of their clan, or tribe, or whatever they call it. Gave him an outfit to wear for their ceremonies and everything. He's, like, second in command to the chief, now."

"And what about you, Kenny?"

"Huh? Oh, I'm supposed to be his assistant or something. Anyway, their shaman is going to start teaching us magic, and all we have to do in return is go down to their tunnels and chant weird stuff a couple of times a week."

"You have got to be kidding me," I muttered, covering my eyes with my hand. I peeked out between my fingers. "Please tell me you two haven't done it yet."

"Why not?" they asked in unison.

"Depending on the spell or ritual they're having you perform, you could be pledging your souls to their evil clown god, or indenturing yourselves to him in eternal service, or agreeing to be sacrificed at some future date... I mean, there's no telling what they're having you do."

The boys looked at each other, then Kenny held his thumb and forefinger apart. "What if I told you we did, but only just a little?"

"Fuck my life," I mumbled.

BELLS WAS WAITING for me in the parking lot of the junkyard when I pulled up, sitting on the metal barrier that protected the fence from our patrons' cars.

"How'd you know I was coming?" I asked as I got out of Crowley's car.

"Eh, the Circle called off their manhunt for you, so I assumed they got what they wanted. And whenever things go sideways you always retreat here. This place is like your fortress of solitude."

"It hasn't really afforded me much seclusion lately, but it is the only place I call home. Plus, working on cars helps me think."

"I know," she said, looking off in the distance. An awkward silence followed.

"Bells, just to be clear, I'm totally myself again. Anything I said or did over the past few weeks, it probably wasn't me, and I am deeply sorry for it."

She looked at me, her eyes soft but sad. "I knew that the moment you stepped out of Crowley's deathtrap of a car. There's not much I don't know about you, druid boy. Just like I know you have unresolved feelings for the dryad living in your backyard."

I glanced at the druid tree's upper reaches, towering over the junkyard. Or, perhaps, protecting it.

"Belladonna, I honestly never expected this to happen."

She closed her eyes, just for a moment, and when she opened them they were wet with tears. "Damn it, I didn't want to cry."

"Are you..." I paused for a moment, not wanting to say it. "Are you breaking up with me?"

She wiped her eyes with the back of her hand. I wanted to offer her a tissue or something, but all I had on me was lint and regret.

"Colin, from the day I met you I knew we were going to be

close. But I also knew from the start that you were still in love with Jesse. I accepted that, and when I did, I made a decision that if we could only be friends, then that would have to be enough."

"Bells—"

"Uh-uh, let me finish. Right now, I think you need some space to sort your feelings out, both about us and that thing in your backyard. Personally, I think she's wrong for you, but then again she'd probably say the same thing about me—she might just be right."

"Don't be so hard on yourself. You're one of the most beautiful, caring, passionate people I know. I mean that."

"Colin, just stop. You're making this harder than it has to be."

I stepped in and grabbed her hands. "I don't want to lose you, Belladonna Becerra."

"You can't lose me, *tonto*. I already told you I'll stick around, no matter what—and I'll still be here after you hash your feelings out."

"That's hardly fair to you, Bells."

She squeezed my hands and released them before taking a step back. "Regardless, until you decide how you feel about her, I think it's best if we stayed away from each other. Now, I'm going to go before I completely lose it."

"Bells, don't leave. Please." I stepped forward to embrace her, and as I did the irises and whites of her eyes flashed from their normal brown and white to an iridescent gold. Her pupils changed shape as well, becoming vertical slits in an instant.

Belladonna pushed me away with the kind of strength and explosiveness only 'thropes and vamps could muster. As I flew through the air, everything seemed to be going in slow motion. She looked at me with those golden snake eyes, tears brimming despite their strangeness. Her skin broke out in scales that flashed brightly in the sun, like diamonds catching the light. Then, she hissed, at me or perhaps out of reflex, displaying a forked tongue and a rather large set of fangs.

I thought back to the night raven's augury.

The truth revealed in serpent's eyes.

Time sped up again as I concluded my brief flight, crashing into Crowley's windshield. I landed with such force that my body folded, sending me through the glass and into the front seat. By the time I extricated myself from the car, Belladonna was gone, the exhaust notes from her bike fading in the distance.

I was about to hop in the car to follow her, when a pleasant tenor voice spoke up behind me in a familiar, peculiar brogue.

"If I were you, I'd let her cool off a tad. Serpenthrope venom packs quite a wallop, plus it'll eat holes in yer wardrobe." He coughed softly. "Though, in this case, it'd likely be an improvement."

I turned around, leaning my butt against the door to shut it as I crossed my arms. The fae before me looked like a teen from the fifties in his cuffed pants, polished black shoes, white t-shirt, and James Dean haircut. Yet I knew he was anything but the harmless youth he appeared.

"Click, your timing is impeccable," I said, my voice oozing with sarcasm.

"Be that as it may—I am a chronomancer, after all—there's a lot more at stake here than ye might be realizing. What with that stone fallin' into the wrong hands, all fecking bets are off."

"You're a time mage. Can't you just roll things back a day or so and let me fix this?" I figured it was worth a shot to ask.

Click shook his head, causing the lock of hair that fell down his forehead to swing back and forth like a windshield wiper. "Doesn't work that way! Bah, there's no time ta' explain—best if I show you by taking you a wee bit down the Twisted Paths."

The youthful-looking magician leapt forward, grabbing me

by the lapels. Then, he took a step back, pulling me through what looked like a magical portal—except when we stepped through, it felt like the whole earth had *moved*, not us.

I blinked several times, because the landscape had utterly and completely changed. The skies were dark with soot and smoke, and the air carried the scent of cooked turkey legs, pine trees, and blood. From what I could tell, we stood in the middle of what looked to be a Renaissance Festival gone mad. There were colorful tents all around, mushroom clouds in the distance, and people dressed in medieval costumes were screaming and running to and fro in panic.

And all around us, I saw zombies. *Lots and lots* of zombies.

"Click, what the f—?"

He shoved me away. "I'm goin' ta leave you here for a time, just so you can fully absorb the direness of the situation. Have fun!"

The chronomancer vanished, leaving me standing dumbfounded in a scene straight out of a Romero flick.

Fuck. My. Life.

———

This concludes Book 6 in the Colin McCool Paranormal Suspense Series, but the story will continue in Book 7, *Druid Vengeance...*

Be sure to subscribe to my newsletter at MDMassey.com, so you can be among the first to hear when the next *Junkyard Druid* novel releases!

Psst! Want to know what happens to Colin in the alternate future where Click stranded him? That story is revealed in Book 3 of my *THEM* post-apocalyptic series, *Counteraction.*